# The Blind Devotion of Imogene

# The Blind Devotion of Imogene

## The Misadventures of Imogene Taylor

## David Putnam

*Dedicated to my lovely wife Mary.*

# Chapter One

Twelve years ago, time became Imogene's enemy. The way it reached into her soul and squeezed the life out of her. Guilt owned the largest part of this melancholy. She needed people around as a distraction or her mind took off, spun out of control with dastardly images from the past.

The day it all started she sat on the tall stool behind the checkout counter in Dentco watching over the empty store, fallen prey to a lull in customer activity. The late afternoon sun blared through the long front window heating up the store, making her want to lie down and a take a nap. She lit a Marlboro, her twenty-third for the day. Seventeen more to go, a self-imposed maximum. The nicotine surge made the world a tinge brighter.

The store owner, Micheal Higginbothom, came in through the front door and futzed around with the sales data retrieval sheets. She ignored him, puffed, and stared too long at the yellow sunlight stretching across the food bins and linoleum-tiled floor, chipped and bubbled. Dust motes sparkled and danced, unconcerned that life flitted past.

Her default thought was always of Wayne and what happened between them. Deconstructing those past events only raised more questions: How much weight can love bear? What is love's tensile strength before it shatters, making it all come tumbling down? And who, in the ethereal world, accumulates stats on such vital information?

Was love supposed to be so demoralizing?

At a time when Wayne was still in her life, Imogene would've given anything for those answers. But as it turns out every person has to decide for herself. Make her own decisions. Choose the wrong path, and love will break bad. Crack like a rotten egg.

That's what happened to Imogene. Only for her that misfortune, that miscalculation came late in life. Right after she'd turned sixty-three. She found out the hard way. In fact, there wasn't a more difficult path than the one she took to discover the depth of love.

Only to have it snatched from her grasp.

These and other blinding revelations first arrived in gritty fashion after she told her new cohort in CIW, Chino Institute for Women. Ange told her how love had dumped her in the slam. Ange informed Imogene in her crude and crass language that the rules of love apply to all equally, no matter the age.

Except when they don't.

Her first day in CIW, Imogene picked up the unfortunate moniker "Miss Bea." Her new friends thought she looked too much like that poor old wretch on the Andy of Mayberry TV program. The one that played on reruns over and over on the prison's list of approved programming. Syrupy fiction about a make-believe hometown in some distant fantasy world that never existed in the first place. Never would.

In CIW that's how names are coined. One half-wit opens her mouth, blurts out some inanity, like the name *Miss Bea*, and the others sitting around pick it up like a bad flu and spread it.

*Miss Bea* of all names.

And like love, there was no inoculation for that kind of inane thinking. Like an IQ booster shot.

That wasn't the worst of it, though.

Imogene never thought of herself as having a tail, and once she got out ten years later, she discovered she'd actually been given one.

Shamed beyond belief.

As if she didn't have enough regret over the thing with Wayne. Enough shame to fill three lifetimes.

No one would ever find out about the tail, not if she could help it. Of all things, a seventy-five-year-old woman, a mother of a beautiful daughter.

A mother with a tail.

Higgy-baby, a nickname he resented, was a bespectacled benevolent employer who let Imogene have a free hand in Dentco "Number One." And according to him, his flagship store.

A flagship, yeah, right. More like a little hole-in-the-wall in the worst part of Fontana.

Higgy-baby was tall with thick prescription glasses. For no good reason he chose that day to stop in to see if "The walls were still standing."

Right. More like to check on the weekly receipts and siphon off some unreportable income. Snatching a handful of bills from the till. He didn't like how every year the IRS stuck their beaks into his pocket and sucked up his hard-earned cash.

When the little bell rang, like it did for everyone who entered the store, Imogene looked up from the inventory printout Higgy-baby was showing her. Her stomach did a little flip, like a dolphin in a SeaWorld show who wanted a dead sardine. Imogene hated sardines. Wayne had loved them, especially the brand that came soaked in tomato sauce. Every time she spotted a tin in the miscellaneous tub, one with the little silver and gray fish surrounded by red, it reminded her of Wayne. How much she'd loved him. How much she dearly missed him. The sight of the tin always brought on a little ache of yearning along with a regret the size of Montana.

The black witch came through the door looking for Imogene. Nancy Do-right.

That's what Imogene took to calling her the first day they met, two years earlier, when she was seventy-three.

Nancy Do-right wore a gray pantsuit that might've fit twenty-five pounds ago. Funny how weight can also gauge time. As fat through an hourglass, so are the days of our lives.

Outgrown clothes stayed the same size no matter the pressures applied from the outside world, a part of life frozen in time.

If the world was truly fair, Nancy Do-right would leave her alone. She'd let Imogene get on with her life. She'd quit doggin' a seventy-five-year-old woman who was doing the best she could with the cards she was dealt.

At the sight of the rotund woman coming through the door the first thing Imogene thought about was the handgun on the shelf just below the countertop on her side. Last resort protection against robbers.

A huge reminder of how far Imogene had devolved. A reminder of what she'd been before the unscheduled trip to CIW. A reminder that shrank her down to the size of gutter scum.

The second thought, a worse one; Higgy-baby was about to find out about her tail. The one she'd so carefully hidden from him for two years.

Imogene hurried around the counter, her open hand out in front, guiding Nancy along. "Yes, yes, the feminine products you were waiting for have come in. They're right over here, ma'am."

Nancy Do-right froze, her back stiffening as she pulled her shoulders back, assessing the situation, understanding in an instant what had happened. Imogene had not informed her employer as required by the state. Nancy looked from Higgy-baby, then back to Imogene Taylor—Miss Bea, trying to decide the best course of action.

Imogene held her breath. Which way would the witch jump?

She chose to follow Imogene to the far corner of the store, where they could talk in private. The black witch apparently had a soft underbelly that had just now exposed her vulnerability. The first thing Imogene did was thank her profusely, hating every word kowtowing to this woman who held sway over her life.

The woman took out a pad with a spiral top and flipped to a blank page. "How are things going? Are you staying out of trouble?"

What a stupid question. Did the woman think she would voluntarily incriminate herself?

"Fine, no problems. I'll be glad when you aren't lurking, looking to trip me up. Trying to snatch away my remaining years. Life is too precious at my age."

She looked up from her writing, angry at the allegation. "I'm not the one who—" She hesitated, looked down at her pad, and shifted back to all business. "You're not associating with any other felons or using alcohol?"

"No, of course not, and I won't. I know the rules." Imogene needed to ease up, or she'd be in handcuffs on her way back to CIW.

"When is the last time you talked with Eugene?"

The question caught her by surprise. Imogene's back went rigid. "Not since POTUS visited Palm Springs last year. Why?"

"Don't you read the papers? The President is visiting again. Los Angeles, this time on a stopover to support the local Democratic candidate. Eugene notified me that he'd be taking you to lunch that day. When he does, don't embarrass yourself. More important, don't you dare embarrass me. I'm giving you fair warning."

Imogene nodded. "I understand. I won't give Eugene a problem like the last time. I'll comply. I only have two years left on my parole." Her tail. "I'm not going to screw it up this late in the game. You can trust me on this." She tried her best to force a smile that fell short of its ingratiating goal.

"You're not going to make it. Two years is plenty of time to screw up. I've been doing this a long time, and I know your type. All sugar and honey on the outside, but on the inside, you're hiding your real self, a woman filled with a seething anger and hate."

Part of Imogene's problem had always been her mouth. How it tended to all on its own just get up and walk away, abandoning the brain control panel. This time was no different. "Tell me something, ma'am. Is there some kinda contest?"

"What?"

"You know, the kind where at the end of every month, your office counts up the number of violated cons, and the winner gets a toaster? Because I have to tell you I've been nothing but nice to you for the last two years and—"

Nancy Do-right's mouth dropped open as if a wild dog had chased an alley cat up her pant leg. She closed her notepad, shoved it in her purse, and stomped over to the counter where Micheal Higginbothom stood watching them both. His eyes blinked behind thick prescription glasses, making them larger than normal.

"No, don't do it," Imogene whispered to no one. "Don't tell him. I need this job." Without a job, she'd get tossed back in the can to serve out her term. Fifteen more years.

She'd far too often taken to whispering to herself. And at the most inopportune times.

At the counter, Nancy looked back at Imogene as if asking her to beg from ten feet away. But Imogene wouldn't do it. She wouldn't beg. The one thing that kept everyone going in prison was pride, and she wasn't about to give up on it now. Imogene held her breath. Would Nancy Do-right blow the lid off the great thing Imogene had going at Dentco? If Higginbothom got wind of Imogene's history, he'd fire her for sure. Do it right on the spot. No doubt about it. He held himself up as a Mr. Law Enforcement type.

Maybe he'd even put the beautiful and much younger Suzie Q in as manager of The Flagship. Just to make extra points with her. In a way Imogene couldn't blame him; she now understood how love operated.

In each and every case, love works its long spidery tentacles under the skin into the muscle, down through the bone to the heart, and encapsulates it. Takes the soul hostage and refuses to let go. Won't let go until it's good and ready.

Nancy turned and faced Higginbothom. Imogene continued to hold her breath. She didn't move a hair.

# Chapter Two

When Imogene refused to beg, Nancy Do-right said to Higginbothom, "Your store manager Mrs. Taylor is on parole. She's an ex-con."

Imogene's knees sagged. For support she grabbed onto the bin piled high with roll-on deodorant, most of them dried and shriveled under the caps.

Higginbothom stared at Nancy through his thick glasses and blinked. He said nothing.

Nancy couldn't violate Imogene without justification. Not having a job, though, was justification enough.

Higginbothom continued to stare at Nancy.

Nancy raised her voice as if he had nodded off. "Murder. Mrs. Taylor committed a murder ten years ago. Twelve, now that she's been out for two."

Higginbothom blinked, still staring at her.

He finally said, "Yes, I know."

He looked around Nancy. "Imogene, can you come here and explain what's going on with this entry. It doesn't make any sense. If I'm reading this right, we have too many canned peas. I told George that when he makes his pickups, the stores will try to pawn off all their peas. I told you to watch for that, so it won't happen again. And now look.

"Unless, of course, they're *Le Sueur* peas. That's the premium brand in the silver can. We never get enough of those. Would you talk with him next time you see him? Please?"

Imogene and Nancy both stared at him. Nancy's head swiveled to glare over her shoulder at Imogene. Imogene smiled. She shrugged and cocked her head trying for, "See, no big deal." Doing a good impression of carefree.

Nancy stormed out. Imogene had made an enemy, and now there was no doubt Nancy would be back to try to violate her.

Through the front window, she watched Nancy go to her car, an old faded blue Dodge. She got in, started up, and exited the Cherry Avenue strip center, merging with the afternoon traffic.

Imogene let out her breath in one long harrumph, moved back to her regular stool behind the counter, and lit up another Marlboro. Her hand shook.

Higginbothom asked, "What was that all about?"

Imogene looked through her cat-eye glasses trying to back him down. When she walked out of CIW with her tail she made a promise never to lie again. But life made that tenet impossible. She decided that doing the best she could would have to be enough.

"Do you really wanna know?"

"I wouldn't have asked if I didn't wanna know, now would I? Why was that woman in my store acting crazy?"

Oh, that's what happened. Nancy Do-right never identified herself as a parole agent. He thought she was some kinda whack-a-do shopper.

She glared at him, blinked several times, and finally said. "That poor woman is delusional. She only likes *Lady Godiva* maxi pads. She gets real crabby if we're out of stock. She says it's the only brand that has enough absorption power to take on her massive flow. We didn't have any, so she's… well, crabby."

"Sweet baby Jesus. Did you have to go into such detail? I don't need to hear all that crapola."

"You asked, didn't you?"

"Sometimes, Imogene, I don't know why I hired you. Really, I don't."

"Yes, you do." She puffed the Marlboro as if it might be her last. "You couldn't find anyone more honest or anyone who'd work for slave wages." She shot him a smile and batted her eyelashes like she'd seen the girls in C block do when they wanted a little extra from the male guard in the control booth. Peanut butter and cheese crackers or stale day-old donuts none of the guards would touch.

Male guards weren't allowed on the mainline, but they could work the control booths. And they did quite often when the female guards called in sick. The males wouldn't give Imogene the time of day. She didn't have *the tits or the legs for it.* This, according to Ange.

Even back when she was with Wayne she never acted flirtatious like that, loose beyond belief. Flashing a little ass or cleavage. But if she learned nothing else in her ten years in the joint, a person had to adapt or get run over. And she was done getting run over, that was for gotdamn sure. She'd gone to prison for something she hadn't done.

Well, she hadn't committed murder like the jury seemed to believe. Poor ignorant cusses. Manslaughter at best. Yes, yes, manslaughter. But only if it came right down to the brass tacks of the matter. Not murder, never murder.

Higginbothom shook like a dog come in outta the rain. "Absorption rate. I'm not gonna get that outta my brain for weeks." He walked toward the front door with a fist full of cash, shaking his head.

Imogene had warned him about his cavalier attitude toward his own safety. Especially how he handled the store's money. Someone on this side of town—the wrong side of town—was gonna chunk him over the head and rob him blind. Ange had taught her how to case a score, and with those criteria in mind, Higginbothom stood out like a blinking red beacon. It was just a matter of time.

On Fridays, he joined the beer-drinking ne'er-do-wells on the side of Cherry Liquor, "tossing the bones." Shooting craps.

Gambling didn't fit with his skinflint lifestyle, making him an enigma of sorts.

"Hey, Boss?"

About to step out the front door, Higginbothom turned back.

"How long have you known?"

"Known what?"

"About my…my tail?"

"You been here what, two years?"

"That's right."

"Hmm, then one year, eleven months, and twenty-nine days." He smiled, winked, and left the store.

Out in the parking lot he got in an old Chevy step-side truck and drove the two hundred and fifty feet over to the side wall of Cherry Liquor and parked. He could easily afford a nice new car, but he was so cheap, as Wayne used to say, "He was waiting for the bible to come out in paperback" before he'd cut loose with any cash to buy one.

Higgy-baby had just gone way up in Imogene's book. He was a much nicer guy than she gave him credit.

No sooner had he driven away than a brand-spanking-new Lincoln Continental pulled up and parked in the red zone right in front of Dentco. Baby blue. Sleek. Out stepped a thug, who the girls in C block would've called a "Beastie Boy," someone who worked for organized crime, the OC. All brawn and without one iota of a brain cell. Ange had said, *When those kinda guys lined up to get their teaspoon full of brains from the Big Man himself, someone jiggled his elbow.*

This guy wore a dark maroon velour warm-up suit with a heavy gold chain around his neck that had to be plucking at all that fur on his chest. In the mild breeze, his brown head hair didn't move at all. Too much Aqua Net. He'd turned his hair into a helmet.

He looked around, taking in all the stores in the strip center: Cherry Liquor on the corner, The Lotus Massage and Tea House (aka Madam Woo's Rub and Tug), A-One Carpet and Tile, Asian Mike's dry cleaner, and a donut shop with real apple fritters. The kind fermented several days before they're fried, giving them that little extra wang.

Cherry Avenue was a main drag north and south, and at five in the evening, cars zipped by one behind another in go-home-from-work traffic. The abundance of cars raised the ambient noise echoing off Dentco's front window, making the glass hum.

Some folks stopped at Cherry Liquor for a Miller High Life and to wait out the hustle and bustle. They smoked unfiltered Camels that Ibrahim, the Jordanian owner, got in LA for half price. Got them with coupons he bought by the pound and passed on the savings as a loss leader to draw in customers to his booze. Flies to a long-dead cow. Everyone who stopped in now smoked 'em. Coupons by the pound, that's how fads got started. Camels didn't have filters and were harsh on the throat. The fools sacrificing a little comfort for cost.

Seven men squatted on their heels, exchanging money back and forth, smoking those Camels and drinking from brown paper sacks. Higginbothom had just joined them, making an eighth. Five-thirty on a dark winter night in Southern California.

The thug should've headed over to Cherry Liquor. Dice was a thug's favorite vocation. Especially once you added the beer and cigarettes. Or, at the very least, he should've headed over to the women in Madam Woo's.

Instead, he turned heel and came into Dentco.

Of all places.

He wasn't there to buy Lady Godiva maxi pads, that was for gotdamn sure.

He came over to Imogene, who watched his every move while she sat on her tall stool behind the counter, taking longer drags now that her nerves had calmed. Trailing in behind him like a kicked dog came a reek of Old Spice. She only recognized the scent because Wayne wore it. The pig wearing Wayne's cologne made her want to give him the boot all the more. Kick him the hell out before he had the chance to corrupt too many memories.

She wasn't normally prone to such aggressive thoughts, but anything that would desecrate Wayne's memory got her back up. And her blood still ran hot over Nancy trying to violate her.

He placed two hands flat on the counter. He leaned in and looked her straight in the eyes, trying for intimidation. She knew all about intimidation from Chino. This turd didn't have it, not one iota. His breath smelled of Juicy Fruit. His jaw gnashed, working the gum, giving it a thousand violent deaths a minute.

He smiled. "You own this rat-infested piss hole?"

She said nothing and stared.

"Hey, I asked you a question."

She said nothing.

Maybe he'd get tired like an incorrigible child who was ignored and walk away.

Not likely; he wanted something and wouldn't leave until he got it.

He reached out and swept the lip balm display and the box of stale Big Hunk candy bars off the counter. The ones marked down to a quarter apiece. They clattered to the floor.

She stared and blinked at him from behind her cat-eye glasses. The older model, black frames with rhinestones embedded in the corners. This was 1973 and she had the glasses going on thirteen years. Chino didn't have eye coverage just basic health. Their definition of basic health differed greatly from the real world.

He leaned in even closer. "Okay then. Let's start over. What's your name, Mama?"

She said nothing but thought about how far her hand was from the .38 Colt under the counter. Thought about how fast she could get to it. Thought about, if she did shoot this pig, how fast she'd end up back in the joint working off the rest of her tail. She couldn't take one more day on the inside. She'd done ten of her twenty-five, she still owed fifteen. Even the thought of fifteen more made her stomach clench.

From the back room sauntered John-Tom, a scary-large, dark gray alley cat that had taken to Imogene. He came to visit one day and stayed. He worked for Dentco now, hunting fat rats that came for the damaged dry goods. He'd heard the ruckus and came out to see for himself and instead found a different kind of fat rat.

The pig looked at Imogene, said, "Scared stiff, huh?" He stood back, nodding. "I can understand that. I know, I tend to do that to people. So, here's the what-for. This joint is ripe for getting ripped off. I'm here to put you and your store under my protection. Put your mind at ease. You understand? You never again have ta worry about getting robbed."

She stared at him; her hands folded in the lap of her worn housedress with a blue paisley pattern as she sat on the stool. She could afford new clothes, but Ange had said, *You dress like a victim, you'll become a victim. Walk and talk like a predator, you become a predator.* In no way did Imogene want to be someone who preyed upon others, but she also didn't want to be a victim. A person who wore nice clothes on the west side of town called out to be mugged.

He leaned in even more. "For that great bit of insurance, it'll only cost ya two hundert a week. What a deal, right? I'll be here every Friday to make the pick-up. Nod if you understand?"

He had a round pudgy face with a large nose. The kind of face that pleaded to be mashed flat with the black fry skillet she had back home.

He raised his hand, pointing an index finger. The gold rope bracelets rattled. "Two hundred, lady, on Friday or this place…" he pointed around Dentco's interior, "might catch fire in some kinda terrible accident. You hear what I'm sayin'?"

John-Tom let loose with a loud meow. Cats didn't understand how to protect a master like a dog, but John-Tom was different. In his heart, he was part cougar.

The pig reached under his shirt for a weapon.

*For a cat,* of all things. He was gonna shoot a dern cat. The man had no intestinal fortitude. She knew the type. But if she pulled the .38 Colt, took him out, three more just like him would appear to take his place. Poof just like that. That was just the way of the world.

To hell with it. Her hand inched down her leg toward the gun on the shelf. If he shot John Tom, she'd throw down on the pig and shoot him six times. Ange had told her again and again, *If he's good for one, he's good for all six. Always. Always let 'em have it until your gun clicks empty.*

Imogene wanted him gone before she did lose her resolve, picked up the handgun and shot him just because. CIW had made her this way, taught her to adapt at all costs or get run over. This pig was doing his best to run her over.

He changed his mind, took his hand from under his velour shirt. "Good. I'm glad you can listen to reason. I didn't want my pals to hear I tuned up a broad old enough to be my mom's mom. You know what I'm sayin'?" He chuckled at his own stupid joke. He was forty-five years old if he was a day.

She'd yet to utter a word.

*Please, please get the hell out before I pump a couple of lead pills into that soft cranium of yours.*

He turned and headed for the door.

She reached, put her hand on the cool wood grip to the .38.

He turned around to look at her one last time.

She said, "What's your name?"

"Ah, the crone speaks. Why do ya wanna know?"

"So I can put it on the check. You know, for this Friday."

His expression crumpled in confusion. Then he smiled hugely and pointed a fat finger, shaking it. "Now you're just messing with me, right? You crazy old broad."

Imogene forced a smile. "Yeah, I am. But I still wanna know your name."

"Okay. You can call me Sam. Sam Giancana. My friends call me The Cigar. You're my friend, right?"

This thug wasn't the real Sam Giancana, though with that round pie-pan face he did look a little bit like him from the black and white photos in the papers. In the joint there wasn't much else to do but read crime novels and keep up with current affairs. Lots of crime novels.

"You bet your ass, Sam. I'm your friend. See you next Friday."

"You gotta mouth on ya for an old bird, don't ya? I'll see ya Friday, Babe."

He walked out of Dentco and down the way, going into Madam Woo's Pleasure Palace.

When no one was looking the devil had blown into their little burg.

The problem was Imogene didn't know the half of it.

# Chapter Three

Thirty minutes later, the OC gangster Giancana was still next door and hadn't come out. A twinge of worry set in. Madam Woo knew how to deal with the Giancanas of the world. It came with the territory.

Imogene pondered whether or not to tell Higgy-baby what happened or to just cover the two hundred herself. Higgy-baby, a paper-pusher, wouldn't know how to deal with that kind of problem. He would, without a doubt, misread the situation. He'd call the cops. Bringing in the cops would just get his flagship store incinerated with a Molotov Cocktail. Lucky he hadn't been there to deal with Giancana, missed him by seconds. He was still over tossing the dice at the side of Cherry Liquor.

Higginbothom had opened another store in Bloomington, the next district over, and spent most of his time there getting it "up to speed." Imogene knew different. He had a silly high school crush on Suz. Said she was the love of his life. He'd told this to Mary Woo, who ran The Lotus Massage and Tea House, right next door. A place Higgy-baby used to frequent quite often before he met Suz, and his life "changed forever." Imogene got Suz the job. She was Imogene's next-door neighbor to the east. So logically Higgy-baby owed Imogene a big favor. He, of course, denied any remuneration for the referral, said he knew Suz' dad, and that her dad had even given him the seed money to start the first store way back when. Higgy-baby had delusions of grandeur, a silly dream that included a chain of Dentco's spanning three states. The Dentco King.

Dentco sold dented canned foods and damaged dry goods, out of date pharmacy products. Sold them to the less fortunate.

Higginbothom had twenty-one contracts with big-box grocery stores to pick up their dented goods for ten cents on the dollar. After which he sold them in his two stores at a forty percent markup. He made far too much money off hungry folks forced to shop in his stores for lack of anywhere else to go. If Imogene had her way, she'd sell the food for the same price she acquired it. But that wasn't how capitalism worked.

Imogene turned on the alarm and locked the door. She stepped over to the Lotus Massage and Tea House, opened the glass door painted over in black, stuck her head in, and listened. Soft Japanese music wafted out on a sweet scent of jasmine. The waiting area was empty. That meant the pig was in the back with the girls, creating who-knew-what kinda havoc. She hesitated, conflicted about going in, grabbing the guy by the ear and dragging him out. But her tail wouldn't allow it. She had to be extra judicious with her choices. Play it safe.

She let the door ease closed and headed for home.

Twenty minutes later, Imogene sat in the dark on the divan in her front window and watched the neighbor's driveway and front yard to the west. She settled in and waited. She had catnapped for the first hour. Staring into the dark had made her sleepy. She always catnapped on the divan, unable to sleep in her room or Wayne's either, for that matter. Their house at 744 East Hawthorne had two small bedrooms and one bath, with a heater built into the floor in the living room that was supposed to service the entire house. Their other house they'd lost in LaVerne had floor vents in *each* room with a central heater.

She waited by the window two days a week. Watching. Then, as sure as God made little green apples, Bernard Lowery, her neighbor, slipped from his house like a thief in the night. He hurried through the side gate, headed for a tryst his wife knew nothing about. Disappeared into the silky blackness.

Friday and Wednesday nights Bernie made the trek over to Delores's house on Campus Avenue. He entered through her back gate, then through the rear door. A door left ajar just for him. He'd ease it shut and stay till the wee hours of the morning.

Love did that to folks, made them half-crazed. Or maybe, in this case, it was just lust. She hoped it was just lust. She, too, had dark designs on ol' Bernard. If she learned nothing else in the joint, you didn't wait around for love to find you. You had to go out, tackle it, knock it on the head, and drag it back to your cave.

How did Imogene know about Delores? She'd tailed him and, on more than one occasion, sat on the street most of the night in her little red AMC Gremlin. Watched and waited. She'd done the same thing before she went to CIW and couldn't believe it was still going on ten years later after she got out. Maybe it *was* love.

But she loved Bernie Lowery. At least, she thought she did at one time. She wasn't so sure anymore. The desire to be with him had been the crux of her entire problem. The ruination of her life. Even after the debacle involving Wayne twelve years earlier, you think she'd have learned. Maybe it wasn't love anymore; maybe it was Imogene's inability to walk away from a goal. She loved Wayne, but she also had a little thing for their neighbor. That's what the bible ordered, right? Love thy neighbor.

Bernie had felt bad about what happened with Wayne. Their own little thing was what caught Imogene between the law and taking it on the lam. Bernie truly felt bad. She'd seen it in his eyes.

But not bad enough to attend Imogene's trial. Oh no, not bad enough for that.

While she was away visiting the pen for ten years, Bernie had watered the huge avocado tree in her backyard at 744 East Hawthorne. She would just die if that tree suffered due to her error in judgment. Every two weeks, he put the oscillating sprinkler under the long drooping branches and let it run for ten hours, deep-soaking the roots the way Wayne wanted his Mr. Majestic watered.

The only time Bernie ever dropped her a line in Chino, he sent a short missive in regard to Mr. Majestic.

Mail in the joint arrived sporadically. The guard would toss the already opened letters onto the inmate bunks.

When Imogene spotted her first letter and who it was from, her heart caught, skipped a little. Finally, Bernard had pulled his head out of his butthole and wanted to tell her he loved her. Tell her that no matter how long her stay in the joint, he'd wait for her. Be there at the front gate when she walked out.

Tears filled her eyes. Her hands shook almost too much to open it. She gently extracted the folded single sheet of paper, angry that a guard had already read it. Inside she found too few words. And worse, not the words she wanted.

*Imogene:*

*This note is to inform you that Mr. Majestic is doing well. I checked with the nursery, who said I needed to fertilize him every year before October 31. September was preferable. Organic fertilizer was best. I have taken up this annual chore, scattering around the base what they call chicken crumbles. Processed chicken droppings. Mr. Majestic is putting out more avocados than ever before. It seems foolish to let such fine fruit go to waste, so each time Mr. Majestic comes into season, I alert the neighbors. Mr. Majestic now supplies the entire neighborhood. You should be proud. I thought this information might give you at least a bit of solace during your long sojourn away from home.*

*Always your dutiful neighbor*

*Bernard*

He sent her a dern letter about chicken shit. The entire note was about Mr. Majestic and nothing about his love and devotion to her.

The night the note came, Imogene curled up on her bunk in an emotional void so dark no light could penetrate.

Imogene didn't tell Ange the problem even though Ange tried her best to find out. Ange's one big flaw was that she thrived on others' misfortune. Plenty of that in CIW.

*It's a dear John, ain't it, Em? Come on. Go ahead and show me already. I've seen a thousand of 'em. Damn straight, if I ain't. No big deal.*

Smothering shame wouldn't allow Imogene to show it to Ange.

One day, when Imogene let her guard down, Ange grabbed the note hidden under her mattress, a place off limits by mutual decree. Before Imogene knew what was happening, Ange had read it. Ange howled so loud it caught in her throat. She coughed and choked, her eyes bulging with mirth.

Imogene was glad she could entertain her friend with a blackness that had taken Imogene to the dark edge of the abyss.

Imogene went a long time without talking to Ange. Wouldn't say a word to her. One night, two weeks later—maybe three—Ange crawled up onto Imogene's bunk and spooned her. Held her in her arms and whispered in her ear that she was *God-awful sorry* and that she should never have laughed. Only when she said it a little mirth slipped out in her tone. She still thought it hilarious. What else could Imogene do but forgive her cellie.

While on her "sojourn," as he put it, Bernie also paid her mortgage. Paid it with money from her social security check. She'd given him full power of attorney to access her checking account. The foundation of love had to be trust. She showed him her trust and hoped he would reciprocate ten years down the line.

Ange had warned that when she got out, she'd find her account fleeced right down to the bare bone.

When she did get out, she found Bernie hadn't pilfered one cent. He only paid what was owed. He was a good, upstanding man, just like Wayne. The twenty-year mortgage finished and was paid off five years into her term. That allowed the social security money to add up and also collect a little dab of interest. She had a nice nest egg when she got out. But she was still required by the state to have a job or be violated. Hence, the job at Dentco was the only place that did not ask about her tail.

Be violated. The state needed to change that term; it was rude.

Bernie's wife Dorothy had a massive stroke some fifteen years prior and required full-time care from a daytime nurse. Bernie loved his wife Dot just like Imogene loved Wayne. A kind of love that was more devotion than tenderness or intimacy.

Bernie would come home after working all day as a bookkeeper and take care of Dot all night. Did it all himself: the bath, the dressing, the feeding. All the while, Dot just stared at him as if he wasn't there. How did he do it, day after day, week after week?

Bernie and Imogene had a "moment" back before she made her mistake and slid into the gutter. Before she dropped right down into the thick of criminality.

Still, Imogene had not deserved Chino. Not for just an accident. A minor little slip.

Somehow, Bernie had found Delores over on Campus Avenue before he'd found Imogene. Loved worked that way. It was a parasite that once scorned had the absolute ability to jump from one host to another. Lower its beak and start sucking up emotional blood until there wasn't anything left. Imogene had been abandoned in that same manner. Now, she was nothing more than an empty husk.

That wasn't fair. Bernie had every right to his chance at love. Imogene just wished it was with her. A rekindling of her emotions that lay in smoldering ruin for too long.

Now she sat on the divan, deciding that she needed to, yet again, work up the nerve to tell Bernie how she felt about him. The last time she'd tried had not gone so well. She just needed the opportunity, that's all. That's why she waited and watched the man next door, waiting for her chance. She'd know it when she saw it. Then, it was only a matter of nerve. To take that first difficult step. To pounce.

# Chapter Four

Sitting in her picture window every Friday and Wednesday night didn't help with Imogene's depression or with letting Wayne go.

After Bernie's shadow disappeared into the inky darkness Imogene got up and shuffle-stepped into the kitchen to the ice box searching for relief from the black cloud that settled on her smothering all else. Schlitz malt liquor, her savior.

Bernie waited on those two nights every week for Dot to fall asleep before he slipped out. Had Imogene not done her stint in Chino, she knew she'd never have had the evil little thought that nagged at her. One she would never in all the world act upon. She wasn't that woman, never had been. Never would be. But the thought lingered just the same.

Even if that dastardly little idea did fester all week and then raised its ugly head every Friday evening. *What if she waited for Bernie to slip out and then went over to Dorothy's? Sneak in and use a pillow on poor old Dot. It would be a blessing. Put her out of her misery. Right? Imogene would be doing the work of a dark angel. Yeah, a dirty angel, but still an angel.*

But that would just release Bernie from his obligation, not his loyalty to his recently deceased wife. He'd cling to her like she was the last life preserver on the Titanic.

Good for him.

That's why Imogene loved him so, his loyalty and compassion rarely found in an upright man.

She took from the ice box the six-pack of Schlitz malt liquor. Talls. Sixteen ouncers. Beer that packed a wallop and would *knock you back on your skinny ass, girl.* This, according to Ange. Someone who had helped keep her safe and sane in Chino. Nice that Ange would describe Imogene's ass as skinny. That train had long ago left the station. She smiled to herself at another memory, one back when Wayne couldn't take her eyes off her skinny ass.

She dearly missed his hugs. It's what she missed most of all. The way he took her in his long arms and held her close, so close they became one. He'd kiss the top of her head slowly three times as if it were a ritual. As if she meant more to him than all the orange and lemon groves in LaVerne. He was a citrus man, a grover, who always had a long fruit knife in his pocket.

In his hug, she'd take in his scent, Old Spice, citrus blossoms, and burnt cherry smoke from the pipe that perpetually hung from the corner of his mouth. He also never went anywhere without a dark gray fedora. The kind with one of those little red feathers stuck in the hat band.

Part of his wonderful scent was sweat that permeated from that dern hat. The hat that made him too dashing made all the loose women down at the pool hall give him the eye. A place where he spent a great deal of his time. The pool hall on Fourth Street next to the Dairy Queen.

When he over-stayed at the pool hall and knew there would be trouble when he got home, he'd pick Imogene up an Orange Freeze, orange soda pop blended with soft-serve ice cream. She could live without them, not her favorite from the Queen. She was more a banana split kinda gal. But the fact he thought to buy her an orange freeze made all the difference. Those orange freeze days, he'd open the house screen door, yell "Imogene," and toss in his fedora to see if it was safe to enter. He'd chuckle like it was a big joke. No matter what kind of tiff she'd worked up over his tardiness, he always made her smile with that stupid hat trick.

But the very idea she'd be lying in wait with a gun to *blast his sorry ass* when he tossed his hat in was ludicrous beyond belief. And that description had come from Ange.

She missed her. While Imogene sat on the tall stool in Dentco, she wrote to Ange every other day without fail.

Ange never wrote back.

In a way, Imogene understood why. What was there for Ange to say?

Imogene was on the outside in the real world, and Ange only had gray bars to look through and write about. Write that the green Jell-O was watery or the bologna in the lunch sandwiches was stale. Or that Leticia got shanked in the laundry because she'd kissed Big Alice from Compton. They'd simply be senseless missives.

Ange wasn't ever getting out of Chino.

Ange came home early from her industrial laundry job, hot, sweaty, back aching, and found her man *in bed with the neighbor woman. So, I grabbed up the gauge and let them both know that I didn't at all agree with their choice of fornication partners.*

They gave Ange life without the possibility of parole. Times two. The state somehow wanted to extract two lives from her friend Ange. Rude.

Ange was never offered a tail. Said she was an ongoing threat to public safety.

Imogene took the six-pack of malt liquor along with a saltshaker into the living room and sat on the divan. A divan she'd purchased with Wayne. Maybe the last time he'd ever held her hand out in public. She'd tatted the three antimacassars draped across the back and faded yellow after ten years of ignoring them.

She popped open the first can and salted the hole and around the rim. The beer foamed up. She took a good long slug, let it cool all the way down her insides. She waited all week for this. She sat back, relaxed, and drank the first one too fast. She popped open the second while stifling an ugly belch. She still possessed some class even if she was a convicted murderer. Murder of all things.

Across the small living room sat Wayne's easy chair. Across from the chair was a console television that kept her company while Wayne toiled in the citrus groves or frittered away his time in the pool hall on Fourth Street.

She smiled and took another glug of beer. Memories—that's all she had left. Wayne, sitting in front of the console television on Thanksgiving Day with his Jap camera up close to the screen snapping pics of the parade in New York. The way he giggled. A grown man, 63 years old, giggling. He said, "I'm gonna tell the boys down at the hall, you and me, we travelled by train to New York and watched this parade firsthand. The color on this set is great, ain't it? They won't know any different. No, sir, they won't."

Back before the stint in the joint, a place where a person was forced to gain life experience quicker—more like in dog years—she laughed with him at the ruse he perpetrated on those wet-brained friends down at the hall.

He purchased the camera when he took her on one of their few vacations. The time they traveled the forty-two miles west to Los Angeles, toured Universal Studios where they had the entire set to *Gilligan's Island* to tour and walkthrough. He snapped five rolls of photos of that phony place. The things people would waste their money on.

He never watched that ignorant show before they took the tour. After the vacation, he never missed a rerun. And that TV station ran Gilligan reruns several times a day. Wayne would sit in his easy chair smoking his pipe, the burnt cherry tobacco rising in a cloud over his head, and he'd point. "See that there, Imogene, that's not a dern lagoon at all; that's really a Doughboy above-ground pool. Ain't that something else. On the TV, it looks just like a dern lagoon."

She sat on her divan, smoked her Marlboro red box cigarettes and smiled, happy that he got such a kick out of something so inane.

Above the console television, hanging on the wall, was a portrait of their daughter painted by a professional painter. Joyce was a beautiful girl. In the painting she wore a green dress with a white collar. She had her hair in the fifties style. The painter gave her red lipstick and ignored the tiny acne scars under both cheekbones. It had been so long since Imogene had seen Joyce she'd forgotten what those little scars looked like. Would have forgotten her face entirely had the portrait not stared down at her day in and day out. Joyce never aging.

Joyce had been smart, the most intelligent kid in her sophomore high school class. Imogene might not have believed her daughter, not entirely anyway. But during parent's night at the high school, all her teachers said the same thing: "Whip-smart." "She's really going places." "She could be the first woman astronaut, the way she does math problems." Imogene listened to those same teachers talk to other parents about their kids to see if they blew smoke up their dresses.

And they didn't.

Joyce was a true wonder. She had it all: beauty, brains, and tall like Wayne. Imogene basked in that knowledge for two more weeks after the teacher told her that. Until the deputy coroner and police officer knocked on their door at 744 East Hathorne, bearing the horrid news no mother should ever endure.

Joyce had been riding on the back of a young man's 350 cc Husqvarna motorcycle. Funny how little details stuck to her memory like fly tape. Not shaking loose no matter how hard she tried to forget that part.

They weren't driving crazy. They'd just caught a green light and took the left turn too fast. Leaned over just a little too far. The foot peg caught asphalt and…and the bike tumbled end over end. With the two riders in the mix.

*End over end.*

That's what the bastard said as he stood on the porch, said it just like that: end over end. Imogene couldn't get rid of the images freeze-framed in her mind, ones created through pure imagination. Her poor little girl caught up in a metal-crunching somersault. Slapping asphalt tumbling, shattering bone and skull, tearing muscle, rending skin from the body.

How horrible.

The last can of malt liquor, half full, slipped from her hand and fell to the tired and worn-out gold high-low carpet. Imogene drifted off into her Friday night stupor.

* * *

She woke Saturday morning, mouth cotton-dry, head pounding. Woke to Joyce in the portrait looking down upon her.

Judging.

Imogene put her hand up to cover her own face. "Please, Baby, don't look at me like that."

Suz knocked on her screen door and came in without being asked. She'd never done that before.

Imogene had left the front door open all night. She'd never have allowed that to happen before Chino. But in the joint a person learned a different perspective of fear, of danger.

Suz stood just under Joyce's angry glare.

Tears streamed down Suz's cheeks.

Imogene's heart skipped a beat. She jumped up, her old knees not agreeing with such a youthful endeavor. She staggered. Suz hurried and caught Imogene before she could take a header. They hugged. Imogene learned from Ange to hug other women whenever the possibility arose. That connection, the most important thing in this world. Solidarity.

"What's the matter? What's happened? Did Higginbothom dump you? That pig."

Suz shook her head, not comprehending what Imogene had said. Her tears dampened Imogene's house dress. For a brief moment, Imogene wondered if she reeked of body odor. She had not taken her normal after-work bath to slough off the Dentco stink.

"No. I woke up, and Daddy…Dad was dead on the kitchen floor. His special coffee mug was shattered with coffee everywhere. E, he's just dead."

"Oh my God, I'm so sorry. Here, sit down. Let me get you a cool glass of water." She set Suz down in Wayne's easy chair and hurried into the kitchen. She took down two green glasses, filled one and drank it down while she filled the other. She hurried back and gave Suz the glass.

She held it in her lap, her eyes gazing out the front window at Hawthorne Street.

Imogene pulled a chair over close and rested her hand on Suz's arm. Her body still told her she needed more water, but she couldn't leave Suz's side.

"Was he sick? Your dad, I mean."

Suz came out of her trance for a second. "What? No. He was just…old." The tears renewed their assault on her cheeks.

In Chino, you weren't supposed to talk about time, or age, it was forbidden. No one wanted to think about all the life that rushed past the front gate as they sat on their bunks twiddling their thumbs or working on a chickenshit hobby craft. When Ange and Imogene did whisper about it after lights-out,

Ange described age as if it belonged in a thick tome containing the law. She related every-dern-thing to the law. Law was what had incarcerated the both of them. *From sixty to sixty-three, Ange had said, you're misdemeanor old. From sixty-three 'til you get thrown down in the hole for your long dirt nap, you're felony old.*

"How old was your father?" Imogene asked Suz.

"Old. He was sixty-two."

Imogene took the green water glass from Suz's hand and drank down her water as well. Imogene had always thought of herself as misdemeanor old and it wasn't until that moment she realized she had long since crossed that Rubicon, going deep into felony old. How had that happened without Imogene being aware of it? Ange had never mentioned Imogene's felony age.

That ten years, that chunk of her life in Chino, had frozen Imogene in time, left her stuck back there before her conviction. And in her mind, she'd never advanced in age. This was an odd feeling that made the air wobble a little like a heat wave. Or it could've just been her malt liquor hangover.

Suz leaned in and hugged Imogene again and cried.

Imogene now had to pee something fierce but would knuckle through it a little longer. Suz needed her.

Imogene whispered. "You don't have to worry about a thing. I'll help you take care of getting your dad…ah, taken care of."

Suz nodded. "That's real nice of you, E."

"What about your mother?"

"I never knew her, not really. I was only six or seven when she died. Cancer or something like that. Dad never wanted to talk about it. He was torn up about her death. I could tell by the way he acted when I asked about her. He really loved her. I missed having a mom. I envied all my friends. I'd sit and just watch the way my friends and their mothers interacted. It only made it worse."

She rambled. Heated emotions.

"Have you called Mike yet?"

"Who?" She pulled back from Imogene's chest, leaving it wet, and looked into Imogene's eyes.

"Higginbothom."

"Why in the world would I call him?"

"Oh, dear Lord, girl. I thought you…I mean…I think he thinks that you and him are—Oh, dear Lord, girl."

Suz sat back, her mouth sagging open. "You mean he thinks that him and I are…Oh my God."

"That's kinda what I just said. Twice."

They fell into each other's arms, laughing until they both cried.

# Chapter Five

Two days later, Imogene slipped into her funeral garb, a black dress made with imitation satin, a black hat with a black mesh veil sewn in, and black shoes with two-inch comfortable heels. The leather on the shoes was a little scuffed. The same shoes she'd worn during her trial. During trial breaks, recesses, and lunch, she was shuffled off to a holding cell like some kind of dangerous animal, one that survives on stale cheese sandwiches and green apples. Ugh.

She'd worn the get-up four times in the past, all for little-known relatives' funerals, on Wayne's side. And now for the neighbor next door, Suz' father, Herb. She wouldn't have attended but she wanted to emotionally support Suz. Being needed was reason enough for anyone to keep on breathing.

She stopped in the bathroom, located not two short steps from her bedroom door. She checked her makeup. Only lipstick. Nothing around the eyes. Everyone knew you didn't use mascara or eye shadow when you attended a funeral. Even if it's only to support a friend. You'd end up zebra-faced for sure.

The bathroom mirror revealed a moth hole in her dress over her breast, toward the top, close to the cleave. Exposing a smidgeon of too-white skin, now made whiter by the surrounding black. And also, of course, allowing a partial age spot to peek out.

"For cripes sake."

She pulled her dress down snugly and used the mascara after all, used it on her breast making sure to cover a large enough area around the skin in the interior of the hole. She took a step back, moved from side to side, turned on the light. She smiled. She couldn't even tell, and she'd been the one to camouflage her boob.

She attached the hat to her gray and white bun and pulled down the veil. She could be an extra in a movie; call her "the despondent widow."

Then she remembered the law had not allowed her to attend Wayne's funeral. Wouldn't let her take a field trip from lockup, pending jury trial.

The bastards.

Her stomach turned a little at the thought.

Ange had ruined any logical thought Imogene possessed before she'd entered the Female Gladiator Academy. Now, if she wanted to sound like a real person, she had to stop and think of her answer. Usually, inserting the second or even the third choice would risk sounding like a con. Ange had made her too cynical and suspicious of everyone and everything. Worst of all, afraid to venture out into the world of dating. Imogene was too old anyway. Who'd look twice at a murderous ex-con. One with a tail ta boot.

No, she had a better chance prying ol' Bernard away from Delores. And given the first opportunity, that's what she intended to do. She'd waited too long a time already, too long. She'd been mulling over ideas about creating her own opportunity. She wished she could talk with Ange about it. She'd know exactly how to handle the Bernard situation. Only her method was sure to leave a lot of emotional wreckage. And even a body or two with physical evidence.

A knock at the door.

Imogene checked her watch. Suz was twenty minutes early.

That girl.

Imogene hurried to the door, a thick, wide one installed back when they used to know how to make a house solid with real wood. The door was painted dark green on the outside and beige on the inside to match the walls and décor, in a muted sort of way. Joyce had always wanted Imogene to change the color of the inside walls said "The puke beige reminds me of a mental institution." She'd said it enough times. Imogene wanted to ask her how she knew what the inside of a mental institution looked like. But that was back when she still possessed her word filter that kept the angry battles down to a minimum. Back when she ate those words rather than spew them.

She opened the door to a man with sandy hair wearing a suit and tie that didn't really match: brown suit coat, yellow dress shirt, and blue tie. He was older with a tan and wrinkled face from too much sun; tennis probably. Older, hell, he wasn't even misdemeanor old, maybe fifty-five. But she wasn't good at guessing ages anymore. Another attribute wrung out of the inmates in Chino for no other reason than why would anyone care?

The man startled, his smile shifting to surprise.

She said, "Whatever you're selling, I don't—" Then her felony old memory kicked in. This was Eugene L. Lujan, a bona fide member of the U.S. Secret Service. Here to take her to lunch because the President of these United States was coming to Los Angeles to support a fellow Democrat running for office.

Ugh.

Eugene recovered quickly. "…Ah, I didn't know we were dressing up."

Stupid words really, nothing wrong with a black dress on a weekday morn. That's not dressing up.

"I'm sorry, Eugene. Nancy told me about this lunch thing, but she didn't tell me what day. I have a funeral to attend. My neighbor's father passed away."

Suz hurried over from next door, a flash of black with scissoring white legs. Came across the crumbling asphalt driveway, onto the concrete walk, and climbed the two concrete steps to the large concrete front porch. "Imogene, what's going on?"

Eugene put his back to the wall and crossed his hands at his waist. Now, he looked like a funeral director. Or just a sappy vulture with a walnut-sized Adam's apple.

"Come on in, the both of ya. Or we're gonna have all the neighbors bumpin' their gums about this little impromptu rendezvous." She opened the screen door and stepped aside to let them pass. She could really give two craps about what the neighbors thought.

All except Bernard Lowery. He was at work at the moment. But he sometimes came home for lunch.

She'd really said it to give her time to decide which way she wanted to fall on this issue: lunch (the third one the President caused) with Eugene, or a dreary funeral with Suz. Of course, she wanted to choose the lunch. Eugene never scrimped on the lunches, not on the government's dime. But Suz was a good friend, her best friend outside the tall barbed-wire fences of Chino. *Outside the Tall Barbed-Wire Fences of Chino* sounded like a great book title.

Once inside, Imogene turned to face her guests. "Suz, this is Eugene, my—"

He held out his hand, "Her second cousin from Arkansas."

If someone asked Eugene how he fit into Imogene's life, he had a prepared answer, one they'd both agreed upon. They'd worked out several tales that wouldn't embarrass either.

Two lunches in two years, they knew each other pretty well. In fact, according to Ange, who kept up on current dating protocols, *'With three dates you get egg roll, darlin'.* Imogene had to ask her what that meant. She broke it down to a vernacular she could understand.

*Sex, baby girl. You automatically get sex on the third date. It's automatic.*

Automatic, her wrinkled old ass.

But that was for the third *evening* date, right? She'd have to write Ange and ask if accumulated lunches could equate to three *evening* dates. And what that number might be. Not that Imogene wanted any part of Eugene. She just didn't want an embarrassing moment to needlessly arise. Him closing his eyes and moving in with those caterpillar lips. Moving toward hers for an open-mouth kiss.

Before her stint in Chino, sex after three dates would've been absurd. That wasn't any way to court a woman.

Since she'd been out, she'd let herself daydream of a wonderous third date with Bernard.

Only Ange never answered her dern letters. If Imogene ever wanted to talk to Ange again, she'd have to kill someone. The way her week was going, that wasn't out of the realm of possibility.

If people only knew what went on when the President came to town, how the secret service acted like overpaid nursemaids, they'd ask who exactly was running the madhouse.

She'd told Eugene she didn't like him using Arkansas, that she preferred Boston. She wanted fake relatives coming from a place of substance and not from some hick fly-over state where people had six toes, talked with hick drawls, and on rainy days dragged their barbeques inside their houses for cookouts.

Even though that *was* where Wayne's folks hailed from, he had none of those traits. All his folks died there, too, without ever having stepped foot outside the state. Real hayseeds.

It irked her that Eugene could smile while he stuck a fork in her like that. He was angry. He was smart enough to realize he was about to miss out on a government-sponsored expense accounted lunch. In exchange for a weepy funeral with crusted-over casseroles at the back end. Mac and cheese, goulash, cream of mushroom, and taters covered in stale chips, that list could go on forever and a day. And don't forget those dern little cucumber sandwiches with the crust cut off. Whoever thought of something like that? They just one day said, hey, why don't we slice up a perfectly good cuke, slap some mayo on, and put it between two pieces of white bread. And oh, while we're at it, cut off the crust. Sweet Jesus, some people needed to get a life.

"Imogene, you never told me you had a cousin?"

"I don't," she whispered to no one.

"What did you say?"

Imogene waved her hand. "Nothing. He comes out here once or twice a year when Goofy gets the urge to see Gilligan at Universal Studios." Goofy being the President of these United States.

"You call your nephew Goofy? Wait, they don't have that set at Universal Studios anymore. They have the Burning House tour. I haven't gone, couldn't ever afford it. Are you going today? If you want to go, it's okay by me, Imogene. Your cousin doesn't come to town very often."

"That's very nice of you, ma'am. I do dearly miss my Imogene." Eugene edged over and put his arm around her.

She elbowed him and stepped away. "Stay out of this. The women are deciding."

"I don't think—"

She raised her hand to slap his shoulder. He shut up.

"Boy, you two are definitely cousins."

"If you only knew."

Imogene caught Eugene staring at her breast. She rested her hand covering the dern moth hole. Made her look like she was saluting the flag.

"Seriously, Imogene, you go ahead. I'm okay with it. Daddy was old, and I'd been preparing myself for this for a long time."

"Sixty-three's not old."

She ignored Imogene's indignant outburst and said, "If you really want to be a true-blue friend, you can help me clean out all of Daddy's crapola in the garage. It's literally piled clear to the ceiling. Looks like a Machu Picchu pyramid I've seen in National Geographic."

Crapola, that's a word Higginbothom used. Did he get it from her or vice versa? Language tics were just like lawn ticks. They crawled on and wouldn't let go. Sucked away any available intelligence until one day, you woke up sitting in the stands watching a NASCAR race, wondering how the hell you got there.

"That deal sounds more than fair, Imogene," Eugene said. "Come on, we really have to get going. I made reservations at the Magic Lamp, and the traffic, who can predict it, right?"

"Are you sure, Suz? I don't want to leave you in the lurch."

"Seriously, it's fine. But you better change or you might scare all the kids at Universal Studios. They might think you're Morticia from The Addams Family."

"Who?"

They were not going to lunch at Universal Studios. No way. The conversation sure spun out of control on that inane topic.

Eugene gently took her arm and escorted her to the door. "We have to go, dear. Very nice meeting you, Miss." He wagged his eyebrows over the top of a Groucho grin. Imogene had seen him do it randomly to other attractive young women.

"Your cousin's a hoot. Is he staying the night? Maybe I can come over later, I'll need a good laugh after planting Daddy."

"Sure, that's fine," Eugene said, continuing to spew words.

*Outta the left side of his ass,* as Ange used to say.

* * *

Thirty minutes later, he pulled his baby blue Dodge government car into the parking lot of the Magic Lamp. The restaurant doors didn't open for another half hour. Imogene took out the long pin in her bun and took off the hat.

"Careful with that. It's a deadly weapon."

She handed him the pin. Eugene had a weird sense of humor that she couldn't read. Did he do it on purpose to keep her guessing or was he really just that big of a goof? Maybe that was why, when the President came to town, he got assigned lunch duty with a felony old woman.

One time after one of those lunches, the next day, when she walked out of her house to her little red Gremlin to drive to Dentco, Eugene's G-ride was parked on the street. She walked up and tapped the window fogged over with condensation. Startled, the stalwart member of the U.S. Secret Service fumbled with the window, rolling it down. His hair was ruffled as if he'd had a toss in the hay with the farmer's daughter—or fought the good fight during an unusually active nightmare.

"Imogene?"

"That's me. What are you doing parked out here?"

"If I told ya, I'd have to kill ya."

"What? Was the President spending the night in LA instead of flying back to DC?"

"Yes, but you didn't hear that from me."

"Humph." She turned and headed back across the street to her yard.

Eugene let go with a harsh whisper. "Imogene? You didn't leave the house last night, did you? I kind of dozed off."

She kept walking.

"Imogene, I'm only three years away from my pension. Tell me you stayed in last night so I can put it in my report."

She mounted her Gremlin, backed into the street, and pulled up next to Eugene's car, his window still down. "Eugene Lujan, did you know you could ruin a woman's reputation by parking in front of her house all night? Next time, I'll report you to your supervisor." She drove off feeling oddly gratified.

Once she set her black hat and veil on the dashboard, she folded her hands in her lap and waited for lunch. Her stomach growled. How utterly rude and embarrassing. She took the red box of Marlboro's from her clutch and lit up.

Eugene said, "I, ah, have asthma, Imogene, remember? Can you please—?"

She pulled open the ashtray and wasted a cigarette. She put her head back and closed her eyes.

The reason she sat in the G-ride with a dopey G-man came from her uncontrollable anger that needed a vent way back when. Life at Chino did not resemble anything even close to life at 744 East Hawthorne Avenue. A true utopia in comparison.

She couldn't help it, she cried the first two weeks after lights out. During the day, she didn't want anyone to see her weakness. But everyone knew. She was a "weepy fish." She heard their rude whispers; they only made things worse.

After the second week her assigned cellie got parole, took her new tail, and skedaddled. In came Angie Belfour, the best thing that could've happened to Imogene. Well, the best thing under the given circumstances. Ange got her straightened out.

The first night after lights out, Imogene again started her weepy jag. Ange stood on her bottom bunk, with her face too close to Imogene's on the top. Sour breath, jailhouse spaghetti mixed with burnt Bugle Boy tobacco. *What the hell's the matter with you, girl?*

"Leave me alone."

*This your first jolt?*

"My what?"

*The first time in the can, the joint? The first time you found your ass trapped in a large concrete box with a bunch of smelly bitches?*

"Yes."

*Listen here. I gotta get my beauty sleep, or I'm cranky all day. Landin' here the first time, it's like...it's like grief. You have to go through the different stages. And this first stage that you can't seem to move past is makin' my ass ache. And I'm not kiddin'.*

*Look, you need a vent. Somehow you need to transfer this 'oh, poor me' regret to someone else, so you can move on.*

"How do I do that?"

*Blame someone else.*

"What are you talking about?"

*Come on, girl, all you gotta do is blame someone else for what happened. Blame 'em for how you got your happy ass dropped right in ta the middle of ugly town.*

What she said did sound like a good idea, like she actually might know what she was talking about.

"Who am I going to blame?"

*Damn, girl, you want me to do the blaming for you? You just gonna lay back and have your cellie do it all for you, huh? That your game?*

"No, I'm not pampered. I've always taken care of myself. Held up my end."

*"Who wronged you that a white bread middle-class bitch like yourself would end up in this den of bitches? That's who you blame. There's got to be someone.*

Imogene shook her head. "I kinda deserve what I got." She was already picking up the Chino vernacular.

*That's your problem right there, girl.* She started chuckling. *You're the only guilty bitch in the whole joint. Everyone else is innocent.*

"I don't think it's very funny. I'm in prison for twenty-five to life, and I'm sixty-three years old. I'm never getting out."

Ange moved in close, not laughing. Stuck her nose in Imogene's face. *Then move it up the line.*

"What?"

*Don't you 'What' me one more time or you won't live to regret it. I'm not kiddin', here. I don't need no, 'What,' bird in my cell. Blame the DA. Blame your PD. Hell, blame the President of these United States for all I care. Just get started on the blaming so we can move on.*

"Huh."

The next day, Imogene started writing God-awful letters to the President. The more she wrote about ugly ways she was going to kill him, dismember him, crush and burn him, the better she felt. After a couple of weeks, she'd stopped crying at night.

Even so, she chose to continue the therapy. She kept writing to the President, a guy she voted for and thought did a halfway decent job. At least for a man.

Later, when she got out, and met Eugene for the first time, she asked him how was she any different? There had to be hundreds, maybe even thousands of deranged folks who sent threatening letters to the President.

"Yes, but your threat assessment reached level gold, one level down from red. You put too much detail in your plans on how you were going to do it. Your threats weren't just general; you had all your plans covered right down to where you'd buy the pliers to pull out his fingernails and teeth. You had the different places you'd pick up the duct tape and other items. How you'd procure C-4 military-grade explosives. That one really put a scare in everyone. The military bases added one more security level to their explosive depots because of your letters. Your meticulously neat diagrams you drew and sent along. You wrote plausible ways in which you'd create a diversion to pull away part of his protection detail, distract them, leaving openings. Valid actionable opportunities."

She'd smiled and remembered all the good times she spent in the prison library reading murder mysteries that allowed her to write those fifteen-or-thirty-eight-page letters with so much detail. Ten years of doing nothing else. She now knew the law, how it worked. Knew things about guns and ammunition, about how to thwart cops and side-step physical evidence. Learned all about the previous attempts on the presidents, the successful ones, and the boners. She had it all down in her head. It gave her something to do. Something to ponder while time ticked on, sauntering by the front gate at Chino without slowing.

Since they already thought she was a murderer, why not play the part? So she continued to send the letters.

The warden tried to shut the letters down, but Ange had turned Imogene on to an underground organization that was happy to mail them. Through another inmate, she'd mail them to an outside person who then sent them on to the White House. She wasn't shy; she signed her name to all of them and even put down her return address, 744 East Hathorne Avenue. Putting the Chino address would've taken some of the fear out of the letters, taking the sharp edge off. What did it matter, she was old and was never getting out. What else could they do to her? Give her green watery Jell-O on Christmas day instead of the special treat, all-you-can-eat, instant tapioca pudding.

The government didn't want to violate her rights by picking her up and putting her in a holding cell each time the President came to town. Not when she hadn't committed a crime. So Eugene took her to lunch. It's America, after all.

The Magic Lamp manager came out the front and unlocked the doors.

Eugene leaned over too close, wagged his eyebrows, and shot her that crooked Groucho smile. "Soup's on."

# Chapter Six

The next day, she opened the front door to Dentco, turned, and looked around the parking lot and strip center. Most all the parking slots were empty. Odette should've been there waiting; she was late. Again. Imogene had no problem working the counter, sitting on the high stool, working the register. Watching for pilfering. Odette did all the stocking, working three days a week. Imogene's knees couldn't handle stocking. Her knee cartilage doing the crunch, rattle and roll loud enough to wake the dead.

George left four large bins in the back. He used a forklift to get them there from the warehouse at the other end of the strip center. The bin contents needed to be priced and brought out to the front or Higginbothom would throw a category five hissy fit. Not a fair assessment; he was just looking out for his business.

With the death of Suz' father and the presidential lunch, Imogene had lost track of The Cigar and what he'd threatened if Dentco didn't pay him the two hundred dollars come this Friday.

He'd firebomb the place, burn Dentco right down to scorched anchovy tins.

She didn't care so much about the fire or even the business, it was her job she worried about. She needed to stay gainfully employed to keep Nancy Do-right from violating her parole.

She really should tell Higginbothom about The Cigar, let him deal with the blackmail. Let him make the decision on what to do. Take it out of her bailiwick. But maybe she was better equipped to handle it. After all, she was a card-carrying graduate from the Women's Gladiator Academy at Chino.

She relocked the door and moved over to the Lotus Tea House and Massage Parlor—Madam Woo's Rub and Tug. She knocked on their glass door, painted over with black on the inside. The action at the Tea House didn't start until after twelve noon, the male population's lunch break, or when the slothful rose after a night of debauchery, ready to start again, trying too hard to die of dissipation.

An eye appeared in a spot on the door—the lower right—where the paint had been scraped away for that purpose. A lot like her black funeral garb with the moth hole. Both masked sex of sorts. The new and the old.

Passing muster as an acceptable visitor, the door rattled with keys on the other side. The door opened to Amy Chin, a pretty gal dressed in expensive satin pajamas with long black hair hanging down past her bottom. Only now, not so pretty.

Evidence of violence blared bright and loud, reflecting off her lovely but now despoiled countenance. Someone had *dotted the I,* as Ange would've put it, socked Amy up, but good. Her left eye was swollen red and welded shut with purple. She stepped aside to let Imogene enter. She acted as if her face didn't hurt and violence had not visited in the form of a fist-delivered airmail by a fat man who called himself The Cigar.

The rub and tug business tended to draw in the lower strata of humans, men looking for quick gratification. Some looking to satisfy an overwhelming need to dominate women, men too stupid to understand and control the deviate yearnings to have a normal relationship. So they sought out pay-as-you-go women. Women cornered in life and forced by societal rules did not report the crimes against their persons. Most of the time, they could wrangle the obstreperous, the wild bulls, manipulate them into a calmer pose. They simply blew warm, moist air in their ears, the same as a cowboy did when he bit a bronco's ear so the rider could mount.

But not for The Cigar. It didn't work for The Cigar.

Before Chino, Imogene had been unaware of this separate world not ten miles from 744 East Hawthorne. Had no idea women, out of sheer necessity, subjected themselves to this type of degradation. Sure, she'd read about it, was aware that it happened, but her mind automatically filed this information away as inert, unusable. Not real because it had nothing to do with her world. Most people did the same.

The tail Imogene sprouted when she left Chino, the tail that precluded her from rejoining her place in her old world and dumped her at Dentco, had opened her eyes to the truth. Shocking revelations that just kept coming at her in waves without end, sinking her deeper into that same mire of degradation, misery, and deprivation with no visible way out.

The sight of Amy's dotted I made Imogene want to get the gun under the Dentco counter and go looking for The Cigar. Shoot him right in his red, bloated nose. "Knock the wheels off his little red wagon," as Wayne would've said.

She followed behind Amy, through the interior reinforced security door, on into a long hall with doors on either side. The Rooms. And on back to the open door at the end that led out into the alley. Moving down the hall past the rooms, a lovely scent of lilac filled the air, masking a blatant despair permanently instilled in the walls.

In the alley, seven women of multiple nationalities sat on milk crates or folding chairs or squatted, smoking menthol cigarettes and joints. Scantily clad in silk boxers, tees, and robes. One cooked up breakfast on a long hibachi. The girls ate well, nice cuts of beef and fish and sautéed fresh vegetables.

These girls weren't eligible for workman's comp, social security, Medi-Cal, or retirement. Truly a disposable class. They lived out on the edge of their world, day to day, without a future. In Chino, at least, the inmates had medical and were partitioned off from the male gender, who sought to exploit them at every turn. Imogene felt sorry for herself over her stint in Chino until she went to work at Dentco.

Now, not so much.

"Well," Imogene said, "What are we gonna do about Giancana? We gonna to let him steamroll right over us?"

No one rolled over Imogene. No one.

Amy leaned against the brick wall. "So, he came to your place?"

"Yes, he wants two hundred dollars when he comes back next Friday, that's in three days. What's the damage for the Tea House? How much does he want?"

"A thousand-fifty, that's one-fifty each."

Imogene thought the cost would've been much higher with the amounts of cash that passed though the Tea House doors, through the fingers of the girls and into Clete's black briefcase.

"Did you tell Clete?"

Clete, short for Cletus, a tall thin black guy who made the tour of the three Lotus Tea House and Massage parlors in the Inland Empire. Made his rounds twice a week, picking up the cash receipts, toting them around in a black briefcase. He'd also hit two more in Orange County and one up in the high desert for a total of six. He always wore a black suit and tie with a white shirt. He made sure all the girls saw the .38 Smith and Wesson he kept in his waistband. As if the girls were the ones he needed to intimidate.

Then he'd take all the cash back to Pomona to the owner who worked out of an auto-body shop for cover. The bossman of the minor criminal enterprise.

Clete could've been too handsome to be a male. But a violent person cut him with a slash that angled down across his face. A wicked disfigurement. Even with the battle scar he looked docile as a cat. Instead of looking mean, he just looked defiled.

Imogene knew Clete's routine. She'd once followed him when he left Madam Woo's, followed him in her little innocuous AMC Gremlin. Ange had schooled Imogene on "scores," how to take them down. Imogene never intended to attempt such a thing. But she wanted the information just the same. She wanted to see if she could do it. She wanted to put to use this new-found knowledge gained from Chino-U. After all, she was a "murderer," and someone the President of these United States feared.

A president fearing a broken-down seventy-five-year-old woman with glass knees. The commander in chief with black helicopters, bazookas, B-1 bombers and black ops guys who could sneak into 744 East Hawthorne, cut her throat and sneak out, no one the wiser. Who would even care? Or notice?

In the back alley to the rub and tug, Amy looked down at the broken and rocky asphalt. "Clete just shrugged when I told him."

"He saw what that pig did to your face, and he just shrugged? Are you kidding me?"

Amy shifted her voice, tried to make it deeper like Clete's, and said, "It's the cost of doin' bitness, Baby Girl. I'm surprised it ain't happened sooner." Amy scratched her crotch and cleared her throat like Clete tended to do when nervous. "The bossman says that as long as the bite stays under fifteen hunnert, he'll let it go. Doesn't need the aggra-vation or the bad press it would take to stop it."

Amy returned to her normal voice. "He also said the bite comes out of our end. Said, 'Pay it, or deal with it your own selves, jus' keep the mayhem to a minimum.'"

Imogene shook her head. "What a bastard. From your *end*, that's one way or the other, right?"

Jenny, the only white girl in the group, said, "He ain't so bad. He's jus' doin' what he's told."

Jenny was sweet on Clete and Clete sweet on her.

To a point.

He apparently didn't care if some thug came in and strong-armed her, strong-armed all the girls.

Imogene said, "What about Ibrahim over to Cherry Liquor, did he get hit too?"

Louisa, a little Guatemalan girl who spoke in broken English was the only one who smoked the loss-leader unfiltered Camels from Cherry Liquor. She flicked her ash, scowled. "A thousand plus a case of vodka. The good kind with the blue lettering on the glass bottles. Ibrahim won't tell me what he pays wholesale, but retail those bottles cost a butt-load."

"I'll say it again: are we gonna to let this guy run us over?" Imogene didn't know why she said it. She was pushing seventy-five and crotchety with creaking joints. It was time for the rocker on the porch. A quilt over the legs. A crochet hook with a balled skein of yarn. And a sixer of malt liquor. Let the people who still care deal with this kind of tyranny.

But Ange had drilled into her, "We live in a land where a half-blind, one-eyed man is king. Now we just need to poke out his other eye." Ange had soured a little on men.

Imogene again looked at Amy's eye, how that pig had marred such a lovely girl who was only trying to get along in an already difficult life.

Amy smiled, trying not to sound condescending. It didn't work. She put her hand on Imogene's arm. "Don't do anything. Ours is a dangerous business. We'll pay him and be done with it."

Louisa said, "What we need to do is knife the fat bastard." She was the firebrand of the group. "My pussy's already going on strike, and now this."

"You want to eat?" Amy said to Imogene. "I'll get you a plate and a setup." She disappeared into the backdoor to the Tea House.

Louisa lowered her voice to a whisper. "A thousand-fifty and Amy's eye wasn't the only thing he took from her."

Jessica, the Black girl, said, "Don't. Louisa. Shut your mouth."

Imogene muttered, "Sweet baby Jesus."

* * *

Odette stood waiting for Imogene, standing at Dentco's front door, when Imogene came back around the front to open up. Odette was back on crank. Meth. The White Devil. She fidgeted and scratched. Imogene paused and stared at her. Odette broke down in tears and came into Imogene's arms, spoke into her chest as if her breast was a public address system. "I'm so sorry, Boss. I'm a weak person. I want to quit that evil crap. I do. It's hard. It's the hardest thing I've ever had to do."

Imogene would fire her, but that would only make things worse for poor Odette.

"No stealing," Imogene said. "You can eat from the bins, but you have to show me what you take so I can cover it. You understand? Higginbothom watches that theft/loss report like it's a matter of life and death. If he catches a discrepancy and you didn't tell me about it beforehand, I won't be able to cover for you. Not again. He won't allow any more theft from you."

"I understand, thank you, E."

Imogene unlocked the door. Odette bent over, picked up the mail that had been shoved through the slot in the door, and handed the sheaf to Imogene.

She took the load of envelopes, senseless ad-mailers, over to the counter. John-Tom ran from the back storeroom out the front door. Off to scout the warehouse for a fat rat that feasted on the Rice-A-Roni, the mac and cheese, and the chicken soup in the foil packets.

Inside Dentco, the air hung thick and a little rancid. What could you expect from dented cans and moldering dry goods? She took off her crocheted shawl and hung it up. She took a seat on the tall stool behind the counter and sorted the mail. Odette got to work.

The letters all belonged to Higginbothom or were useless business solicitations.

*All except one.*

Oh, dear Lord.

She'd used Dentco's address for her crazy, demented idea. Just in case Nancy Do-right did one of her spot checks at 744 East Hawthorne and checked her correspondence. Imogene even used a pen name to further muddy the water.

The return address came from *Delacorte Press, New York.*

*A letter to me from New York?*

*What do you think of that, Wayne? Huh?*

*A little girl from the Ozarks getting a letter from New York? Big doings, if I do say so myself. Calls for creamed corn with chicken and dumplings tonight, wouldn't you say?*

Her hands shook as she held it. Never in her life had she thought they would even give her the time of day. Not a broken-down old woman with a tail. She looked up and out the front window, checking for Nancy Do-right's light blue Dodge, or that fat pig, The Cigar.

Or even good ol' Mike Higginbothom.

She only cared if Higginbothom discovered the contents: a rejection for sure. She couldn't deal with one more thimbleful of humiliation. And sure as God made little green apples, it had to be a short note, a horrid little rejection asking Imogene to *"Please learn how to write before resubmitting."*

She shoved the letter under the open box displaying the Big Hunks that The Cigar had swept off the counter a few nights before. Shoved it under there to keep the letter close at hand. She tried not to look at it, tried to let her eyes follow Odette around as she stocked from a basket she brought from the back. A long brown Slim Jim hung from her mouth, disappearing an inch at a time as she chewed. Chewed and stocked Jolly Green Giant corn niblets, chewed and stocked half-mashed boxes of mac and cheese. Chewed that stale Slim Jim she'd pilfered and had yet to declare to Imogene.

Odette was no bigger than a minute. Wayne would've said, "That girl turns sideways, she'll disappear." She wore tired dungarees that needed washing and a sunny yellow blouse with colorful flowers in a vase embroidered on the front. Her shoes…her shoes…dear lord, looked brand new. If Odette was back to chasin' the dragon, how could she afford new shoes? She couldn't. She'd stolen them. She was farther gone than Imogene imagined. And she had been clean for three months, a lifetime for an addict.

She'd have to keep a close eye on the cash register. She could trust Odette implicitly. She just couldn't trust that dern ol' dragon who was now on Odette's back clawing at her throat.

Imogene again sneaked a quick glance at the Big Hunk box. The Delacorte letter was calling to her. But she knew, once opened, the excitement of the unknown—the possibilities filled with hope and desire—would dissipate in a puff of thin air. And if she'd learned anything from her extended vacation in Chino, it was a girl couldn't live without hope.

This letter represented a crap-pot full of hope.

Only a fool would open it, risking so much. At least that's what her inner voice kept telling her. If she played strictly by that rule, the envelope contents would never see the light of day. From that moment forward, it would sit in a place of reverence where it could be viewed daily. Project the hope like a lighthouse beacon.

What price tag could a person even put on that kinda hope?

Hope as a belief was one area where Imogene and Ange parted ways.

According to Ange, "Hope is for suckers. If you have hope in one hand and a steaming lump of crap in the other, which one you think'll start smelling first? Stinkin' up the whole room, the whole cell block. I'm here to tell ya. It's the stink test, Imogene, you damn fool. How many times I have to tell ya. Every time you have any kinda question, you give it the ol' stink test."

Well, Imogene gave The Cigar the stink test, and it came back rancid. She grabbed the .38 from under the counter and headed to the back room. Precept number three in Ange's criminal checklist; always, *always* test your gear. Imogene had that list permanently etched in her brain. A crook's ten commandments to caper by.

She picked up two thick phone books, old ones stacked waist-high against the one wall in the back room. Higginbothom loved all books, collected them, and couldn't even part with the dern phone books. She set them up on a rolling desk chair and rolled it to the far side of the room. She came back and raised the pistol that shook in her hand, as if alive with spirits long dead. People killed by the little hole at the end of the barrel that belched flame and lead and separated the human husk from the soul.

Sure, she'd fired rifles and shotguns. Had to learn how, living adjacent to citrus groves most of her adult life. Wayne kept guns handy for snakes, hobos, and the like. Not that she'd ever shot a hobo. Had to brandish a 12-gauge twice when the bums refused to scat after she'd fed them a hotdog sandwich with plenty of mayo and a vanilla malt with a sprinkle of nutmeg on top.

Imogene turned to look and caught Odette standing in the doorway watching with a weird sort of look in her eyes. Excitement maybe. Eagerness.

No, it was more than that; it was an evil glint. Odette liked the power of the gun, the way it tamed the world that stood before it, cowering. Ange used to say, *The thing about death is that it's contagious. Don't go anywhere near it unless you got the cure.*

"You gonna shoot that in here?" asked Odette.

"Check the front door. Is anyone in the store or coming in? I gotta see if this thing works."

Odette checked. "It's all clear." She licked her lips, her eyes wet with excitement.

Sweet Jesus, the things you found out about a person when you picked up a black piece of steel that made weak men beg, and bold men die.

Imogene turned back to aim at the books and pulled the hammer back. In her head, Ange walked her through how to fire it without *jerkin' the sight picture off target.* Imogene took a breath and began to slowly squeeze the trigger.

The gun barked and jumped in her hand. Simultaneously Odette let out a little squeak, put her hand to her chest. "Oh, my."

The girl dern near had an orgasm.

Imogene walked across the room to the phone books. She'd hit exactly what she'd been aiming at. Confirmation she could shoot a pistol.

But according to Ange, "Shootin' a swingin' dick is far different than shootin' cans. Believe it. When the time comes, don't think twice about it. You think about it; he'll take the gat from you and stick it right up your ass. Or other places more painful. When you yank your gat, you keep pullin' the trigger till that bastard is barking in hell."

This was one of Ange's more colorful descriptions that again described her total lack of love for the male gender. She more than once espoused that nicotine, heroin, and even rock cocaine were evil drugs, but testosterone was the devil's redheaded stepchild. Get rid of that hormone, and the world would be a peaceful place. There would no longer be a need for guns or war.

"Come on, Imogene, let me give it a go, please? Can I, please?" Odette licked her lips again and again, her eyes wild with excitement.

Imogene held the gun out to her. "Once. That's it. You swear?"

"Yeah, yeah. I understand." She took the pistol. Her hand left a sweat streak across Imogene's palm and fingers.

Odette had had some training as well. She immediately spread her legs in a shooter's stance, turned, lined up on the phone books, and fired. She missed, totally. Hit the drywall to the side of the chair, leaving a little black hole difficult to discern from a distance. She looked over her shoulder at Imogene and cackled.

Just as Imogene realized, oh, sweet baby Jesus, the other side of the wall belongs to the Lotus Tea House and Massage Parlor.

No. No. Noooo.

Someone over there pounded on the wall.

Odette turned, the wild look in her eyes now magnified to that of a crazed person who'd just outrun the men in the white jackets swinging the butterfly nets.

Dear Lord, what if Odette hit someone on the other side?

The poor girl.

Someone grievously injured all because Imogene had wanted to test fire a gun. Indoors of all places.

What a fool she'd been for handing the gun to Odette. A tweaker. Thinking it out loud now sounded even worse.

Just that quick, the squeezing of a trigger—by someone else this time—had changed Imogene's life. The world around her downshifted, grinding the gears, as the event drove her right over the cliff.

The police would be called. Nancy Do-right would find out and cackle like Odette had when she fired the gun. Nancy would put the cuffs on Imogene, shove a one-way ticket to Chino in her pocket and kick her in the ass getting on the corrections bus. While she half-sang, "Another one bites the dust."

Sweat broke out on Imogene's brow and ran into her eyes, stinging, as the moment stretched out long and gooey like pink saltwater taffy on a candy-stretcher.

# Chapter Seven

In the backroom of Dentco, white smoke rose in an even fog bank toward the ceiling.

Bam. Just like that, life had shifted yet again. Driving Imogene—also known to her friend Ange as Miss Bea—driving her back full speed deep into a life Imogene tried her best to shake loose and escape.

Reality kicked back in. Time grabbed hold and now shifted into high gear.

Odette cackled again, turned back. The gun in her hands solid as a rock.

Odette fired.

She shot the screen to the old console TV that let loose a little glass/mechanical fart, a kind of huff as if finally released from a life of servitude. She shot the big school clock on the wall. Hit it in the pie-wedge center of three-fifteen, stopping time. The exact time school used to let out when Imogene was a young girl.

The clock swayed from side to side, angry, threatening to fall to the floor. Odette raised the gun and shot the fluorescent light that crackled and sparked, one side going dark. Broken glass fell to the floor.

She swung the gun around—

And pointed it at Imogene.

Dead on.

Pointed right at her face.

Some say, once confronted with one's own death, life will pass in the mind's eye at the speed of light.

That's not what happened in this case.

Imogene checked herself and realized she was not at all afraid, not one wit. She'd somehow subconsciously made her peace with this world. Just let it go; it no longer mattered. Maybe it happened when…when Wayne had passed on. Left her holding the dirty bag of life. Left her to live, to survive all by herself. Not fair at all, Wayne. Not fair.

Imogene slowly let a smile creep across her face as more women on the other side of the wall that separated Dentco from The Lotus Tea House and Massage banged hard with hands and hard objects. A staccato noise, a muted echo that squeezed passed the ringing in Imogene's ears from all the gunfire.

Odette's wild-eyed expression shifted to scared, then to a weird smile that imitated Imogene's. Odette swung the gun around and fired the last bullet into the two-gallon tin can of *Goldens Boston Baked Beans* sitting on the floor by the couch. Higginbothom had been saving that can for his family picnic next July. George, Dentco's driver, had never before gotten that large a can of baked beans, and Higgy-baby was as proud as a new father. He wanted to show it off to his family as if he had a wife who birthed a kid. As if a wife could crap out a can that size.

Silence rolled over the both of them.

The pounding finally stopped.

Seconds later, the bell on Dentco's front door jingled. In came seven frantic women running to find out what had happened in the back room. Of course, they could only assume The Cigar had returned and, after a verbal argument, shot it out with the bullheaded and crotchety Imogene Taylor. Miss Bea.

The seven Lotus Tea House women crammed into the threshold from the front to the back, afraid to venture any further. They looked in awe at the gun smoke, the damaged TV screen, the shot-to-hell clock, and the Boston baked bean juice that glooped out onto the floor into a glistening brown puddle.

The gun continued to click as Odette pulled the trigger again and again.

The entire scene—or maybe it was that all the girls from next door were unharmed— somehow tickled Imogene's fancy. She started to laugh.

Odette caught the mirth virus and followed suit. Soon, all the women in the doorway laughed along. Laughed until they burned out, turned, and left, one at a time, without obtaining a logical explanation. Accepted the visual facts as presented. As if Imogene had always used her back room for a shooting gallery.

Imogene took the gun from Odette without a word, carried it to the front counter. She reloaded it and took her seat on the stool. She put the gun back on the shelf, confident now that she'd fulfilled Ange's third commandment. Odette cleaned up the Boston Baked bean juice and returned to stocking the bins out front. Everything back to normal as if nothing happened.

An hour later in walked Micheal Higginbothom, the Dentco dented food magnate. Right off, he put his nose in the air, sniffing. "What's that smell? Imogene? You're not cooking something in the back, are you? That's acrid smoke. Code enforcement walks in I'll get a big fat ticket."

Imogene said nothing, her eyes locked on the Big Hunk box, the one with the letter from Delacorte, the one that held behind its thin paper flaps the sum of all hope in Imogene's world.

Higginbothom walked on by and grunted over, not getting an answer to his inquiry.

She took her eyes off the Big Hunk box and watched him disappear into the backroom. She counted to herself, waiting for the tsunami to hit.

One Mississippi. Two Miss—

The yell could've been heard down to the Hole-in-One donut shop, waking Jimmy Wo-Fingers Wade, the donut fryer, out of a dead slumber. "Imogene Taylor, get your butt in here. Now."

Imogene slid off her tall stool and strolled into the back room. Odette fled out the front door to parts unknown, abandoning two hours left on her shift.

Coward.

Higginbothom stood, one hand on his hip, the other pointing at his television, the one with the exploded screen. He liked to sit on the couch in the backroom and watch ancient reruns of Sheriff John's Cartoon Time on Nickelodeon. He couldn't watch it at the Bloomington Dentco store. He didn't want Suz to find out. See him as some kinda weak sister.

"What?" Imogene said, trying to blend heavy exasperation into her tone for being summoned from her post, leaving no one left to protect the store.

"Look! Can't you see it? The TV, it's ruined. The screen's blown up."

She looked up at him, her eyes blinking more than normal. Suz said it was how she got him to do whatever she wanted.

"Well, what happened?" he asked.

The blinking thing wasn't working for Imogene. "What happened about what?"

"The television. *The television.* Look!"

"What? Boss, that happened a couple of days ago."

"What happened a couple of days ago, Imogene? Answer me straight and quit with the dodge. You're starting to test my—"

"Atmospheric conditions."

"What?"

*"Now see, you're doing it, too. Saying, 'what,' all the time. I think the 'what.' bird has—"*

"Imogene, explain."

"I've told you a hundred times that leaving the air conditioning off to save a few pennies would cause problems. The afternoon sun out there hits that front window and acts the same as a giant magnifying glass, burning up red ants on the sidewalk. It's cool back here all day until about three in the afternoon. Then bam with the help from that front window—the magnifying glass—it jumps in temperature all at once. That sudden swing can cause a violent shift in the atmosphere, and voila. It ruined your precious television. I tried to warn you about not using the air conditioner. You really can't blame this on me."

She again blinked through the thick prescription of her cat-eye glasses.

She'd pulled that little tidbit of propaganda outta the left side of her ass, as Ange would've said.

In the day room at Chino, Imogene had overheard a couple inmates playing Go Fish as they spouted one inanity after another in a verbal game of one upmanship. One of which was an excuse used in front of a judge: how a jewelry store window imploded all on its own while the jewel thief (the inmate) stood next to it. The jewelry of course then fell out the window onto the sidewalk, easily dropping into the finders keepers realm. The judge didn't believe her. No way did Imogene think repeating a portion of that story would work, especially not with someone of Higginbothom's intelligence. After all he did own two businesses, both "going concerns," according to him.

He opened his mouth to rant and closed it. He looked from Imogene to the television. "Ah, ta hell with it." He turned and fled.

His luncheon with Sheriff John's Cartoon Time now ruined, beyond repair.

Higginbothom never came back that day, and neither did Odette.

Quitting time.

Imogene locked the meager daily receipts in the floor safe, set the alarm, and headed home.

When she turned onto Hawthorne from Campus Avenue, Bernard Lowery had just pulled into his driveway, home late from work. He got out and stood by his open car door. Her heart pitter-pattered, an emotional effect she never really believed in until it happened to her. But what the heart wants, the heart wants.

Not since Wayne, anyway.

Imogene leaned over and waved. She honked when ol' Bernie didn't see the wave. He crouched down a little as if to see who might be driving the little red AMC Gremlin. The big goof. Who did he think was driving?

She made a quick turn into her driveway right next door, one house to the east. That's when he recognized the car and shot her that wonderful lazy smile. He waved. Imogene got out and hurried over to him, the letter from Delacorte in her clutch purse. As she crossed her lush grass yard headed his way, she fought the urge to show him the letter, explain the wonderful hope it contained. Hope bright enough to make her purse glow warm. Pure imagination. Paper can't heat up all on its own.

But he wouldn't understand. And he'd, of course, ask the insipid little question why she didn't open it.

Her answer: "I never plan to open it."

He'd look at her aghast, as if she were from an alien planet.

Leaving her no option but to keep the letter a secret. To keep the hope alive and well.

"Hello, Bernie, how are you doing?" He stood with his back ramrod straight wearing his standard khaki pants and long-sleeved baby blue shirt that brought out the blue in his eyes. He kept his balding head covered with a dark gray porkpie hat that he couldn't really pull off, not stylistically. He looked more like an accountant trying to look like Popeye Doyle from *The French Connection*.

"Hmm, ah yes, hello, Mrs. Taylor. I thought I should tell you a large Black woman came over last night and was making inquiries about you. She was rude and quite indignant."

She reveled in his speech, his vocabulary, so articulate and refined.

"Whoever could that be?" she said. "I mean, I don't know why anyone would be asking for me." She wanted so badly to once again live in the other life and not in the one thrust upon her by an overly insensitive and callous judicial system that liked nothing better than to cast aside women from society's lower socioeconomic neighborhoods. Toss them in prison.

But she knew the who and the why. Dern that Nancy Do-right. She hadn't liked the way Imogene had treated her the other night in Dentco. The way Higginbothom didn't play her silly game and told her that he already knew about Imogene's disgraceful tail. Now Nancy wanted to spread her poison throughout the neighborhood, as if everyone didn't already know Imogene now carried the shameful moniker: *ex-con*.

For cripes sake, she'd been gone and in prison for ten years. The neighbors all watched the way Bernie kept up her yard, trimmed her privet hedge, watered, and cared for Wayne's temperamental dichondra patch next to the lee side of the front porch where the sun rarely kissed.

The first day Imogene got out of Chino before she even went into the house at 744 East Hawthorne, she kicked off her black orthopedic shoes, sat on the porch edge, and ran her toes through that wonderful dichondra. Soft and cool to the touch, releasing wonderful memories of Wayne, his long, lanky self, replete with cherry tobacco scents.

Bernie had this thing he did with his eyes; he could smile with them. He did it again once he'd revealed what had been bothering him in regard to

Nancy making her inquiries. Imogene let out a little gasp and put her hand up to her chest as her face flushed hot. She was nothing but a silly ol' hen. Delusional with desires too far out of bounds to attain.

Bernie reached out and gently touched her hand as his eyes continued to delve deeper into that desire, her need to go further with this man. Taunting her to break through her stunned silence and say something of merit. Tell him that he didn't have to go so far for love when he sneaked out on Wednesday and Friday nights. Love resided no further than her front door. Her body shook off a shiver at the thought.

He'd recently turned seventy, five years younger than her. Once a man and woman passed sixty, five-year increments meant nothing.

He finally spoke, breaking her trance. "You want to come in for some Hydrox cookies and milk?"

Seriously? After the moment they just had, he wants cookies and milk, for cripes sake? Ange had said, *All good men need to be prodded. You can lead 'em to water, but you have to bonk 'em on the head to make 'em eat.*

Imogene wasn't entirely sure what Ange meant by her mixed metaphor, but it seemed to sort of fit the situation unfolding on Imogene's front lawn. In fact, they now stood not ten feet from her bedroom window. The irony.

Another chill caused a shiver to run up and down her legs and back.

She didn't want to go into his house, not with Dot in the chair in the front room. Once the in-house nurse left for the night, Bernie would be tasked with his wife's care. Dot would sit there staring at Imogene with those dead eyes. Dot would ruin the moment, in fact, blow it all to hell and gone.

"Why don't you come over to my place instead? I have homemade pecan pie and whipped cream." Beat the hell outta store-bought Hydrox any day of the week.

His eyes still on hers he wrapped two fingers around two of hers, holding on, not letting go. He'd only done that six other times in the past two years since she'd been out. This was definitely a Dear Diary moment. More manuscript. She'd included a character in her book who looked and talked just like Bernie. The character helped the protagonist in the plot to assassinate an out-of-control President hellbent on flying the country right into the ground.

"I have to relieve the day nurse," Bernie said. "I'm already late. Come on, come have some Hydrox with me. We can talk. Please?"

Imogene was torn. In her heart she knew his invitation went beyond those dern Oreo cookies he tried so hard to up-sale. He had something else in mind, something she wanted as well. She yearned to be held in an intimate way. Something more than a friend's hug.

Just not in the same house as Bernie's wife. Lordy.

No, she couldn't do that to the woman. That was one step too far and would fling her the rest of the way into the moral abyss.

Never to climb out.

Even though Dot would have no knowledge of what was happening. According to Ange—Imogene had told Ange all about the situation—Dot was nothing more than *a warm tater—no sour cream and chives—sittin' on that dumb ol' couch.*

Rude, on so many levels.

"I'm sorry, I just can't."

His eyes shifted from adventurous to sad. Then pleading.

How did he do that?

She willed her fingers to disengage from his. They wouldn't obey. He stood close a moment longer until his eyes let go of hers.

The same as if some kind of science fiction tractor beam had shut off. She was once again free of his unworldly influence. Her feet moved all on their own, backing away. With each step, guilt over what she had almost done, the mere thought of it, was like a kick in the gut by Bessie, the old gray mare.

He smiled one last time, tipped his porkpie, turned, and headed into his house to tend to his wife, the tatter on the couch.

The spell broken, she could think clearly again. Why, when around that lothario, did she always act like a silly schoolgirl with her first crush? He had Delores on the next block, his Wednesday and Friday. What did he want with Imogene? Did he want her for his Tuesday and Thursday?

She always experienced disgust right after an encounter with him, green vile disgust, until it gradually, over several hours, began to fade. Once at the halfway point, desire and lust again took the baton, running slowly at first, then hitting an all-out sprint for the finish line. Until she could barely stand it.

She hadn't hit that *particular* finish line in more than ten years and wondered if she even remembered how. Bernie wasn't no Schwinn.

At least she hadn't with another person, anyway. A few times Ange had politely solicited Imogene's physical affections, said it was simply a "When in Rome" situation. Imogene told her she hadn't lost anything in Italy and that she had no desire whatever to go in that direction.

Imogene turned and headed into the house, disgust morphing into anger. Why did she let herself in for such an emotional rollercoaster ride? In the throes of anger that gripped her, the voice of Ange in her head suggested, *You don't like it, why not lure your precious Bernie over some night? Tell him to climb in that side window to your boudoir. Tell him you got some of the sweetest cherry pie he'll 'ver eat. Then cap his sorry ass. He's the devil, Imogene, trying to make you another notch on his headboard. Wants you to take up his lothario slack for two days of the week. I say do him in and come back to Chino wit me.*

But was he really? What if he really just wanted to share his Hydrox. Enjoy a nice neighborly conversation. And did not have dark and lascivious intent toward her body?

She had not played the boy-girl game since before Wayne had turned her head that night five decades ago. Sat on the hood of his first beat-up old Studebaker truck, parked skewed on the dirt road in front of the diner, strumming his banjo to beat the band. The blue tick hound Lulu, in the bed of an adjoining truck, howling over the bleating screech he took for music.

She could easily be imagining Bernie's kind gestures as flirtations. If she told Suz, her neighbor on the other side, she'd have an opposite view than Ange. She'd say, "You're just in love with him because of loyalty. You've mistaken loyalty for love. That's so easy to do. He took care of all your affairs while you were…away. He is loyal to a fault to his wife, Dot. Loyalty can be a huge aphrodisiac. It's loyalty, E, that you've mistaken for love. You have to walk away from it; he's married."

She had not told Suz about Delores over on Campus Avenue. Hadn't told her about the Wednesday and Friday rendezvous. That little tidbit would sour her on Bernie in a big hurry.

Could Imogene even fault Bernie for his Wednesdays and Fridays? After all, he was a man with normal male urges, no different from Imogene with hers.

Imogene stepped up onto her porch, stuck the key in the lock.

"Imogene?"

Suz came walking over across Imogene's driveway in front of the Gremlin, stopped at the porch, and looked up at her.

"Can I talk to you for a minute? I don't wanna be a bother if you're busy?"

"Sure, come on in. I have some fresh pecan pie and whipped cream."

# Chapter Eight

Imogene sat on the divan smoking a Marlboro and sipping a large mug of black coffee. Suz sat in Wayne's easy chair with an untouched plate of pecan pie in her lap, the whipped cream melting, returning to white liquid.

Imogene had turned Suz down flat. Suz kept on, though, doing everything short of getting down on her knees to beg. It wasn't Imogene's fault Suz let slip about the mess her recently deceased father left behind in his garage. Imogene had said she would help, but that was before Higginbothom nosed in, sniffing around the love of his life. Nothing against Higginbothom, but she caught a large enough dose of him at Dentco. Apparently, so had Suz.

Out the front picture window on the street appeared one of the two Dentco big box trucks driven by Higgy-baby. He ground the gears, pulled forward, and backed into Suz' driveway, not two feet from the side of Gremlin. Suz let squeak, "Oh my God. Imogene, what am I gonna do?"

The old Imogene would've offered some back-home bromide that fit the situation, something with blue tick hounds or how fresh churned butter wouldn't melt in Suz' mouth. But since her stay at Chino, none of those came even close to being real.

Suz juggled her pie plate and did a snake-slither out of the easy chair, staying out of view of the picture window. She lay flat on the gold high-low carpet, now twenty-plus years old.

Love made people stupid.

"Oh, for Pete's sake." Imogene struggled up out of the divan, her legs barely doing the job. Age, chicken dumplings, and malt liquor had crept up on her quietly like a bobcat on a hare. She stomped over to the big wooden front door, opened it, and stepped out on the concrete porch. "Micheal?"

He stepped out of the truck cab, shock plain on his mug. He'd been so wrapped up in becoming Suz' knight in shining armor he'd forgotten Imogene lived next door.

"Imogene?"

"That's me. Now get that gotdamn eyesore outta my front yard before I call the cops on ya."

"But Imogene, this isn't your drive, it's—"

She used her middle finger and thumb to flick her lit Marlboro his way, the white cylinder leaving a smoking arc in his direction. "I'm callin' right now. They'll tow that bad boy in a hot second. Can you afford a two-hundred-dollar tow bill?" Of course, he could afford it; he still had the first dime his mother gave him for lunch money, foregoing food to add funds to his already bloated piggy bank.

He waved his hand in the air, "Okay, okay, I'm going. Don't get your big panties in a wad."

Then, all of a sudden, he decided to stay. He raised his chin in defiance, maybe realizing that his lovely maiden could easily be in her home window watching him turn tail and flee over a simple verbal threat. He'd stay and challenge the bluff of law enforcement intervention.

"Big panties? I'll show you big panties, you little pipsqueak." She stepped down off the porch, tromped through Wayne's dichondra, and turned on the hose spigot buried deep in the gardenia branches. She grabbed the high-pressure nozzle and hurried toward Higginbothom, depressing the handle. The stream searched out its target like a spotlight in a dark sky. Higginbothom didn't move fast enough. The water found its belligerent target. He yelled as he tried to remount his Dentco box truck, "You're fired, Imogene. I swear to God you're fired for real this time." He got in and slammed his door. Water spray continued to hit the window. Through the blur, he stuck his face close to the glass. Water had mussed his perfectly coiffed hairdo. Cheap hair dye ran in his eyes. He was fit to be tied. Maybe he really meant it this time, and she no longer had a job. That would mean a long stint back in Chino. Over what? Rescuing a neighbor caught up in a predicament, Imogene had no business getting involved in the first place. Poor choices were what landed her in the joint.

Imogene kept the spray on his truck as he started up and drove away. She turned the water off and noticed, in her haste, she'd dug a divot in Wayne's dichondra. She smoothed it over with her foot, turning angry all over again. She looked down the street to see if the Dentco truck had turned around, if so she'd hurry inside the house and grab her ball bat behind the door. "Big panties, my achin' ass."

Down the block at Campus Avenue, the truck turned south. He wasn't coming back.

Imogene trundled up the two steps to the concrete porch, out of breath from the encounter. Women of a certain age weren't supposed to be using water hoses to scare off white knights.

Inside, Suz had gotten up off the floor and hugged her. A second too long for Imogene's liking. She hoped Suz wasn't from Rome like Ange.

Suz stepped back but didn't let go of her hands. "Now come on, let's go sort out some of that crapola in my garage."

"What?"

Suz put on that pouty bottom lip that worked slicker 'n snot on Higgy-baby, but not on this old gal, no sir.

"E, you promised to help me, remember? That's how you dodged the funeral so you could go to lunch with your cousin from Arkansas."

"Boston. That dumbass is from Boston. All right, let's get this over with."

"Thank you, E."

She'd told Suz a dozen times her name wasn't E, but did that matter? Just what she wanted to do, sift through old man crap. A lifetime of someone else's memories that only meant something to him. Maybe she should call Higginbothom back, load up his truck, and take it to the dump, sight unseen. That's the only option that truly made sense.

She followed Suz out the front door, back out onto the porch. Suz stopped. "Aren't you going to lock your door?"

"Why?"

"Seriously?

Imogene stared at her like The Cigar had stared at Imogene.

Suz finally shrugged. "Okay." She stepped to the edge of the porch and peeked around the corner toward Campus Avenue. Imogene walked by her and down the two steps, taking hold of her hand as she passed. "Come on, little girl, let's get this over with."

Suz said, "Okay, take it easy. Slow it down just a tad, would ya?"

But she came along anyway.

Suz's driveway mirrored Imogene's. The backyard sat much lower than the house. They walked down the steep drive toward the detached garage. Imogene held onto Suz's hand, not for the comfort of a human touch. For that, too. But more to keep from falling on her big panties keister.

Suz opened the garage door to a bleak darkness and disappeared into the gloom. The naked light bulb hanging from the ceiling crossbeam came on and swung back and forth, casting eerie shadows over the six-foot-tall pyramid of cardboard boxes, old wooden crates, and other crapola. She was right, it did look a little like Egypt—or was it Machu Picchu she'd said?

Despair crept on Imogene with insidious intent. She dealt all day with food discarded by the well-off. She sorted and sold it to the less fortunate. She absolutely didn't need to come home and deal with someone else's discarded junk. To sort it and sell it to folks even further down on the socioeconomic scale. The thought of the massive chore took her emotions one step closer to that edge she tried so hard to stay away from. The edge, where if she just took one step closer, she'd fall forever into a permanent blackness thick enough to drown in.

To take that step, all she needed to do was say screw it and go shoot someone like The Cigar. Do something to better the world. Make a sacrifice. One that would return her to the security of Chino, to CIW where she'd never have to make another decision. Right, wrong, or indifferent.

And if, while in Chino, she couldn't take it there anymore, the world coming down on her in a similar soul-crushing fashion, Ange might again grab that opportunity to crawl up in the top bunk and spoon with her the same as Wayne used to. He never hesitated back when the cold froze their lemon grove or the sun scorched the avocado trees. He'd whisper words she couldn't help but believe, "Everything will be all right, and nothing else matters but us. Right, Imogene?"

Nothing, except time that encompassed that day, that hour, that minute—CIW time. There, you had to live in the minute or eventually lose your mind. There, you hear the ticking in your head as the second hand circumnavigates the clock face. Again and again.

That time, never to be retrieved. Lost forever.

Unlike in the real world outside Chino's walls, out in the vast open freedom, where time shape-shifted and all but turned invisible. That was a different kind of time, one folks took for granted. Folks who didn't understand the breadth, the width…the darkness of time. As if those folks' number would never be called by the Grim Reaper. Some who were forever standing in the wings, waiting for those with their dopey grins and their glorious ignorance.

Imogene sat and slid over the closest crate of books: the Encyclopedia Britannica. The A's thru M's. Dust rose, infected her nose, made her sneeze. She got up, dragged the box out into the driveway, came back and again sat.

"Bless you, E."

Imogene raised her hand and waved, reached into the next box. Her hand came out with five magazines: *National Geographics*. She put them back and slid the box closer to the door with the other one. "You're going to run these boxes up to the top of the driveway. Then you're going to put up a sign that says, "Free.""

Suz stopped, her eyes searching Imogene's.

Imogene said, "What? You wanna keep all these old magazines?"

"Ah, well, no, I guess not."

"Do you want to put them in your car and make a thousand trips to the dump?"

"Okay, I get the idea. You're right. I guess I just have to get used to the idea of breaking away from…getting rid of…" She choked up. Tears filled her eyes.

"Oh, for Pete's sake, girl."

Suz daubed at her eyes. "Of course you're right, that's a good plan. Go ahead and take that box up, and I'll make the sign like you said."

Imogene shot her a crooked grin, "Baby Doll, these old knees barely made it down that slope hauling this old body. This part has to be on you. I'm sorry, I wish I were younger."

"No, you're right. I got it. I need the exercise. But I'd rather not do it piecemeal. Let's get a big bunch separated before I take them up."

"Suit yourself." She pulled another box over closer, labeled like the last one, "Educational Mags." She opened it to double-check and found it filled with old Playboy magazines. She shoved that one over toward the National Geographics.

Suz picked up two bundles of newspapers tied with twine, carried them out, and set 'em on the crumpling asphalt driveway. "Do you really think people will come and take all this crapola?"

"Not if it's sitting there by its lonesome. But once you put up that "Free" sign, it'll trigger this weird need in the human brain. There are some folks who just can't walk away from anything that's free. You wait and see if I'm not right."

"But even back here, in this out-of-the-way neighborhood?"

"Along with that weird part of the brain, that latent need to collect useless crapola, the word goes out telling others with the same disease. Because that's what it is, an illness. Look at all this crap your dad collected. He was one of 'em. Go ahead, put up the free sign, and see what happens."

Imogene worked at sorting, moving her seat closer to the pyramid as she ate away at the base, eroding the mountain base. Suz did the same, but on the other side. She said, "E, you mind if I ask you a question?"

"Only if you quit calling me E."

"Oh, now you're just being silly. But really, please?

"I guess I'm a captive audience and don't have a choice. Fire away with your inanity."

"Okay, this question is strictly girl to girl." She paused.

Imogene waited, curious to hear. She was sure it would have something to do with Imogene's ugly tail. How she came to have it? What it felt like to have one whipping around behind her, devastating all in its path. Clearing away the real world and keeping her firmly anchored in the one she'd come to abhor.

"How do you know if you're in love?"

"Ah, for cripes sake, girl. You're kidding me, right?"

"I don't think I am. No. I'm sure I'm not. I don't think I've ever been in love before. At least, not that I know of. I mean, I've really liked someone to the point of thinking about him all the time. Is that what love is?"

"If you love someone, you know it. It has to work that way, or there wouldn't be any procreation. Love is pure nature. Cupid fires that dern arrow right into your ass, and you can't pull it out even if you wanted to. Most of the time, you don't want to."

Imogene wished she could reach back and pull out the one in her own Big Panties ass. The one with Bernie's name on it. Break it in half, bust the spell, and good riddance.

Imogene shook her head. "Love is something you have no control over. You fall into it face first. You're walking along, minding your own business, trip, fall, and bam. You go face-first into a big pile of steaming horse apples. Only in this case, you come up with this huge smile on your face and you can't explain why. And you don't care at all about the horrible smell. That's the best description of love I can think of."

How the hell had she gotten into such a silly conversation? It was the first time she'd ever thought about love that way, and it really set her back on her heels. Brought back that dreadful ache in her chest over the loss of Wayne. All over the stupid desire for Bernie.

From the other side of the Machu Picchu pile, Suz said, "I read somewhere that eagles mate for life. You think that's true?"

Suz had somehow read Imogene's thoughts about Wayne, how she would never forget him. Never fall out of love with him.

Never.

A lump rose in her throat. She couldn't answer that bullshit question about the eagles. She could only sit there still as a post as memories of Wayne flashed past in her mind's eye.

Suz went silent, not moving any boxes. Then: "E, would you mind telling me how you met your husband?  I met him twelve or thirteen years ago when I was only ten.  I can easily see how you could love someone like that, unconditionally, I mean. Tall, handsome, with those large hands. And tan. My goodness. How did he get so tan?  I used to come over to your garage. He let me watch him make those full-size soap box derby cars for the neighborhood boys to drive up and down the sidewalks. The time and love he spent working on those cars was amazing to watch. The best thing, though, was that he'd talk to me like I was an adult. He'd answer any question I had about anything, no matter how silly. Sometimes, I think if he didn't know the answer, he'd just make it up. Please tell me, E, I need to know how you two met."

Imogene had already slipped back into that long-lost memory, the one she'd tried so hard to suppress after the court trial. She had to forget about him just to survive in CIW. But now she gave herself to the remembrance, let the smells, the lighting, the events play back like an old color movie. She started talking, the words carrying no meaning to her as she traveled on the back of that memory to a lovelier time.

# Chapter Nine

A lice Louise Putnam had the world by the tail. Until her beau TK—Ted Fredrickson—left her over money. The lack of. She found out quickly how love stood tall on the foundation of cash. Without it, love sank slowly, choked, and drowned in a quagmire of penury and greed.

The five J and J Department Stores in Arkansas, owned solely by her father, failed under the smothering weight of too many mail-order catalogues and their cheap prices. Their ten-cent bars of lilac soap, two-dollar Iver Johnson pistols, three-dollar girdles, and their complete kits to build a house priced for a song. How could a store with any kind of overhead compete?

Alice's dad shot himself in the head on a fine spring morning with the birds chirping outside the open window to his upstairs office. An office in their ten-bedroom Victorian-style home out on the edge of town on the *right* side of the tracks.

Nine months after the sheriff's auction, where every last possession had been picked over and sold, leaving them virtually penniless, her mama died of a broken heart. No money remained, not even to plant her next to her father. She had to go in a pauper's grave in a potter's field. Without a headstone and only a number to locate the plot. Too horrible to contemplate.

Grief weighed heavy on Alice, but she soldiered on. What else could she do? She took a broken-down room off an alley, a sort of lean-to attached to a boarding house that catered to visitors who came to town to see the monstrous lake, to fish, water ski, or just boat. People with spare time, who didn't have to work just to eat.

Her new room cost two dollars a week. But for that low rental price, she also had to clean the other rooms, make beds, and scrub the floors. Her hands and knees, now perpetually pink, grew callouses. Her achy bones and joints constantly reminded her of the life that had kicked her out of the car and left her for dead.

For her regular job she worked in Ozzie's, the local diner, slinging hash and eggs with bone-in ham rounds and biscuits and white sausage gravy. Platters of food that, in the past, she would never have touched.

Now her stomach growled when she balanced one on each arm and one in each hand, the greasy aroma calling to her. When the crabby and ancient owner, Maude Gibbs, left the diner on errands, Les, the fry cook, would fix her a quick little plate of food. He'd say he accidentally filled a wrong order and wink at her. She'd turn her back to him, ashamed of the way she'd scarf it up no better than a mangy cur dog.

If she ever let her guard down in the diner, the truck drivers pinched her ass and called her "hon" or "baby cheeks." Two regulars proposed marriage every two or three weeks. Silly men with schoolboy crushes. Even so, they still only left her a nickel tip.

They'd make salacious comments loud enough to hear as she walked away. Ones like "That mamacita has legs clear up to her shoulders." Or "I wouldn't kick her outta bed for eatin' Saltines." And "Her thighs are so sexy, they can't stop touching each other."

That last one didn't make any sense. She didn't have chubby thighs.

Alice had never eaten in a diner. Didn't even know Ozzie's existed. Located out on the *wrong* side of the tracks. She also just thought all waitresses took the same abuse.

The other two women who had worked at Ozzie's for years never had a smile for Alice, never said a word to her. Even though they talked to each other and joked with the customers.

Rude.

Alice started out in a financial hole. The price of two diner uniforms, with two aprons and two hats, were deducted from her pay. Which meant for four weeks she worked for tips only and at the benevolence of the fry cook for meals. Tips were dimes, sometimes on rare occasions a quarter. She did her best to smile and act nice while dodging periodic lascivious pinches or slaps on the bottom.

Friends from her old life would come in, take a table for six or eight, whisper when she came close, and laugh out loud when she moved away. This was the first time she'd realized the vast expanse that existed between two totally different worlds. Worlds that somehow coexisted without her knowledge in her own hometown.

Even her best friend, Lisa Howard, pretended like she didn't know Alice. Treated her as if she had contracted some kind of highly contagious African monkey disease. One where if they ventured too close, they too, would fall down the same rabbit hole and come out the other end working at Ozzie's Eats.

How far had she fallen? An easy answer. All the way to the bottom.

The minute she saved enough, she'd move out of that hell-hole of a town. At least find someplace where nobody knew her. This, her new goal in life. A pitiful one.

Until the tall, handsome man she'd never seen before walked into the diner.

He sat at the counter, where he ordered the hot plate special. She caught him glancing at her while he ate his country-fried chicken dinner with greens, taters smothered in gravy, and a slice of fresh blueberry pie with a scoop of vanilla ice cream. He stayed long after he finished his supper and kept drinking coffee. Cup after cup, she poured with him, watching her eyes. He reminded her a little of Gary Cooper with his tan and his big hands. Long, graceful fingers. That lazy smile.

What she didn't like was the way he dressed. Clothes that screamed laze-about. Bum. That he didn't have two dimes to rub together. She would not, under any circumstances, leap out of the frying pan her daddy dumped her in by putting that two-dollar pistol to his head. By which he'd tossed her into the fire. She'd not give the bum any play.

Even if the man at the counter did have brown eyes that smoldered, had lips that begged for attention.

When he finally got up to leave, he put down four pennies as a tip.

*Four dern pennies.*

She looked down at the paltry gratuity and shook her head as if saying, "What did I expect from the likes of you." She left the pennies on the counter, turned, and poured coffee for some of her regulars who at least appreciated her. When she turned back, he stood on the wrong side of the counter, not inches away. His eyes on hers.

His breath smelled of burnt Ozzie's coffee and vanilla ice cream. Not at all unpleasant. His duds had the scent of citrus blossoms.

After all that coffee, his bladder had to be ready to burst. His arms hung down to his sides, loose.

Five long seconds passed. He finally moved. His two fingers reached and took hold of her two fingers.

Her heart skipped.

Her dern heart. Traitor.

She turned angry. She couldn't allow a bum like him to crawl up into her vulnerable emotions and set up camp. She'd only be worse off. She needed out, not buried deeper.

Still, she stood there breathless. The regulars on the counter threw jealous verbal snipes at the tall man who was making a play for their favorite diner girl.

Over at the register, Maude Gibbs, who most called MG or Machine Gun out of earshot, spotted the irregularity in her smooth-running business and yelled, "Hey Slick, get the hell out from behind there. That counter is for employees only. Move your skinny butt."

The tall man didn't waver. He kept looking into her eyes. "I'm sorry about the tip. I had no idea I'd come in here and meet the woman I'm gonna marry."

Her breath caught again, not at his arrogance but at the raw truth buried in his words. Even though she denied it and shook her head no. She didn't want to believe in that truth, not from that raggedy-ass bum.

But the way he'd said it with such calm assurance, it had to be true.

"My name's Wayne. I'll be back in five days. I'm workin' a grove the next town over, and the man owes me sixteen weeks of wages. We're pickin' right now. When he gets his, I'll get mine. I'll be back with a whole pocket full of folding money. Then I'll sweep you off those beautiful feet of yours. You wait and see if I don't."

Ralph, who sat at the counter and drove a regular route delivering lumber to the local vendors, said, "Buddy, a fool, and his money are easily parted. Better men than you have tried to crack Cleopatra of the Ozarks. Some hick dressed like you with a rope for a belt ain't got a Billy goat's chance in hell. So, so long, pal, and see ya later. The little lady has coffee to pour."

Maude Gibbs, still not leaving the till, yelled. "Les, get your cast iron fry pan and run this yay-hoo off. Conk him over the head if you have to. Jus' get him movin' outta my cafe. We got hash to sling, and he's clogging up the works."

Wayne still hadn't looked away from her eyes. He squeezed her fingers. "Five days. Can you wait five days? I'll be back to court you proper. Okay?"

Her face flushed hot at the statement. "Go on, git," she said. She couldn't take much more of the embarrassing attention with the entire diner focused on her.

On the two of them.

Les came from around back with a meat tenderizing hammer, the one he used to soften up the chicken fried steaks, or no one would be able to choke 'em down.

Wayne backed up, still holding her eyes.

She looked down and spotted the rope for a belt that Ralph had pointed out. It made her angry all over again that she'd almost considered giving Wayne his chance to whisper in her ear and turn her head.

No way would she go for a picnic or even so much as a walk down Rosewood Lane with someone who spent his money on expensive chicken dinners and blueberry pie with vanilla ice cream. Not when he couldn't even afford a dern old belt.

Then she remembered the four cents he'd left as a tip.

"Get out, you good-for-nothing stumblebum. And don't bother coming back in five days or ever for that matter. Get out."

A cheer went up from the locals. Happy their Cleopatra would continue working the diner.

He still had not lost his smile and backed up to the pass-through, turned, and walked over to Maude Gibbs. He gave her the dollar twenty-five for his meal as advertised on the wall.

"What's that pretty girl's name that you have working for you? You must pay her well the way she draws in all these men folk."

Maude shoved the till's drawer shut. "Be on your way, you wet brain good-for-nothing, and don't be comin' back. There's nothing here for you."

Wayne had still not lost that sappy smile. He turned, caught Alice's eyes, and gave her a two-fingered salute, just like Gary Cooper might do. "Goodbye, my *Imogene*. See you in five days." He turned and fled out the café door.

*Imogene?* The man had sunstroke.

Everyone had stopped eating as they watched the silly drama play out, the one with a stumblebum as the star. Some of the men, sweet on her, stood. They put both hands to their hearts and spewed romantic entreaties mocking Wayne.

Through the windows, Wayne ran toward the road just as a stake-bed truck loaded with empty wood crates drove past. The truck slowed. Wayne, running, reached out, caught a slat, and swung up into the back. He waved to Alice, shooting her that same sappy smile.

Alice put her hand on her chest, her heart racing. It wasn't for Wayne. No one had ever treated her that way. Wayne acted so sure of himself, as if he was some kind of savant and could see them together as a couple in the future. Both of them and two kids on a goat farm out in some to-hell-and-gone town. A place nothing more than a little black dot on an obscure map in a hollow no one ever heard about.

That wasn't Alice in Wonderland crapola, it was more a nightmare.

But rest assured she'd never see him again, and good riddance to bad rubbish.

Ralph leaned across the counter. "Imogene, can I get me some more coffee? And why don't ya get me a big slice of that crumble-crust apple pie, ana thick wedge of cheddar cheese to go with it. Would ya, Hon, please? While you're at it, will you marry me?"

Callin' her *Imogene*. The raw nerve of some men.

Two other men said similar things, ordering extra food and suggesting marriage as well. They too called her by her new handle.

Imogene? What was wrong with that dern Wayne, making up a name for her on the fly.

Maude raised her voice over the din. "Alice, come here please."

Sweet baby Jesus, she was going to be fired for causing a ruckus. One she'd had no control over. She moved with heavy feet toward her boss and tried to put words together, reasons why she should keep her job.

Nothing sounded good. She'd never had to beg for anything in her life and she wasn't going to start.

Maude brusquely took her by the arm and turned them toward the glass front door, her back to everyone else. Maude whispered—and she *never* whispered, "Okay, I'll give you a nickel-an-hour raise. But don't you dare tell the other two girls. You hear me?"

Alice took this new twist no different than if Maude had administered a stinging slap across her face. In the five months since she'd been living in a shack and working her fingers to the bone, she'd learned one thing for sure, and that was how to think on her feet. An attribute needed to survive in this new alien world.

"Make it a dime, or I'm walking out right now."

Maude clamped her jaw and spoke through clenched teeth. "Then walk, you big-titted milk cow. You'll never work here again. And I'll see to it no one else will ever—"

Alice started for the door, untying her apron.

"Wait. Wait, damn you. Okay, a dime." The word "dime" came out a harsh utterance as if expelling poison that clung to her tongue.

"And I get Sunday off."

With Sundays off, she could bake pies and cakes and sell them in the town square after church let out. Make twice what she made at Ozzie's in one day. A daydream. Maybe even three times as much. She'd just have to co-op Les to let her in the kitchen after hours and…and he'd also have to show her how to bake. Fry-cook donuts.

Maude's face instantly flushed and bloated. "Fine. Now get your ass back to work, Missy."

Alice hid her smile. Any gloating would get her fired for sure. She poured coffee, slung pie slices, flirted with the men at the counter, and received the highest tips ever. Jealousy did that to men, an attribute she'd store away to use later on.

For several days after Wayne had visited the café, Alice started actually saving some money. Whether he meant to or not, Wayne had raised the ante in Ozzie's Eats. Try as she might, she couldn't stop thinking about that tall drink of water. She tried to fool herself that she really wasn't counting down the days to his return.

The word had gone around town about what had happened, and on the fifth day, the café was packed to the gunnels. This time mixed with more women who also desired that tidbit of romance in their lives. Needed to believe it still existed. At least somewhere in their world. A need equal in necessity to the air they breathed.

The day finally arrived. Alice had never worked so hard and fast trying to keep up with all the orders. She forgot all about Wayne. Maude actually had to leave her money perch and help serve. That had never happened. Noise inside continued to rise.

Until all at once, the café turned quiet.

She looked up and spotted the cause.

Outside in the dirt turnout in front of Ozzie's, Wayne sat on the front of a parked beat-up old Studebaker truck. He wore a dusty gray fedora that made his nose look bigger. He strummed a banjo and sang a barely audible song with "Imogene" in the lyrics. A little ditty he'd obviously made up. In the next truck over, a blue-tick hound howled, his nose in the air.

The diners all laughed at the scene.

A new customer entered the overly packed café. When the door opened, Wayne's words and music floated in. He was God-awful. The hound sounded better.

But the man had a whole lotta heart. And was shameless in his endeavor.

When he finished, he shot her that same two-fingered salute. Then he simply got back in that old Studebaker and drove off.

She didn't think she'd care, but she did. Once he drove out of sight, a big hole opened in Alice's chest and didn't close again until he came back five days later.

He pulled up, driving that same stake-bed truck. He didn't get out. He honked and waved for her to come on.

She smiled large enough to break her face. She untied her apron on the run out of Ozzie's Eats and never looked back.

* * *

Telling the long story to Suz in her garage while sorting olio and knick-knacks saved by Suz's father from decades past gave Imogene the answer. She realized how a person could tell if she was in love.

Of course, in relating the story Imogene didn't tell Suz her real name was Alice Putnam. No one knew that secret, one buried deeper than the Snows of Kilimanjaro. Or at least under six feet of dirt that now resided over the top of ol' Wayne.

Imogene stood, stretched her tired back. "You want to know how you tell if you're honestly and truly in love?"

Suz slowly stood, her expression open, as if she were about to receive the most important information of her young life. "Yes, I do. Please, do tell."

"First, you have to tell me who this beau is who sparked your fancy."

Suz shook her head and looked down at her feet. Her voice, a squeak. "I can't."

"Lordy, it's that dern Micheal Higginbothom, isn't it?"

Suz's head jerked up with a faint smile on her lips, anxiety in her eyes. "Am I a total fool, Imogene?" She wrung her hands.

"No, of course not. The heart wants what the heart wants, and to hell with everything else." Said it even though she'd have probably steered her away from him. There was something about Higgy-baby that set off a little alarm in the back of her brain. An instinct she couldn't quite explain. Higgy-baby always came off harmless as a pup and she could only hope she was wrong.

No matter. Cupid's arrow was buried deep in Suz' backside, and there'd be no turning her back now.

Imogene pointed into the dark toward the street. "Then why did you have me run his sorry ass off?"

Suz looked down at her feet. "I don't know. I…I guess I'm just scared. I hadn't even thought of him that way until you brought it up. Now I can't think of nothin' else."

"You've caught a bad dose of it, that's for sure. I'd say run for your life, but that doesn't do any good."

She looked up, a little scared. "You think so?"

Love could do that, terrify a person.

Imogene said. "Yes, I do. And the answer to your question in this case is another question. Do you ache inside when you're away from him?"

Stunned, Suz eased down onto the wooden crate, her eyes staring off into the distance. "Oh, Imogene. No. Dear Lord, no. I am smitten, for sure."

Imogene patted Suz' knee. "I know the feeling, kid. Love ain't fair. Someone needs ta catch that little Cupid bastard and knock the wheels off his wagon."

# Chapter Ten

The next day, Imogene came out the front door of 744 East Hawthorne on her way to Dentco. Before she could close the door, agitated movement caught her attention. The driveway over at Suz's place swarmed with *those* people. The kind of folks that can never walk past something free without stopping and filling their dern pockets. Load up. Throw the heavy items over their shoulders to tote away the crapola. Come back with their cars, excited beyond belief at this new treasure trove.

Eureka. Junkyard gold.

Many of them were old enough to have lived through the Great Depression or the Dust Bowl that forced thousands to migrate west. Wayne had been one of those people with the same ailment. It took Imogene a couple decades to wring it from his garbage-pickin' soul. He'd struggled with the terrible junkman's affliction that raised its ugly head two weeks before she ever saw him again.

He sat in his easy chair, rocking and smoking his pipe with cherry-flavored tobacco, filling the air with gray smoke, and reading the classifieds from The Daily Report, the local rag. He looked up from the paper. "Imogene, lookee here. Brand new snow skis for sale. Half-off, over to The Valley Department store. Half-off, can you believe it? What a deal. I'm thinkin' I should—"

"Dern your sorry hide. You never snow skied in your life. You never even seen snow, you chucklehead."

The fire in his eyes extinguished, adding yet another little pebble to the guilt pile that had begun to smother her. She'd treated him poorly ever since he lost both of their citrus groves up in LaVerne. Twenty acres each. The groves and the wonderful house, a dream fulfilled. Lost the life she'd come to love.

Wasn't his fault. Blight, weather, and market price ran them out. Wayne's one-two-buckle-my-shoe kinda bookkeeping hadn't helped matters. They lost their huge two-story Victorian, all the furniture, both cars…every dern thing. If they'd only dropped out once the downturn started, they might've retired in style. But Wayne wanted to hang on. "It has to come back. It just has to, Imogene."

Only it didn't and tossed them headfirst into the lower socioeconomic strata where all the GUM resided, the great unwashed masses. If not for the slow, agonizing decline, she wouldn't have been so bitter. At least, that's what she told herself over and over. Tried to convince herself she wasn't a selfish little brat.

But she was.

Maybe that was why fate took a heavy hand with her. Her selfishness, her stuck-up attitude. Stuck her in CIW to get her mind right. Oh, it was right now. She knew exactly how the cow ate the cabbage. A hard lesson. She needed to work on her attitude, be more open, more giving. More forgiving.

Their downfall wasn't all Wayne's fault, not really. Maybe it was both their faults. The seed money to start the groves, buy their big house, the two cars, came from their first venture into criminality. In all likelihood, dipping their toe in the water of moral turpitude poisoned them for life. At least it did for her. And she guessed for Wayne as well after what happened to him. She couldn't seem to shake that evil bastard fate that kept right on her tail, waiting for her to step off the trail to get slapped down.

Ange had said, *Once you take a bite of that sour apple, there's no goin' back. You're in it up to your ass, baby. In it forever and a day. Till they fit you for that cold dirt nap.*

Too old to start over, they used what little money remained to buy the small two-bedroom house at 744 East Hawthorne, paid cash for it. They had enough left over in the savings account that if they lived frugally, they could in two years make it to social security age. Let the government swaddle them in their fiduciary responsibility. She didn't blame Wayne for hiding out at the pool hall, not the way she treated him.

But the loss smashed on the rocks her big dreams of their retirement. A cruise around the world, stopping at mind-blowing exotic places. Meeting new people and—well, all of those wonderful things the well-heeled did in their twilight years. Card games, shuffleboard, book clubs, that whole stuffy social scene. The kinda thing she never stopped yearning for.

All that kinda money was gone, with it the dreams.

Living with an ugly tail and working in a broken-down shop called Dentco in no way fulfilled anything close to that retirement plan. At least she still had the house and wasn't living out of a grocery buggy under a freeway overpass. She tipped her hat to fate; she'd learned her lesson all right. Learned to love what she had and not to demean others.

Imogene pulled her front door closed, walked across her porch, and down the two steps, far enough out from the junk pile to see a card table set up on the sidewalk with a little blond-haired girl about eight years old selling lemonade and big fat avocados.

Imogene, her pocketbook hanging from her arm, crossed her lawn and walked behind the Gremlin, arriving at the stand to the right of Suz' driveway entrance. "How much for a cool glass of lemonade?"

"Fifty cents."

"Why, that's a ridiculous price. I'll give you a dime."

The disheartened little girl lost her smile, nodded, and poured a paper cup full. Imogene tasted it and puckered. The person who mixed the bitter concoction had gone light on the sugar, cutting back on the most expensive part of the overhead. Imogene still gave her a satisfying "Mmm."

The little girl smiled. "You really like it?"

"Of course, why wouldn't I?" Imogene had been trying hard to shed the old CIW skin in search of who she'd been before her deeper dive into her criminality. Talking nice to an eight-year-old helped toward that end. Refreshing actually. More so than the terrible lemonade. She took a dollar from her billfold and handed it over.

The little girl's eyes grew large at the sight of paper money after dealing all morning with tight-fisted trash-pickers.

"You can keep it."

"Thank you."

"You're welcome. Those are really nice avocados. How much are they?"

"Two for a dime. They're selling better than the lemonade."

Imogene picked one up to examine. A Hass that had most assuredly come from her backyard. From Mr. Majestic.

The little girl lost her smile, fear creeping in. "You…ah…you can have all of those you want. I…ah…found them."

"They look like they might've come from my backyard."

Her eyes started to tear up. Her chin quivered.

Imogene set the green fruit back on the table. "It's okay. You can have all you can carry."

"Really?"

"Of course, there's plenty for everyone. That tree's as big as a small house and twice as tall. What's your name? Mine's Imogene."

"I'm Darla."

"Hello, Darla. Do you know how to use a push mower?"

She shook her head. "Come over this Sunday, and I'll show you. I'll pay you fifty cents each Sunday you mow my yard."

"Are you kidding?"

"No, I'm not."

"That would be great. Fifty cents. That's two dollars a month, right?"

Imogene smiled. "Yes, it is, and it comes with lunch. A hot dog sandwich and a vanilla milkshake."

"Wow, I'll see you this Sunday. Thank you."

"Now watch yourself. I have to back up my car."

She nodded then looked down the street to where she lived, watching out for her mom. Darla must've cut school to take advantage of the sales opportunity. A true Hawthorne Street entrepreneur.

Imogene got in her car, glowing with goodwill.

When thinking about reverting back to her old self, she remembered something Ange had said.

Ange had mimicked the CIW councilor. *Rehabilitation is all about giving back to the community you have harmed.* Ange said that part haughtily, with a sarcastic tone, her nose in the air. Then continued in her gritty style, *Ta hell wit all a them. They're the ones who put me in here. I ever see the light a day again; you can bet your sorry ever-lovin' ass I'm not givin' nothing back. I'll be takin' all I can grab with both hands and both feet.*

Ange's words always sparked a muse for Imogene. Thoughts that spun around in her head even though she might not be directly thinking about a problem or issue. Ideas all on their own would drop down into a slot and lock into a gear. And that's what just happened. She got out of the car, walked back into the house, and made a phone call.

* * *

One she'd wished she'd thought through before acting. But who could see into the future to steer 'round those serious chuck holes in the road ahead? The kind that derailed people's entire lives. And crushed others.

The day slogged on and on, sitting on her stool at Dentco, watching the shoppers weave in and around the bins. Most all would complain about an expiration date, or a box more torn or mashed than the rest, working Imogene for a deeper discount. She couldn't blame them and understood where they were coming from. She'd been there, living in that lean-to and working in Ozzie Eats for a starving wage.

But she'd decided long ago to hold a hard line on prices. Once she started down that path, there'd be nothing but trouble.

Unless it was a mother with dirty children hanging off her like fleas on a blue tick hound. Imogene would pay for their food out of her own pocket and even throw in ten dollars ta boot. The first time she did it, she worried she'd opened a floodgate and they'd be lined up out the door.

Didn't happen.

The next time that same mother came in without the children, her clothes were still worn to a frazzle but cleaned, her hair combed. She again profusely thanked Imogene for her kindness and refused to accept another handout. Too proud.

Imogene had hurried to fill a bag with similar items the woman had purchased and rushed out to catch up. Leaving Dentco unattended. A major, "Bozo, no, no," according to Higgy-baby. She told the woman, "These are damaged goods we can't sell."

The woman laughed. "Aren't all the things in your store damaged?"

"Why, no," Imogene smiled. "Is that what you think?"

The woman laughed some more, accepted the offered handout, and thanked her. She didn't look like a woman who laughed too often.

Later that same day, a phone call from Higginbothom broke up the teeth-cutting monotony. He said he had to work in the Bloomington store because Suz had taken the day off to sort out her dad's stuff in the garage. He wanted to know if George was out in the warehouse, that he wasn't answering the warehouse phone. Would Imogene lock up for just a few minutes, run over there and see what was happening. Call him right back.

Imogene said, "This is some kinda test, isn't it? If you told me once, you told me a thousand times, never, ever leave the store for any reason. You said that if you caught me with the store locked up and me gone even for one minute, that it would be instant termination. Mr. Higginbothom, are you trying to get me to do something, so you can fire me?" She smiled at the silence that followed. Higgy-baby would be squeezing the phone, his face bloating red from aggravation.

"Imogene?"

"Yes, boss."

"Imogene, I didn't fire you for hosing me down yesterday when I should have. Now—"

"Ah, excuse me…ah, Sir. How could you fire me for something I did on my own time at my own house? I bet you FEPA won't approve and will slap you with a huge fine. You don't want a huge fine, do you?"

"FEPA? There's no such thing. *What are you talking about?*"

"You're kidding, right? You've never heard of the Federal Employee Protection Agency?" Imogene smiled and put her hand over the phone in case a smirk slipped out. She derived far too much pleasure from pulling his string.

"Imogene, there is no such thing as FEPA. Now get your butt over there and check on George. He could've dropped a pallet on his head or something. He drives that forklift like it's some kinda go-cart."

She hadn't thought of that. Poor George.

"Oh, right. Why didn't you say so in the first place? I'll call you right back."

George was fine. She found him taking a midday nap on an army cot he'd recently installed in the warehouse office. She didn't understand how he could sleep among all the rats scurrying about. The sour reek of his BO must've acted as a repellent.

She waggled his foot. He wouldn't stir. She might've been concerned had he not been snoring loud enough to rattle the pictures on the walls and exhaling Old Grand Dad whiskey. The empty pint bottle on the floor just under his hanging hand.

The sight of him, the cot, the whiskey bottle, smacked her hard with soul-crushing nostalgia. Oddly, flashing images of the first days together with Wayne. She'd suppressed those kinda feelings for ten years while in CIW. That or go stark raving mad. Out two years dragging her ocelot tail around, and the nostalgia she'd thought gone forever had finally made an appearance. Her knees weakened. She eased down in the desk chair opposite the cot and welcomed the warm tingles all up and down her body. This wasn't her regular memory, images of her historical past. This wave of nostalgia came with sights, smells, and, most important, the wonderful first touches from Wayne. Their first kiss. Their first night together. The shocking reality of Wayne, how he in no way fit the image she'd created in her mind. The nostalgia, pent up for so long, washed over her in warm waves, almost orgasmic in nature. She smiled. Closed her eyes and let it happen. Welcomed it with open arms.

# Chapter Eleven

Alice Putnam sat next to Wayne as they tooled along the Arkansas road. The humid wind blew in the open window, mixing with her hair, giving it a fuller body. She loved the feel of it, adding to the sense of exhilaration. She sat with her leg touching her romantic knight who'd just rescued her from a life of drudgery at Ozzie Eats. She knew this wasn't entirely true but let the dream fester a little longer. Enjoyed it before that ugly beast Fate stepped in and popped it like a dish-soap bubble.

Wayne kept his arm around her except when he brought it down to shift the Studebaker truck, then put it back. Each time he touched her, she sensed his love, his desire. And in a weird way, an honesty she shouldn't have been able to detect at all. She snuggled in close hoping at least a portion of her dream turned out to be real.

He kept taking his eyes off the road to look at her, his eyes on hers. "Gawd dern it, you are beautiful. How the heck did I get so lucky?"

She didn't know what to say. It had all happened so fast. The very idea of running off with someone she didn't know echoed in her brain like a ringing alarm clock. Stop. Go back.

Run for your damn life.

"Say something, baby. Say anything. You haven't said a word since you got in the truck."

She wasn't in love with this man, how could she be? She was in love with the idea of what he could be. A Gary Cooper in their very own movie. She'd jumped into his truck because of the risk factor. The risk that a life with Wayne couldn't be any worse than what she had back at Ozzie's Eats.

In her mind she worked on the issue like a dog with a bone, pondering the pros and the cons. She hoped she got it all sorted, the justification why she rolled those dice.

"Pull over."

Wayne lost his smile, the one that lit up Alice's world. "Whaaat?"

"Just pull over. Right there. Pull over in that little turnabout."

He stared at her, fear filling his expression as if Alice had kicked him in the teeth. She took hold of his nose, pulled on it. "Pull over, tall man, or lose your sniffer."

The truck had drifted to the wrong side of the road while he looked at her and tried to overcome the shock of how she'd crushed his world with so few words. She squeezed his nose some more and wagged it up and down. "Hello? Pull the truck over."

He yanked on the wheel too hard. The truck went up on two wheels, almost going over. He righted it, pulled into the little turnabout, and stopped. One foot on the brake and one on the clutch, the engine in high idle.

She let go of his nose and stared into his walnut-colored eyes.

His voice cracked. "Now what? Are you getting out? No, don't. I'll drive you back."

She stared, not really hearing his words, and said, "I just need to know something. And I need to know it right now before we go any further."

"Okay…I guess. I'll tell you anything you wanna know."

"I'm not talking about with words."

"Not words…then what?"

"Wayne? Kiss me, you foolish man."

He hesitated. She realized he was afraid of women. Didn't have any experience with them.

She put a hand on each side of his face and pulled him into a kiss. He gave her the Clark Gable treatment, keeping his lips closed. She pried them open with her tongue and greeted his. He tasted of burnt cherries. Her body up against his, he shivered like a dog just in out of the rain. He grew more intense, moving closer to her. Leaning over. She dove deeper into the kiss and realized she'd made the right choice. Wayne was exactly what the doctor ordered. A little ache opened inside her, one she had not felt with Ted. A yearning to be with him.

Mama had told her: "Some women have a way of changing boys into men, and some men into boys." That kiss shook her right down to her socks. Scrambled all logic. She didn't know which way she had changed Wayne but change she did.

He straddled one of her legs, his excitement now rock-hard against her. They both breathed hard through their noses. She put her hand on his chest and tried to move him back a smidge. When she couldn't budge him, she turned her face to the side, broke the kiss, and chuffed to get her breath back. "Wayne? Baby?"

His feet came off the pedals. The truck lurched and jumped and lurched, chugging to a stop.

He moved away, his tan face flushed. "Did I do something wrong? I'm sorry. I didn't mean to—"

She smiled, reached out, and took his hand. "No, of course you didn't. You just don't know your own strength, Honey. Go easy. That's all. Just take it a little slower. A girl's gotta breathe, you know." She smiled.

She had more experience than she wanted to admit with Ted before he'd tossed her over for money, the lack thereof. She'd fought Ted off until she, too, wanted what he did. Just as much as he did. They became true lovers. Seven times. Just enough for Alice to realize she loved being with a man. Enough to realize Wayne wasn't like most men. Nothing at all like most men.

"Come here."

He took her in his arms and kissed her again. And man, oh man, could Wayne kiss. It had been too long. She wanted to take him right there on the truck seat. But she wasn't a slut. She could wait. Waiting could make it all the sweeter.

Someone tapped on the side of the truck close to the driver's window. They broke from the kiss.

A uniformed Arkansas state trooper peered in, his eyes ogling Alice's naked thigh. Her dress had pulled up during the first kiss and from the jumping truck when Wayne had left it in gear.

"Everything okay in here?"

She pulled her dress down. Like shutting the blinds on a peeper, the cop instantly turned professional.

"Yes, fine, Officer," Wayne said.

"You broke down or something?"

"No. Aah, we just stopped to have a little chat."

"You might want to find a better place *to chat.* And in the future turn your truck off before you start *chatting.* You almost jumped right down that embankment."

"Yes, sir. I will, sir."

"Now, let me see your driver's license and registration. Son, you from around here? I don't recognize you."

Wayne's body stiffened.

Something was wrong.

"I aah, forgot my license at home."

"Step out of the truck, please."

Alice watched Wayne. His moves suddenly turned furtive. He was thinking about starting the truck and running. The cop saw the same thing. He put his hand on his gun. "I won't tell you again, step out."

Alice leaned over Wayne's lap, one hand out of view of the cop, and grabbed a handful of Wayne's crotch to take control of him. He'd wilted over the threat that stood close by. Wayne grunted. Even with the threat, he again started to grow hard in her hand.

"Hey there, Harold?" Imogene said, "How's your wife Essie?"

He bent at the waist and looked closer. When he'd first walked up, the sight of her naked thigh had befuddled him, and he'd not looked further to discover its owner. "Who's that?" he said.

"It's me, Alice from Ozzie's Diner."

"Oh, hey, Alice. Didn't see that it was you." His entire demeanor shifted. "You okay? You know this Yay-hoo?"

A low groan slipped past Wayne's lips. She squeezed harder to quiet him.

"He's not no Yay-hoo. This is my fiancé."

She shouldn't have said that. Harold lost his little daydream that he, too, could one day be in the front seat of a truck kissing a diner-dolly like Alice.

"That right. Well, I guess congratulations are in order. But I'm still gonna have to ask you two to step from the truck. I'm not gonna ask nice again."

In her hand, Wayne started to yet again wane. To wilt.

She leaned further until her head stuck out the window. "Um, Harold, we're in an awful big rush. We're on our way to get married."

Wayne kissed her naked shoulder at hearing the liar's tale she'd just fed the cop. A move to let her know he was game.

"Alice—" the cop said.

"Harold, Agnes at the diner said to tell you—that if I saw you before she did—that she'd love it if you'd come in again for another order of her grits."

The cook had overheard Agnes talking with Willa about how Agnes had "cooked Harold's grits" in the front seat of the prowl car parked behind Ozzie's. Twice.

Harold took a step back as if slapped, the color leaving his face. "Ah…is that right? I ah…guess you're right. I am kinda hungry right now. You two get on and have a nice weddin'."

"Thank you, officer." She leaned out further and with her free hand waved to him as he walked back to his prowl car. His head was turned to look over his shoulder. She climbed off Wayne and sat beside him.

"We really gonna get married?"

"Hush up a minute." She pulled the mirror down to watch Harold. To make sure he didn't come back. He started up, made a U-turn, and headed back up the highway.

She moved the mirror back. Wayne tried to move in and kiss her again. She put her hand on his chest and pushed him away. "Whoa there, Cowboy. First, you tell me what the hell's goin' on?"

"What are you talking about, Imogene? Nothing's goin' on."

"I don't know you more than a minute, and I can read you like the Sunday funny papers. What do you have going on? Tell me right now, or I'm getting the hell outta your truck and walkin' back."

"That's okay, Imogene. I'll drive you." His tone again shifted to discouraged.

He in no way wanted to give up the secret he so carefully held.

His hand went to the starter button. She grabbed it. "Quit acting like a child and just tell me. It'll be no big deal. I promise."

She thought he might start to cry. Wayne could not only kiss like nobody's business, but he was sensitive as well. The way his fear of losing her caused him such a conundrum was cute. But then, maybe he was too much of a cream puff for her liking. Like Mama had said, maybe that kiss had changed him from a man into a boy.

"I ah…"

"Just tell me, Sport." She'd developed a defensive language and demeanor out of self-defense working at a diner filled with rude and crude testosterone-fueled men.

"This truck, it's stolen."

Alice's mouth dropped open. She pulled back and swung, aiming for a hand-tingling slap.

Quick as a snake, he caught it midair. His expression shifted in an instant to confidence. "Please don't hit me, Imogene." He pulled her in and kissed her like nobody's business. She struggled at first, but man, oh man, could he kiss. She fell into this one that snatched her breath away. He held her in a tight hug. In that moment, love with its spidery tentacles reached down through her skin, down past muscle and bone, and took custody of her heart.

He broke first, started the truck, stuck it in gear, and popped the clutch. The back tires screeched. She sat back, staring at him, trying to catch her breath. She in no way took him as a person who'd steal a truck. The idea of it gave her a little tingle up and down her entire body.

He said, "We can't stop and get married until we get outta the state. That all right with you, Sweetie?

She nodded, still not able to put two words together. She had never in all her life experienced a *Wayne* before. She wasn't a fool and knew the idea of being in a stolen truck, the intrigue, the constant threat of being caught, added to his allure.

He said, "Stick your hand under the seat. I got you a weddin' present."

She did as he asked and found a cloth flour sack. She pulled it out and looked inside.

Money. Lots and lots of folding money all in a fluff.

And a gun.

A little Iver Johnson .32, one of those two-dollar pistols sold in the catalogs. The same kinda gun daddy had used to take his own life. A .32: a small lead pill with the absolute ability to steal away someone she loved with all her heart and, at the same time, change her entire world. And now here, another one sat in her lap mixed among the paper money. The good and the bad.

They drove for a while, the flour sack on Alice's lap, both her hands resting on more money than she'd ever seen in one place. What had he done to get that kinda money? And the truck.

And the gun.

Did he have to shoot someone to get it?  In all her life, she had never envisioned a scenario anywhere close to this one with her in a stolen vehicle tooling down the highway holding a bag of money and a gun. A latter-day Bonnie and Clyde. Only in this case, it was Alice…no, Imogene and Wayne. Somehow, it didn't have the same ring to it. A year ago, before her entire world came tumbling down, she would've jumped outta the truck when Harold pulled them over and run down the highway screaming like her hair was on fire. Not now.

This somehow felt right. And no way should it have.

After an hour or so, she finally righted in her mind all this new information about the man sitting next to her and decided: he'll do. She said, "Wayne?"

"Yeah, Babe."

"Why do you call me Imogene?"

He took his eyes off the road. "Why, that was the name of my first dog. She was a real beaut, Imogene."

Imogene figured it had to be something like that.

# Chapter Twelve

Five o'clock on the dot, Imogene finally locked up Dentco, turned on the security alarm, and drove the little Gremlin home. She made the turn from the street into the driveway just as Suz lugged a box up her steep driveway. A couple of those people, trash pickers, came out of the throng to take the box from her. They could've gone through it right there but instead chose to carry it to a large van parked out front so no one else got a gander at the contents. They'd now resorted to loading it sight unseen, saving the treat for later in the quiet of their own home. The seven or eight folks must've developed a system and took turns taking the boxes as they rose up outta the garage carried by the stalwart Suz.

Twenty after five on a dark winter's night, Suz's tee shirt stuck to her with sweat under her arms and down the center of her chest. The girl had a great work ethic. Unrelenting. Climbing that steep driveway from the garage carrying weight was like a train going up a steep grade.

On the return trip, Imogene followed her down to the garage, her knees screeching in agony. Suz pattered on about all the recent discoveries in their modern-day archaeological dig left behind by her father. Things Imogene would never in the world think to keep. She pulled up a box to sit on to help go through more of the junk. The tall pyramid was a mere shadow of what it used to be. The base and the height eroded down to a ten-foot circumference and, in places, only two to four feet tall. Halfway done. Imogene wanted nothing more than to sit on her divan, smoke a Marlboro, and drink a Schlitz Malt Liquor 16 oz.

"You were right," Suz said, "I don't have to worry about hauling a thing away. Apparently, this crapola is gold. She moved her hands up to each side of her face and shook them, imitating a crazy person.

"Why not have them come down here to the garage, let 'em scurry about, and carry the stuff up that steep incline? Save you the trouble and heartache."

She let a tired smile creep out. "Are you kiddin'? I'm giving my legs the workout of a lifetime." She slapped a rock-hard thigh, then moved over to a tall tool bench cluttered with boxes of every size and shape. All the stuff she'd decided had value and wanted to keep. Imogene held her tongue and said not a thing about how Suz was only perpetuating the same hoarding problem. Maybe it was in the genes she inherited from good ol' dad.

Suz picked up a green felt hatbox trimmed with a faded gold cord and brought it over. "I don't let them down here because I gotta keep control. Look what I found. A box of love letters from Dad and Mom back when they first met." Her bottom lip started to tremble, her eyes filled with tears. "These are so, so beautiful. I had to stop and read each one. I about wasted the whole day. I never knew my mom and now I got to see her for the first time, hear her lovely voice. No wonder Dad never wanted to talk about her. It must've hurt like crazy to reopen that kind of loss. He had a nickname for her. You wanna guess what it was?"

Imogene took out a pack of Marlboros from her dress pocket, the second pack of the day, and tapped it hard against her palm to compress the tobacco. She tore off the cellophane cover, opened the flap, and pulled one out. She stuck it in her mouth and lit it with her Zippo. She was too tired to play youthful games and said nothing. Though a thought did flutter across her brain: those letters would be great fodder for a book if she chose to write another. That idea blossomed into the next. She still had the unopened letter from the publisher. Her little dab of hope.

"It was Dolly," Suz said when Imogene failed to reply. "His nickname for her was Dolly. Can you even imagine having a name like that? When you get a chance, you should read these. She was such a kind and caring person filled with so much life. He loved her dearly. Go on, take one now, and read it. I promise it'll make your day."

Even though Imogene wanted to, she couldn't. She pushed the box away as if it contained a live cobra about to strike. Love letters would remind her too much of Wayne. What had happened between them? What she had caused. The very idea made her stomach churn and threaten revolt. She gulped down her rising gorge. "I'm sorry," she said, "I'm all full up on Gothic Romance stories. Maybe a little later."

Imogene pulled a box over and opened it. More receipts. The man kept receipts for everything he'd ever purchased: gas, groceries, masking tape, tools, and wood. Why, for God's sake's?

Suz bent at the waist and peeked in. "The crazies up there will even take this box. I have to tell you, E, I didn't believe you about these guys, but you were right on the money. Oh, money." She sniffled, swiped at her tears, reached into her shorts pocket, and pulled out a handful of folding money. A thick wad. "Two-dollar bills and silver certificates. Some are collectibles worth a lot. I almost let the box go up there to the horde. I gotta open every box, E."

She walked over and set the hat box down, came back, and kicked the biggest box at the very bottom of the pile. A barely visible corner and part of one side. More a crate that anchored the entire lot. The pyramid core. "I can't wait to see what's in this baby."

The visible side section had tall letters stenciled in black spray paint: *"Danger! Never Open! Don't do it."* Like something out of a cheap horror movie. One that made Imogene and Suz the archaeologists risking life and limb, possibly doomed by a long-forgotten Egyptian curse from the tomb of Tutankhamun.

"Fact is," Suz said, "I'm ready. I wanna see what's in it right now. It's big, and I'm in the mood for a little bit of danger. How about you, E?" She took boxes off the top and laid them in the recently cleared area.

Imogene stood and smoked, not wanting to get in the way. Not wanting to tell Suz that she'd had enough danger and didn't want to flirt with disaster. "You sure? You really think you should just jump in headfirst without at least taking a moment to think about it? What if it *is* something dangerous?"

"Dad had to be making a joke, writing on the side like that."

"I don't remember your dad as a jokester. He was stern and taciturn."

"You didn't know him like I did. You couldn't. He rarely socialized. But he did have a well-kept sense of humor. Trust me on this, E."

"I wouldn't count on it being anything we're going to laugh about. Just give it to the locusts up there and be done with it."

Suz hesitated and looked at Imogene. Suz smiled. "Oh, quit being such an ol' fuddy-duddy. Come help." Suz dove back in with a fevered pitch, moving the rest of the boxes from on top of the crate. Visible goose flesh from the cold rolled up and down her naked legs. She'd started work in the garage in the heat of the day. Now, her choice of dress could easily allow a strong dose of ague to ruin her next few days. She needed to change into long pants.

"What did your dad do for a living?"

Suz didn't flinch or slow down. "Oh, for twenty-five years, he worked at a dynamite factory in Rialto. A line supervisor with full run of the place."

Imogene grabbed Suz's shoulder and spun her around. Suz giggled. Come on, quit it, E. I'm just teasing. He was a private contractor for Lockheed. Worked for them for forty-one years. An airframe specialist with thirty-six classifications. Hardly ever took a vacation. Don't know if he ever did take one. In one of Mom's letters, she accused him of being a workaholic. Now, give me a hand with this. I'm telling you, Dad was just making a joke about it being dangerous. He was a homebody and would never put anything in a box in our garage that could harm anyone. It's a joke. I'm sure of it."

She'd cleared a path all around the crate, the pyramid now a thing of the past, the garage floor a sea of boxes of every shape. Suz stepped up on one and walked across the other boxes like stepping stones in a pond. At the tool bench, she retrieved a pry bar and returned. "Come on, E, get over here and give a girl a hand."

Imogene's curiosity rose and fought against her will to be gone. Curiosity won out over good sense. She wove her way to the crate that looked to be three by four by three feet high. A rectangle of sorts. She lit another Marlboro; the still air in the garage grew clouded.

Suz tried to wiggle the pry bar tip under the top edge. No soap.

Imogene's imagination spun out of control. Could the contents be some type of stolen nuclear device Suz's father took from the government? A bomb agents of the government had been hunting for forty years. This could easily be a Fat Boy and Little Man situation right there in a detached garage on Hawthorne Avenue.

"Wait a minute," Suz said, "Look at this, E. The crate isn't nailed closed. Dad used wood screws and even counter-sank them. Look at this. He put glue in the screw heads, so a driver wouldn't work. Now, he's really got me wondering. How about you?"

"Seriously? I'm thinking we call those predatory locusts down from the top of the driveway and let 'em jus' take it. You haven't lost anything that you need to find, right? Suz, this is obviously a Pandora's box that we should leave alone. I'm not kidding."

She looked at Imogene, disappointed.

"Pshaw. I didn't tell you that after all the years Dad put into working, I never knew him to spend money on anything extra. We had our bills. You know, the everyday kinda things like groceries, the Edison and gas bill, the mortgage. So you know what I found missing? A big fat savings account. I thought all his accumulated wealth might be stuffed in his mattress. Or something like that. But it wasn't. All I found was some dead bed bugs. It has to be in this box. He probably converted it to gold or silver and stashed it all in this innocuous-looking crate. Then, piled everything on top to discourage your everyday burglar. Brilliant if you ask me. He was like that, a real Brainiac."

Odd how they had such diverse opinions, Suz' being the rose-colored glasses, cup half-full bullshit.

"So, you were lying when you said you were just out here looking for memories. For mementos? When all this time you've been out here treasure hunting?"

"Oh, E, do you think any less of me? Truly?"

"Don't be silly. You're my friend. Right now, a hare-brained impractical thinking friend, but still a friend."

Suz smiled, went over to the workbench, cast about, found a big hammer, and returned.

Every fiber in Imogene's body told her to run for the hills and not look back.

Suz banged and banged on the box denting the wood but not making any headway in opening the large enigma. One that had to contain an evil black cloud ready to escape and poison their very souls, banishing them to—

As if Imogene didn't already have enough to worry about, letting her mind create things that weren't there.

Imogene held up her hand, "Maybe we should take this box's obstinance as a sign and shut this whole shebang down for the night. Sleep on it. We'll have clearer heads in the morning. Whatta ya say? Huh?"

Suz stopped and stared; her chest heaved from the exertion. Sweat ran in her eyes.

Imogene looked up the driveway. Shadows of the seven or eight trash-pickers lurked just at the edge of the light. Imogene and Suz in the well-lit garage would be easily visible from their vantage point. They now had to have the same curiosity about the enigma's contents.

Let 'em stay there. When this little Fat Boy goes off, it'll level 'em all. Serves 'em right. Level the entire neighborhood. Maybe the entire city.

Then, the real world stepped in and kicked Imogene in the teeth. Made her realize her error. Ange would've yelled bloody murder. *What the hell? You're a couple a rubes, simple minded marks standing here in this light just waitin' ta be plucked like a couple a fat dumb turkeys.*

Was Ange right? Had the trash-pickers heard everything that had been said in the garage? Did they now know that the precious and precocious Suz had a pocket full of recently discovered cash? Imogene stood and stared. The real threat wasn't in the mysterious crate, after all, but up there at the top of the driveway. How many had there been when she pulled up? Had there been more than the seven or eight she'd seen? How many did they have to deal with? Didn't matter, a couple-a-three men could overpower the both of them. Imogene picked up the hammer Suz had discarded when she swapped it for a sledge.

Suz said, "No way could I sleep tonight knowing this was down here."

"Then maybe we should at least close the garage doors."

Suz had gone back to pounding, stopped, and looked at her queerly.

Imogene nodded toward the threat at the top of the driveway.

Suz smiled. "Now you're thinking, E." She moved over to the double garage doors and pulled them shut. The bottom edges dragged, scraping along on the rough asphalt. With the doors closed, the cloying scent of mold, mothballs, and moldering paper grew stronger, mixing in with Marlboro smoke.

Suz stood on two boxes filled with magazines, lording over the beat-up but unyielding crate, her chest still heaving.

Now Imogene didn't know if the closed garage doors was a good idea after all. The pickers could come down and lurk in the dark, lie in wait close by. Use big rocks to knock them senseless.

Suz went on the move again, climbing like a spider monkey over to a darkened corner, and returned with a breaker bar almost too heavy for her to handle. She climbed on top of the crate and, with both hands, lifted the breaker bar in a pile-driving motion. Her arm and shoulder muscles bulged. Her face bloated red from exertion.

The second before she let fly, Imogene thought that if the box did contain old dynamite, bleeding nitroglycerin tears, poor ol' Suz was going to be blown right up through the roof of the garage. Wouldn't do so well for poor 'ol Imogene either.

Suz brought the breaker bar down with everything she had, striking the crate right between her feet.

The wooden sheet that comprised the lid couldn't hold up under this new onslaught and splintered with a loud crack.

Imogene cringed, pulling her shoulders back and ducking her head as she squinted her eyes.

Suz let out a little squeal of pleasure. She dragged the breaker bar around and worked the edge into the split. She used it as a lever and pried open the broken pieces. The wood cracked and screeched. She worked the bar in again and started to pry—

The scent hit them both at the same time. Suz jumped off the crate and backed up; her face scrunched up in a rictus of revolt. "Imogene, oh my God. That's not a big bundle of cash after all is it? It's not gold or silver, is it?"

Imogene realized it *was* the black death after all. A cloud released that would steal both their souls. Some ancient Egyptian curse that—"

Ange in Imogene's head yelled, *"Dumbasses. It's a body. You uncovered a damn body. Ya penny-ante fools."*

The odor wasn't putrid and wet, but dry and musty yet still unmistakable.

Imogene grabbed Suz's arm. "Put it back. Get some nails and nail it shut. Do it now."

She shrugged away from Imogene. What's the matter with you? It's just some rotten—" She stopped mid-sentence after looking into Imogene's eyes. Suz froze for a second as her mind tried to accept the meaning. She jumped back. "Oh my God. E! That's…that's a dead body in there, isn't it?"

"Hush, child, keep your dern voice down. Of course, it's a body. What'd you think it would be, buried at the bottom of a huge pile of meaningless crapola in a crate marked, 'danger, do not open?' This crapola is nothing more than a mask, a costume to hide under."

Imogene was a fool for thinking it could be anything else other than Pandora's Box.

And yet they now stood ass-deep in a Pandora's Box conundrum of their own making.

# Chapter Thirteen

"Imogene, whatta we gonna do?"

Her past CIW self wanted to say, "Who's we, Kemosabe? You got a mouse in your pocket?"

At least she'd started calling Imogene by her name instead of just E.

Before Imogene could answer, Suz's hand flew to her mouth as shock set in. The reality of having a dead person in her garage for two decades. Or more.

She backed up until her legs hit a box. She fell on her bottom atop a box. One filled with Playboy magazines marked "Research," in fat felt tipped pen.

"Imogene...Imogene." She couldn't catch her breath.

Imogene stepped around the boxes to get over to her. "Stop it. Stop it right now. Don't you dare collapse on me? We can't, under any circumstances, call paramedics for you. You understand. Are you hearing me? Snap out of it."

Suz's mouth opened and closed like a fish thrown up on shore. Imogene didn't have a choice; she slapped Suz hard across the face. Suz fell on her side on top of some other boxes. Both hands covering her eyes as she wept. But at least she took in huge lungs full of air. Suz wasn't accustomed to the criminal life, wasn't used to finding a long-dead person in a crate her father had hidden in the garage for decades under piles of crapola.

Huh, maybe what happened with Wayne wasn't Imogene's bad luck after all. Maybe the entire street was jinxed. They'd gone and built the housing tract over an Indian burial ground.

Suz pulled her hands down as far as her chin. "Imogene...do you think—

Do you think… it's my…my mother? You know she just disappeared for no logical reason, and we never heard from her again. Dad loved her according to the letters but also acted weird anytime I asked about her. Who else could it be? It's mom."

"Oh, dear Christ on a cracker." She hadn't thought of that scenario. Now, it was Imogene's turn to panic. What *were* they going to do if they couldn't call the police? Under normal circumstances, that would be the logical course of action. At least for Suz. Parole tails and dead bodies didn't mix. Imogene would end up in prison for sure.

And that wasn't going to happen.

"Imogene, could you…could you take a look and see if it is my mom?"

The girl was off her nut. How in the world would Imogene be able to tell if it was Clara? She'd never seen the woman and had only heard Mel—Suz's father—talk about her. On top of all of that, who even said it was a woman? Imogene got up and inched her way over to the gaping black hole in the crate, the cigarette between her fingers knocking ash into the dark void. "You have a flashlight?"

"What? Oh, yeah. Of course." Suz sounded as if she'd returned at least halfway back from the jagged edge of total emotional collapse. Imogene needed to help Suz to keep her hands busy. Suz wandered in a daze over to the workbench, cast about until she located a large flashlight with a huge battery as part of the body. She turned it on and handed it to Imogene, not coming close enough, reaching out as far as her arms would go. Not getting any closer to the crate than necessary. Imogene had to do likewise to fetch it.

She held her breath and moved the dull yellow beam into Pandora's Lair. She took a breath and stood up straight. The contents weren't so bad after all. The body *was* a woman as evidenced by the long black hair gone to white streaks in places. The face stared up at Imogene but wasn't at all scary. The poor woman's skin was so desiccated and shriveled it resembled one of those dried apple dolls Imogene had seen the poorer children playing with on the streets where she'd grown up.

"Your mom have black hair?"

"What? I never saw her, remember?" Suz said, "How would I know?"

Imogene took her eyes off the poor woman in the crate and looked at Suz. "Didn't your father have photos or even a portrait of your mom?" The question sparked an image of Joyce's portrait up on the wall in the living room that looked down on Imogene every hour of every day. Maybe that wasn't healthy after all. Maybe Imogene needed to take it down.

More tears ran down Suz's cheeks. She shook her head and whispered. "Oh my God, that is mom, isn't it? Daddy doesn't have pictures anywhere in the house. Imogene, if he loved her, like he said in the letters, how come he doesn't have any pictures?" She let out a long, keening wail.

*Sweet baby Jesus.* Something Ange used to say. *Snap out of it. We have to figure this mess out.*

She stopped her keening as easily as if it were a faucet. "Whatta ya mean? Imogene, we need to decide what we're going to do. We have ta call the police. Don't we?"

Suz didn't know about Imogene's tail and what it meant to have one. Shame wouldn't let Imogene tell her now. Suz knew about the prison time but not the tail. The parole term that kept Imogene standing on thin ice on a warm winter day, the sun beating down, the perpetual loud cracks and pops in the dead calm quiet.

"Look, you call the police this will all fall back on your dad. You wanna tarnish your father's reputation? And all this mess right here will hit the national news. Heck, it might even go international." Imogene did a mock news woman's voice. "Murder most foul. 'Lady-in-a-crate,' found after decades in a garage on Hawthorne. Victim's daughter was unaware her estranged mom had gone no further than fifteen feet away. Daughter, Suzanne Davis, now held for questioning in this morbid incident. A quiet neighborhood ripped apart by a gruesome murder."

Suz's expression shifted to confused as she tried to absorb this new shocking information. "Then what do you suggest we do with...Mom? We sure can't give her to those people up at the top of the driveway."

"We can bury her in the backyard under Mr. Majestic." The words came out of Imogene's mouth before she had a chance to give them a reality check.

The idea was wrong on so many levels.

"E, are you kidding me? Seriously?"

"What choice do we have? You want the street blocked off for weeks on end with newsies, TV trucks, lookie-loos? This place will be a carnival with carnies hawking cotton candy and candied apples. They might even put up a Tilt-a-whirl in the middle of Hawthorne. And what's worse, do you wanna sit in a hot and stuffy police interview room for five hours without a pee break? No food or drink. No one to talk to except dumbass cops while they batter you with the same questions over and over?" Imogene knew that last part from personal experience.

An ex-con with a tail for murder would be their one and only suspect. She had to convince Suz that burying her mom was the smartest move.

"Think, Suz. The police aren't going to believe that all this time, you didn't know your mom was out in the garage." That little dig hurt to say, but it needed to be said. Imogene didn't like conning her best friend in the world. Imogene also didn't want to find her own butt back on the bus to CIW for another stint, fifteen years this time instead of ten. Or worse. Even longer for a new murder beef. Cops tended to hang murders on the closest suspect, then dust off their hands for a job well done, eat a donut, and drink coffee.

And even if you are cleared of any wrongdoing, you'll still carry around the stigma. It'll hang off you like skunk stink. Trust me, I—"

Imogene caught herself going too far and almost let the proverbial cat out of the crate.

"I...I guess I agree with you. Mom would be...I guess better off buried under Mr. Majestic."

"Yes, yes, it's a nice cool place, away from the heat. Much better than a graveyard out in the open with the sun blaring down on her, day in and day out. All those folks walking by looking down at her. Walking over the top of her."

Suz finally let a half-smile creep out. "And this way, she'll be close. I can talk to her whenever I want."

"Yes. Perfect. Why didn't I think of that one?"

"Okay. How are we going to get her over there into your backyard?"

"We'll have to close up the garage like we're done for the night. So the people up there will head home. Then I have a dolly. We'll come back and just dolly her over to the tree and dig a hole. How does that sound?"

Tears renewed their flow. She nodded.

"What? Suz, are you okay?"

"I guess. It's just that I didn't find out until tonight what Daddy called Mom. Remember in the letters? He called her Dolly."

Imogene muttered under her breath, "Sweet Baby Jesus."

They turned off the light, closed and locked the garage doors and walked up the driveway. Suz's hot breath created a white vapor in the cool air. Imogene's cigarette exhale blended with Suz's breath, one acrid, one sweet.

A tall skinny man in khaki pants and shirt with a sharp pointed Van Dyke beard stepped forward. He wore round-framed prescription glasses. "Are you done for the night?" He was the throng of pickers' spokesperson.

Suz started to say something. Imogene put her hand on Suz's arm to silence her. Imogene said, "Folks, that's all for a couple of days. Come back on Saturday."

"That's the day after tomorrow."

Imogene kept walking, holding Suz' arm. She'd melted back into a trance-like funk, her eyes glazed over, obviously thinking about her dead mother being in the garage all these years. Her dad, a killer.

"That's right," Imogene said over her shoulder.

Behind them, the tall man said, "What about that big crate? We'd be happy to bring it up for you."

Imogene turned heel and jumped back toward them. "Look, you heard what I said. Leave now, or you won't be invited back. You understand?"

"Whoa there, grandma. Take it easy."

Suz rushed past Imogene and shoved the tall man in the chest with both her hands. He stumbled back, almost falling on his butt. "Get off my property, now. Or I'll call the police and have you arrested. Don't come back. None of you. You're rude. You're all rude people. Go on, git." She'd yelled her tirade with fists clenched down at her side, her red bloated face stuck out.

Suz had committed battery and was subject to arrest. Imogene had studied the law while locked away at CIW. They had a brilliant law library where she did a lot of research for her novel, *Peekaboo POTUS*.

She put a hand on Suz's shoulder to restrain her. This wasn't at all like Suz.

"Go!" Suz yelled.

The pickers started filtering back across Suz's front yard to their cars on the street. They waited until the last car started up, turned on their headlights, and drove away. Imogene escorted Suz into Imogene's house and sat her in Wayne's chair. She got her a tall, cool glass of water.

Imogene sat in her usual spot on the divan where she could see all at once, out the front picture window, Suz in Wayne's chair, and the portrait of Joyce up on the wall. She lit up another Marlboro.

They sat in silence thinking about the crate in the next-door garage. The one with the long-dead woman. Imogene didn't wanna go back to prison and yet here she sat teetering on the razor's edge of step one, discovery. After that step two, arrest. Then three, the judicial system that would toss her willy-nilly back in the joint. Number four, the correctional system for the rest of her life.

Twenty minutes later, or it could've been forty, a sleek black and white patrol car pulled to the curb directly in front of Imogene's house at 744 East Hawthorne. Her heart pounded in her chest and behind her eyes. How did they know? How had they found out about the crate so soon?

The thought to take it on the lam out the back door died before it could flourish. Not with her old heart. Not with broken-down glass knees.

This was it. There was no getting around it.

A blue-uniformed policeman got out and came around the front of his car, following his flashlight beam. He sauntered across her thick grass lawn. Came up the two steps onto the porch to the front door. He did it the same as a hangman might without moral compunction.

He rang the doorbell. That's when Suz startled out of her trance and looked over at Imogene, who lit the last store-bought cigarette she'd ever have. CIW only allowed hand-rolled Bugle Boy tobacco bought from the commissary. It tasted like crap.

The doorbell rang again.

"Imogene, aren't you going to answer it?"

"It's the police."

"It's the *who?*" Before Imogene could stop her, Suz jumped up, took three long strides over to the door, and pulled it open.

The policeman was a mere shadow on the other side of the screen. Everyone took a breath and paused, one that went on for hours.

"I'm Officer Art Johnson. Are you the woman who lives next door? I was told by the victim you walked over here."

Imogene wanted to run across the worn high-low carpet to slam the door. Delay. Delay. Give her a minute to urgently tell Suz what to say. Really more, what not to say.

"Yes, I am." Suz said, "Would you like to come in?" Suz opened the door and held it for him.

Asking the police into Imogene's house was absolutely wrong. Suz had no right. If Ange had been there, she would've gunned poor ignorant Suzanne Davis.

The uniform stepped in. The first cop to do so in the last twelve years. The last time had not gone well.

In the living room, the cop stood not more than a hundred and fifty feet from a murder victim folded up in a crate. A victim begging to be found and justice served.

He looked to be about twenty-five years old. His uniform perfect, the creases in the dark blue pants sharp enough to shear paper. The badge polished to a high sheen. Same with the shoes. Pure professional. The Government standing tall in Imogene's home for no other reason than to restrict her freedom once and for all.

He was too young and wouldn't know what had happened at 744 East Hawthorne the night they hauled Imogene away. He would've only been thirteen at the time.

He took a notebook and pen from his pocket. "Ma'am, can you please tell me what happened in your front yard about one hour ago?

Imogene stood up too fast and swooned from lightheadedness. "Suz, wait.

Don't."

Suz said, "I got this, E. Don't worry, I'm fine."

"But Suz?"

"Imogene, please."

Suz turned back to the cop. "My father passed away and left me a huge mess in the garage."

"I'm sorry to hear about your father," he said.

Imogene backed up. Her legs hit the divan. She plopped down. The gray ash from her Marlboro fell into her lap leaving a little gray skid against the faded paisley pattern.

Suz continued. "So, me and Imogene over there are sorting through all of this junk."

Imogene squinted her eyes closed and concentrated, trying to send her thoughts across the room to a young and naïve girl who knew nothing about how the real world worked. How you would never, under any circumstances, admit that for decades you had a dead body hidden in your garage.

"I carried the stuff up from my garage and set it in my front yard. I planned to rent a truck to haul it all off. That's when these rude people show up all on their own without solicitation."

Imogene opened her eyes in time to see the cop smiling. He was cute with dimples. Suz stood there in her tank top and too-short shorts. Both damp with sweat. Her legs and hands and arms marred with dirt from the archaeological dig next door in her garage that had revealed a mummy of sorts.

He interrupted her. "So, these people who you did not invite into your yard were trespassing, is that correct?"

She laughed. "Yes, that's exactly right." She playfully shoved his chest with both hands.

Imogene cringed, waiting for the black baton to come out and knock the bejesus outta poor naïve Suz. You never laid hands on a cop, not unless you wanted your teeth scattered on the ground like Chicklet's gum.

But that didn't happen. He smiled, took a half-step back. "It sounds like you were justified in shoving the trespasser. Did you tell him to leave, and he refused?"

Suz shot him that killer smile with her own dimples. "You sound like you've heard this sad story before."

"I have. Can I get your name and date of birth for my report?"

"Yes, of course—"

He left a short time later after giving Suz his business card and asking if he could call her.

They waited thirty minutes before going out back to dig the mom hole.

Four hours after that, Imogene spread the final shovel of dirt displaced by the buried crate underneath Mr. Majestic's long drooping branches. She tamped down the grave one last time for good measure.

She had never in all her life been so tired.

For the entire duration of the digging Suz never shut up. She rambled on and on and on. Imogene tuned her out or risked a brain implosion. Had the ground been hard they would never have pulled it off. They barely made it as it was with the soft soil.

Imogene thought of all the cozy mysteries she read in the CIW library. The ones with unrealistic dead bodies dropping all over the place at the most inopportune moments. And the near misses of getting caught by ignorant cops. And here she was in exactly that same kind of predicament. Though minus the talking cats, knitting needles, skeins of yarn, or recipes. More important, this wasn't make-believe, this was the real gawd dern deal.

Finished, Imogene didn't say a thing. She picked up the two shovels and the dolly and wheeled out from under the drooping branches into the moonlight. Her house wasn't too far from the tree, but she wasn't sure she could make it. Fatigue hung on her like a hundred-pound lead weight, pressing her right into the ground. She dragged her burden along and dropped it at the concrete steps that led up to the backdoor. She looked up at the ten steps and asked herself again, was this what seventy-five-year-old women were supposed to do? Where was the rocker on the porch, the grandkids, the husband to harangue her?

She took in a deep breath and trudged upward. Suz waved and said something inane about nice grave digging or some such then disappeared up Imogene's steep driveway on spry legs three times as young as Imogene's.

Three times as young, dear lord, age was a nasty mistress.

Ange, for the umpteenth time, whispered in her ear. *The only way a secret is kept a secret is if only one person knows about it. Off her, Imogene. Just like I showed ya, take a thick-bladed knife, go over, knock on her door, and when she answers gut her like a pig. Do it right now before you lose your nerve.*

"Don't be ridiculous, Suz is my best friend."

She'd done it again, talked to herself.

*Then what am I, chopped liver?*

"Ange, give it a rest, would ya please? I'm dead on my feet."

But what Ange had said made a lot of sense. She had planted the seed. Imogene could only hope it didn't sprout leaves.

She forgot that she didn't sleep in her bed anymore, that every night for the last two years, she'd catnapped on the divan, half-sitting, half-lying down. Instead, out of old habit, she fumbled into her bedroom, flopped on the bed in her dirty clothes, and fell fast asleep.

While on the edge of consciousness before deep REM sleep, her body shivered and shook. She cried out several times, trying to keep from falling down that God-awful rabbit hole, the one with the memory of Wayne and what happened that moonlit night. But her exhausted body gave up the fight. She slipped over that edge, dropping, dropping into a black oblivion.

# Chapter Fourteen

On the day twelve years ago, Wayne had again stayed late at the pool hall with his drunken and obstreperous friends. He didn't call to say he'd be late. Dinner sat on the table cold and solidified. The grease in the Swiss steak had congealed, fat turned to white globules. She sat on the divan, looking out the picture window, smoking her Marlboro.

At five twenty-one on the dot, Bernard, the neighbor, arrived home from work and pulled into his driveway. Two minutes after he entered his house, out came Poppy Liu wearing her white nurse's outfit, her long black hair like a raven's wing that reached down to her bottom and glistened in the fading sunlight. Poppy, the home care nurse. She got into a beat-up Volkswagen van, beige speckled with rust spots, parked at the curb. It started up with a soft clanking. The engine wasn't long for the world. She lived alone in a studio apartment and sent the lion's share of her earnings to her folks in China so that one day they might join her. She had no family in the States, so she didn't mind staying late when Bernard got stuck at work.

Imogene did a slow burn over Wayne's frequent tardiness and puffed the Marlboro faster and harder.

On occasion, she'd surprised him at the pool hall. Found him at the bar talking to men and women of the wrong ilk. The kind of women who frequented pool halls in the late afternoon. The cool darkness shading their features and masking their youth's early demise, their salacious intent obvious. Imogene didn't feel threatened even though Wayne could still turn a woman's head with his Gary Cooper good looks.

Didn't matter to those kinds of women that he wore a leg brace on each leg from bad knees. The poor man's pain-riddled soul. He looked like a kid with polio. The doctor had shot him up too many times with cortisone, or he wouldn't be walking at all. Shouldn't have been driving, for that matter.

Back in the day, anytime the weather turned bad and a freeze was predicted Wayne would walk the groves all night, keeping the smudge pots lit to warm the citrus trees, or the precious fruit would drop. Walking those uneven rows year after year played hell on his joints. He came home in the afternoon after the sun did its job and took over from the smudge pots. Home thirty-six hours after he left for work. He was black from head to toe, reeking of burnt oil, looking like a raccoon. He enjoyed it, though. He took to the task as if a soldier alone to fight a vicious battle, always coming out the victor. The man had a strong work ethic. She envied his ability to own something that gave such splendid self-worth when all she had were her Marlboros, the divan, and the front picture window where she watched the Widow Weaver across the street perpetually tinker in her flower garden. Primping and pruning those dern yellow roses. Award winners at the county fair in Pomona.

The day the Swiss steak sat cooling on the kitchen table her anger continued to rise. Wayne had too often made the choice to stay at the pool hall rather than come home and have dinner with *her*. The more she thought about it the angrier she became.

Her mind shifted all on its own to Bernard and his situation with his wife, Dorothy. An inanimate hunk of humanity that took up space and kept a good man from getting on with his life.

She got up from the couch, spry and agile for someone sixty-three years old. Wayne took her for granted for the last time. She pulled out some Tupperware and boxed up the Swiss steak, the mashed potatoes, green beans, and scratch biscuits. She put the whole shebang into a brown paper grocery bag along with the fresh blueberry pie she'd just baked. The entire pie. She trundled it all over to Bernie's front door and knocked before she lost her nerve.

When he didn't answer right away, she pivoted on her heel to flee back to the safety of the divan, the Marlboro cigarettes, her big picture window, and Joyce looking down from the portrait, her long-deceased daughter lording over her.

Bernie's front door jerked open. "Imogene, how nice to see you."

She froze and turned around slowly.

She had gone before to Bernard's with some other of Wayne's dinners left to molder on the dining room table. Only this time was different. At least she thought it might be. They had stood and talked in the front yard many times in the past, and it almost made her think that good ol' Bernie might've had a thing for her. The fact that he had the time to invest in conversation, with her of all people, gave her solace.

She would never act on his flirtation. Or at least she never thought she would.

Seeing him standing in his doorway smiling actually scared the hell outta her. What the hell was she thinking?

"Imogene? Would you like to come in and talk for a minute?"

She stood motionless and stared at him, the bag of food growing heavy in her hands.

Three times in the past, when they met, he reached out and took hold of her two fingers with two of his and just stood there staring into her eyes. His simple touch shot tingling needles up and down her back and legs. She knew he was a Lothario, and that he had a woman stashed over on campus; good ol' Delores. But to Imogene, that somehow made him safe. A safety net she thought she needed if she were to take this little misadventure to the next step. She just needed to accept with salacious intent his invitation and finally go inside his house.

She hesitated at this newest invite as she tried to decide if her need to crush her wedding vows in one fell swoop came from a misplaced desire for this man. Would it matter if it was anyone else besides Bernie? Could it be any man? Was it her subconscious that wanted to get even with Wayne for the heartache he caused? Neither excuse justified crossing over that ugly, selfish Rubicon.

In the past when Bernie made the invitation she knew that if she so much as crossed the threshold to his front door that would be it. The destruction of the last barrier. She would become Bernie's Tuesday/Thursday girl. She'd become the Hawthorne Delores.

Bernie stepped to the side, his arm out to usher her in, that Cheshire cat smile grinding away at Imogene, holding her back. His smile is a little too lascivious. A little too lecherous. Had he not smiled—no, it was more a grin—had he kept his expression neutral, only using his eyes to lure her into his web, she would've easily made that wrong choice.

She stood there wavering, ready to step in or flee.

She closed her eyes for just a second and played it out in her head. Ran the tape fast-forward. The way she would pass him to go into the house. His hand on her back guided her into the lair. The place filled with a wonderful scent of cinnamon mixed with a hint of antiseptic rubbing alcohol. Dot would be in her modified chair where Poppy Liu left her. Dot's face was pure blasé, unimpressed with the world, unimpressed that her husband Bernie had just invited a hen into the house to cluck around right in front of her.

Bernie would recognize Imogene's trepidation, the conflict of his wife being in the same room. A step too far for Imogene. He would pick up Dot with ease because Bernie was all man. Wayne had not picked Imogene up in decades. But that wasn't fair, he had bad knees and leg braces. And to be honest she had packed on a couple of side passengers the size of throw pillows on her hips.

Bernie would hurry back and escort Imogene over to the couch where they would sit. He would offer her a beer, a Schlitz Malt Liquor that she had seen him with in the past while mowing his lawn on hot summer days. She never drank beer. In her world women just didn't; a social divide of sorts. He would get her one, and she would like its bitter effervescence.

He would look into her eyes and take two of her fingers into his two, once again sending those wonderful tingling needles up and down her back.

Then he would slowly…ever so slowly…lean in. She would focus on his gray eyes until he closed them. She would peep at his lips, moist and ready to meet hers. She would quickly lick and moisten hers. The very last thing she would do was close her eyes.

Yes. She was ready.

Just that one last step stopped her. It was Bernie being the neighbor.

Bernie, being the lothario. It was the flare of horribly painful emotions once Wayne found out. And Wayne finding out was inevitable, especially with the nosy Widow Weaver right across the street.

And most of all it was the disabled Dot in the same house.

All for what? To feel a man's arms around her. To once again experience a lust-filled kiss. To have a man touch her in an intimate way.

Even with all of those issues, in that moment, the scales balanced out even.

She opened her eyes and took two steps closer, her heart pounding out a merengue.

He reached out as if to help her with this one final hurdle to cross his threshold, where he knew he would add yet another notch to his scorecard.

"Yes, I will come in. But first, could you make that sure Dot isn't—"

Out on the street a car horn interrupted her. She started to spin. Her breath caught in her lungs. It was Wayne, he came home and caught her. Oh, sweet baby Jesus. He knew. He read her mind, saw her intent. He could read her from a mile off. He knew she had made up her mind and had already taken the next step. Had agreed to enter the lair and Bernard's unwritten love contract.

Instead, out at the curb sat a black and white patrol car with two policemen. One got out and walked up Bernie's driveway beside his car and right toward them.

Had something happened to Wayne? Was Wayne okay?

"Excuse me. Do you live here?"

Bernie found his voice first. Or, under the tense circumstances, maybe the lothario in him hadn't allowed his voice box to bind up like it had with Imogene.

"Yes, of course." He said, "How can we help you, officer?"

"How long have you two been standing out here?"

Was it against the law to have an affair with a neighbor? Had the police been Johnny-on-the-spot just that quick before their tryst had even started?

"Only a minute or two." Bernie said, "Why, what's going on?"

"There was a robbery. A shooting. The suspect's on the loose. He's armed and extremely dangerous. We're asking everyone to go inside and stay there until we catch him."

Imogene's hand flew to her chest. "Oh, dear Lord." She took several steps and headed for her house when Bernie said, "Imogene?"

She turned. Was her valiant knight going to invite her to stay with him until the danger passed? Of course, he would.

He held open his hands and nodded to the bag of food in hers.

Her mouth sagged open in shock. She threw the bag to the ground. The Tupperware containers popped open, and the paper bag instantly turned tomato sauce red. She turned and fled but not before muttering under her breath, "Dern yay-hoo."

She had almost made the biggest mistake of her life. Fate had intervened and saved her.

She ran up the two steps to her porch and into her house. She closed the thick green door. She locked it. Stood with her back against it. Her hands clinched to her chest trying to catch her breath. That's when guilt descended upon her thick as a hot fog on a lonely night. Even though she had not so much as stepped across the threshold of Bernard's lair.

But she had still made the choice to do it. She would've done it had she not been interrupted. In her mind, that counted the same as the act itself. Her throat thickened, and tears burned her eyes. She hardly ever cried.

The last time was when Daddy had blown his head off with that two-dollar mail-order pistol. She promised herself then that she'd never cry again. Though promises were like belly buttons.

The last time was at their wedding when they made a brief stopover in Vegas while fleeing Arkansas in a stolen truck and a bag full of money. Standing in that little chapel holding Wayne's hands, staring into his eyes, she promised herself she would not cry and failed miserably. She actually blubbered, happy beyond belief, and so much in love…well, she had a concept of love, but when Cupid's arrow finally buried itself in her bum, she had no idea it would be so all-consuming. They had gotten to know each other on the drive west. In the motels where they stayed overnight, she never insisted on two beds. Wayne, all on his own, chose them that way. The first night in the same room in separate beds, she couldn't sleep knowing he was only a couple of steps away. She wanted him, bad. They talked all night in the dark, getting to know each other. The second night in the motel, after she thought he might've fallen asleep, she slipped out of bed and into his. She cuddled up to his warm body that was hot as a cook stove in July. Wayne said, "Imogene?"

"Yeah, Wayne."

"I love ya, Imogene."

"Me too, Wayne. Me too. You know my name is Alice, right?"

"I know, Babe."

She wouldn't let him at her until they made it official. He never asked and patiently waited. But after the little ceremony in Vegas, oh dear Lord, they got after it like the last two rabbits on earth.

No, that wasn't true, the thing about the crying. The last time was when the cop knocked on their door and told them about Joyce's motorcycle accident. A night not easy to forget. That was the last time she wet her cheeks. That night, something in Imogene died. The emotional mechanism that created tears shattered, never to be repaired.

She came out of her self-pity long enough to realize the backdoor stood open, the screen door shut. "Oh, dear lord." She hurried across the living room floor straight into the kitchen and grabbed a hold of the door to slam it. But hesitated when she saw him down in the lower part of the backyard. A man in a black leather jacket. Just a flash of him at the back wall. Headed toward Mr. Majestic behind the garage. She slammed the door and locked it. The man had a swarthy look about him with slicked-black hair. Someone Wayne would've called a misguided youth." Misguided her ass, you rob and shoot a citizen, you get dumped into the violent felon category and get permanently stamped armed and dangerous.

Hiding under Mr. Majestic was a perfect place. He could scurry up into the high branches that towered forty feet above the ground. In the dark, with that black leather jacket, they'd never see him.

She hurried to the phone and dialed the number for the police, her fingers shaking almost too much to work the round holes in the dial. The entire time, she stared out the window over the kitchen sink to make sure he hadn't changed direction and headed for her backdoor.

Within minutes blue uniforms swarmed her house and the houses on either side, the Davis' and Bernard's. Plenty of good guys in blue to chase the one bad guy in black. Run him to ground and make him pay for terrorizing the entire neighborhood with his selfish nonsense.

In a roundabout way, besides terrorizing, he'd also been the one who'd kept her from crossing over that threshold into Bernard's lair. Saved her from her bad choice.

But they didn't catch the robber. They somehow missed him.

After an exhaustive search, one of the cops knocked on her front door. The Widow Weaver across the street stood in her kitchen window, watching all that transpired at Imogene's house. The ol' gossip.

Imogene turned on the porch light, went to the big picture window to make sure, then opened the door. The kind officer took her statement and asked for a description as best she could remember. He confirmed that her description matched who they were looking for.

She swooned and had to sit. A violent criminal on the loose in their neighborhood. Hawthorne never had so much as a kid's bicycle stolen. What was the world coming to?

She didn't want him to leave, asked if they had checked the avocado tree really well. She told him Mr. Majestic, ever so tall and wide, had plenty of places to elude the police. He tried to console her saying not to worry, that there would be a huge police presence in the area all night. Told her to keep her doors locked and her outside lights on. She couldn't help but feel patronized.

He left.

Imogene called the pool hall and asked for Wayne. Either he wasn't there or the man who answered lied to cover for him. She opted for the lie. She was beginning to believe all men lied, that it was part of their genetic make-up. She told the liar that if he saw Wayne to tell him to come home immediately, it was an emergency.

She hurried into her bedroom and rooted around in her closet, tossing shoes over her shoulder, littering the floor with them. She discovered the hat box, green with gold cord fringe and tassels. She opened it and found what she was looking for. The old linen flour sack with the .32 caliber Iver Johnson. The two-dollar pistol Wayne had when he picked her up that fateful day in front of Ozzie's Eats. Forty years ago.

Would the bullets still be good? Would they work if she had to pull the trigger and shoot the swarthy man if he came for her? Came to hide out in her house until the heat cooled off?

# Chapter Fifteen

Imogene rolled over and sat up, gasping for air. Heart pounding. For several long seconds, she didn't know what room or even what house she was in. Her first inclination was that she sit on the top bunk in her cell at CIW. Ange down on the bottom. She wanted to ask Ange where she'd been for the last two years.

A screwed-up default memory because she spent too much static time in that small cell, not creating any new memories. Just the same old one. Ten years of walls and bars and cackling women who smelled of B.O.

Her eyes adjusted to the dark. This wasn't CIW. It wasn't the living room either, at 744 East Hawthorne.

But *her* bedroom. *Her* bed. The one she had at one time shared with Wayne in a much happier era.

Two seconds later, real time flooded back. The dead body in the crate. That same dead body is now buried under Mr. Majestic. And the fact that hours ago, there had been a cop standing in her living room inquiring about Suz's assault from earlier. A close call for sure. Too close.

In that moment Imogene realized she would not be an endearing character in one of the many cozy mysteries she read in CIW. She was too selfish and narcissistic. But she really wasn't. She just came off that way. After prison, she viewed life through an entirely different lens.

A cadaverous gray dawn seeped through the crack in the curtains. She slid off the bed, her stomach queasy and in need of a strong antacid. A handful of them. She put her hand on the wall for support and walked on shaky legs to the bathroom. She took off her soiled clothes and let them drop to the floor.

An aching pain radiated from every muscle and joint. She climbed into the tub and stood under the hot water. The humidity mixed with her Marlboro lungs brought on a coughing jag that made her go weak in the knees and crave that sumptuous first cigarette of the day. She eased down and sat in the tub, the cascading waterfall snatching at her breath. She stayed that way until the water turned cold and shocked her back to a technicolor reality.

Twenty minutes later, she sat dressed on the divan, smoking that first Marlboro, her muscles already freezing up from all the exercise in the previous night's misadventure. Out the front picture window, the day grew brighter. Mrs. Weaver came out of her house wearing a dumbassed bonnet, ruffled apron, and gloves, looking like a photo right out of Town and Country magazine. She went to work on her dern roses.

Imogene stood, went out on her front porch, and stared her down until she got tired of the witness intimidation and went back inside.

Imogene returned to the divan, smoked, and drank coffee until it was time to leave for work.

With the key in the lock at Dentco, she suddenly remembered it was Friday. It was gawd dern Friday. Giancana The Cigar would be in for his two hundred dollars of extortion money. How had she let time slip by her like a sneak thief in the night?

Ange would've castigated her for sure for the grievous error. *Playin' your dumbass games wit dumbass rubes; cleaning a garage without pay, burying a body that don't even belong ta ya. Bonehead. Bonehead. Pull ya head outta ya ass before it's too late or the man is gonna drag ya down again. Drag yo sorry ass back to See-Eye-Double-ya.*

Ange was absolutely right; a dead woman in a crate could draw a person's attention away from common everyday activities. A common task like paying a crummy organized crime gangster protection money.

Once inside Dentco she punched in the alarm code while squinting through the cigarette smoke. She took her seat on the stool to wait out the day. Deal with all the stress that came with waiting for that punk-ass gangster to come in and strong arm her. The mere idea of the extortion made her angry beyond belief. If he walked in right at that moment, she'd shoot him for sure. According to the law, she had "priors."

The bitter and acrid metallic taste of the nightmare rolled back on her. Twelve years earlier, when she stood in the front yard talking to Bernie when the cop car pulled up. Then, the swarthy man in the black leather jacket in the backyard. Her sitting in the dark, scared to death clutching the .32 Iver Johnson pistol, ready to shoot at shadows. The event in the dream, as real as if it just happened.

She opened her clutch purse for her Marlboros, pulled out the pack, and spotted the envelope. The letter from Delacorte Publishing. Still unopened. The sight of it should've let a little light into her overcrowded life and finally mixed in a strong ray of hope. No matter how small, it would be welcomed. Queue the angel harmony music.

Especially after what had happened the night before with the crate. *"Danger! Never Open! Don't do it!"* Written with three exclamation points, for crying out loud. Any sane person would've walked away from that whole mess. But no. Not Suz.

And what did Suz go and do? She violated the stenciled edict as if some insolent child had written it. Imogene made a fist and pounded the counter. It wasn't Imogene's fault; she wasn't the one making the poor choices. Suz owned that one and now The Cigar had the next one that barreled at her like an out-of-control freight train. Life had been so easy just a few days ago. What she wouldn't do to have that old grind back. The simple life with the only dodge in play being good ol' Nancy Do-right trying to violate her. If the Nancy option sounded favorable, life had really turned rotten.

The bell rang over the door. In walked Suz bright and sunny as if she hadn't buried her estranged mom of two decades in the backyard under Mr. Majestic. CIW-Ange would've said, *No brains, no headache. She's a tool wit out a tool chest.*

Suz walked past the counter where Imogene sat. She waved and said, "Good morning, E." She kept going toward the back to start work.

"Hey?"

Suz stopped. Still smiling.

"What're you doing here today? You're not on the schedule."

She shrugged. "Mike called me at home just when I was about to leave to come over here. He told me not to come to the Bloomington store today. He said I could have the day off. I sat at home for a couple hours and decided to come in here. I just couldn't stay at home, E."

Something was wrong.

"Why did he do that?" That wasn't like him, not telling Imogene ahead of time and sending his future wife (according to him) over to the Fontana store.

Suz shrugged, began to whistle, and continued into the back.

Imogene had developed a nose for trouble and this situation stank ta high heaven. She slid the phone on the counter over and dialed the Bloomington Dentco. It rang twice before Mike scooped it up, "Yell-low. Dentco. This is Mike." His voice came out with a rasp as if he'd caught a cold or had been punched in the throat. He also let slip a couple little grunts that punctuated his sentences.

"Higginbothom, what the hell's going on?"

"Imogene?"

"Why'd you send Suz over to this store?"

"If you haven't figured it out yet, I'm the owner, and you're the employee. I get to make all the day-to-day decisions. Sometimes, even major, important decisions that affect this five-city operation. And believe it or not, I'm not obligated to clear it with you first." He hung up.

"Suz?"

She stuck her head out into the doorway from the back. "E, did you know there are bullet holes all over back here in the walls and such? Have they always been here, and I just missed 'em? The TV is even busted. Did someone shoot the TV? What's going on?"

Imogene ignored her questions. "Did you have some kind of row with Higgy-baby?"

Her expression turned serious as she stepped further into the doorway. "No, why?" Had she already forgotten that they had a mutual crush on each other?

"Then what are you doing over here when you're supposed to be over there?"

She shrugged again. That shrug was getting annoying. That or Imogene's nerves were on edge from lack of sleep. Or it might've been that Imogene had Suz's mom buried in her backyard.

Suz changed her voice in an attempt to sound like Higgy-baby. "It's my five-city operation, and you are merely a cog in this great machine."

"Pompous ass. Five-city operation." Imogene muttered.

"What?" Suz came closer to the counter.

"Where does he get five cities?  His stores are in down-on-your-luck Bloomington and Fontana and they're both in the county area, not even in any cities."

"I think he's counting the cities where he has grocery store contracts. That's the only thing I could think of. You should be nicer to him, E. He really is a nice man."

There it was: the crush raising its ugly head.

"Oh, for heaven's sake's. Please come here. I need to talk to you."

She came closer yet while working on her perpetual smile and unable to bring it to full power.

"Look, I don't think it's a good idea for you to be working here today. Why don't you take the day off? Go home and relax; put your feet up."

"E, are you kidding? I told ya, for right now, I'd rather be anywhere besides that house and garage. At least for now. I don't want to be by myself." Her chin started to quiver. The waterworks weren't far behind.

"Okay. Okay, take it easy. Why don't you run over to the Hole in One Donuts and pick us up some coffee and fresh apple fritters?" Imogene handed her a ten from her purse. "And buy yourself something pretty."

"What are you talking about?"

She was too young to catch the old movie reference. Suz took off, but not with the usual spring in her step. Dead bodies could do that to a person, dampen spirit and mind. Imogene went out the front door and pretended to be on a Marlboro break. It hurt to move. She walked up and down the front of Dentco's long window and peeped at the parking lot. Monitored the comings and goings, waiting for The Cigar to show up. She didn't want

Suz anywhere around when he arrived. Suz was like dangling a bright lure in front of a game fish. More like prodding a Great White shark. With Suz in the mix The Cigar might cause a scene forcing Imogene's hand. Forcing her to pull the gun. She didn't want Suz to endure that large of a chunk of the real world. The irony of that statement after burying her mom in the backyard made Imogene smile.

Suz took her time talking to Hank over at Hole in One. Imogene could see her through the Hole in One window.

Not many cars came to the Cherry Avenue strip center in the mid-morning hours. It'd pick up again in the afternoon-early evening. That's when she expected Giancana just before dark. He was the kind who preferred to move in the shadows. A creature of habit.

While she stood puffing the Marlboro, the red neon "Open" sign for The Lotus and Tea House Massage Parlor went dark. Madam Woo was closing shop to play dead. What a horrible mistake. That wasn't the way to handle the problem. Giancana wouldn't take no for an answer. That's not how his game was played. Giancana would expect a percentage of his victims wouldn't understand. Those were the ones he'd make an example of and do it in the most violent manner possible. The rest of the sheep would then fall into line and, "baa, baa, baa."

She hurried over and knocked on the blacked-out glass door, her knock raising with intensity every second. No one answered.

Imogene turned and scanned the parking lot. A car had pulled up and parked but it wasn't the baby blue Lincoln The Cigar drove. The driver got out, a chubby white guy in Levi's and a blue chambray shirt. He walked around to the front of Cherry Liquor. A strange place to park when there were closer places. Two minutes later, a white panel van with "Landry's Laundry" painted on the sides pulled into the parking lot and stopped. The driver, dressed in all white garb, got out and walked to the Hole in One. He flirted with Suz who still stood at the counter gabbing while the new guy ordered coffee and a pink frosting-covered cruller. Imogene was getting paranoid. Paranoia, according to Ange, caused mistakes; *nerves of steel always carry the day. Eat a paranoid sandwich, and you die just like that.* Ange snapped her fingers.

She dropped the Marlboro and ground it out. She walked slowly back to the Dentco door and stopped. Two other cars pulled up to the Lotus Tea House. The drivers, innocuous men with faces easy to forget, got out and went to the Lotus Tea House door and shook it.

Not today, fellas. You'll have to go elsewhere for your rub-and-tug.

They turned, remounted their cars, and drove off. While she watched them, a homeless person who reeked of body odor snuck up on her. He side-stepped around and entered Dentco. He or she wore too many raunchy clothes with a hoodie down over their brow that kept her from identifying gender. She entered behind him, girding herself for the confrontation sure to come when the idjit stole something and tried to get away with it. Behind the counter she kept a bin of food too damaged to sell. Higgy-baby had disagreed but let the bin stay after she told him, "We don't give 'em something, they'll just rob you blind." You'd think Imogene kicked his puppy at the thought of losing that smidgeon of money to the needy.

The new non-customer moped around the far side of the store pretending to take interest in the personal hygiene bins, toothbrushes, dental floss, toothpaste and the like. Imogene watched him in the fish-eye mirrors she insisted Higgy-baby invest in. The man had no sense of security.

She was watching the idjit closely when the bell above the front door rang. She spun around to look.

In walked The Cigar. He was early. He parked in the red zone right outside the front door, and she missed it. Her senses dulled from the lack of sleep, muscle fatigue, and probably emotional trauma.

Today he wore a powder blue velour gym suit with a black stripe down the legs. He looked like something out of a gangster B movie. The mere sight of him brought back the memory of Amy Chin's dotted eye where the pig had slugged her. Her eye was swollen purple to a slit.

Imogene tackled her rising anger and snuffed it out. Had to in order to survive the day. Hell, survive the next couple of minutes.

"Hey, Grandma, what's cookin' good lookin'?"

Movement caught her eye not too far outside the front window. Suz had chosen that moment to return from the Hole in One carrying a bag of donuts and two large coffees in a cardboard tray. She was almost to the glass door.

Nothing Imogene could do about it now.

The Cigar snapped his fingers in front of Imogene's face. "Hey, knock knock, anyone home?" He tried to bang his knuckles on Imogene's forehead.

She grabbed his hand. "Touch me, and it'll be your last conscious act." She didn't like touching slime like him, his skin dry and coarse like a snake's.

He lost his smile. Fear flashed behind his eyes, fleeting like a phantom with a cape and cowl to hide in the dark recesses. He quickly regained his stature returning to dipshit gangster. He yanked his hand away. "Gimme my money before I reach across this counter and beat ya like I own ya."

In walked Suz, smiling and munching on a fritter. She spotted The Cigar and recognized the conflict from both their postures. "What's going on here?"

A long, ugly smile crept across The Cigar's face. He took a step back out of range of Imogene's slapping hand. "What, who do we have here? Hey there, Baby Doll."

Imogene opened the cash register that dinged. An international sound that meant money. She pulled up the cash drawer and reached underneath for the envelope she'd prepared ahead of time. "Here, take it."

But with men like The Cigar, sex always trumped money. He snatched the envelope like a monkey after a banana. He crumpled it in his fist and shoved it in his sweatsuit pants, never taking his eyes off the luscious Suz Davis.

Even unsuspecting victims recognized a predator when one approached. Suz froze, looked at Imogene for help then decided to go it on her own. She raised her chin and tried to back away. The Cigar grabbed her elbow and yanked hard.

Suz let out a tiny eek. She'd been snared by an apex predator with no way out.

"Why don't we take a walk into the back and have a little get-to-know-The-Cigar session?"

"No. No. No." Imogene muttered. "Not gonna happen, fat man." She reached for the .38 Colt Detective Special. There would never be a good enough reason for going back to CIW, but this one came dern close.

Before she could swing the gun into action Suz swung her free arm and doused the pig with two hot coffees in the Styrofoam cups.

He staggered back, his hands going to his wet, steaming face. "Bitch. I'll kill ya for this. I swear ta God I'll kill ya." His hand snaked under his baby blue workout top. Chrome flashed. A gun. A big one.

Imogene's brain had given the command to her hand to shoot the bastard, but her hand wasn't cooperating fast enough. Not near fast enough. The Cigar was going to shoot her best friend Suz then bring the gun to bear on Imogene. The only witness.

From out of nowhere, the homeless person appeared with a large automatic pistol he thrust into The Cigar's ear. His other hand gripped his throat. The homeless man shoved with his body until he had The Cigar pinned against the glass counter that shook from the collision.

The homeless man yelled with saliva, spattering The Cigar's face. "Move, dirtbag, and I'll blow your friggin' head off."

# Chapter Sixteen

The hoodie had fallen back on the valiant homeless man whose wild eyes at first made him difficult to recognize. But she did.

Eugene.

Her own personal Secret Service Agent. She'd called him and asked for help, but he'd said he couldn't get involved unless it dealt with a crime that came under the agency's direct purview. A dipshit gangster with a gun didn't fit that criteria. Nothing anywhere close.

Dentco's door burst open. In ran the man wearing all white who'd driven the Landry's Laundry van. Behind him came the man who had gone into Cherry Liquor. They rushed Eugene and The Cigar. They grabbed The Cigar and threw him to the ground. Mopped the spilt coffee on the floor with him. They got him cuffed and stood him up. His Aqua Net hair crumpled and mashed in places made him out a clown. They started to drag him from the store all three a roiling turmoil of struggle and obstreperous language. Elbows and knees and kicks.

Imogene shook off the shock that froze her thought process. "Wait!"

Nothing happened. They didn't listen to her.

"I said, wait! Dern you."

Eugene used his big-boy voice. "Everyone, freeze."

The two men stopped struggling. One put The Cigar in a pain compliance wristlock. He hopped on one foot, then the next. "Leave go of me. Let me go or pay the consequences."

Eugene said, "Go ahead, Imogene."

"Look in his pocket. He came in and offered me something. He said he wanted me to be his shill. To shill something. Whatever that means. I told him to get the hell out of here. That's when he started to get rough with my employee. Go on, check his pocket."

"You guys got nothin' on me. I'll be out before you get the paperwork done. I got a lawyer like you've never seen before. He'll sue you for everything you got. That's money in that envelope. That's all. A guy can't have money? You guys are penny ante flatfoots. I've been arrested by the FBI. You guys are just chickenshit locals who don't know your asses from a hole in the wall."

Eugene walked over to him, not breaking eye contact, not the least bit afraid. This was a side of Eugene Imogene she had never seen before. She liked it. Those sparkles rolled up and down her back. She was a silly old woman.

Eugene grabbed a hold of the Cigar's blue velour pants pocket from the outside and yanked hard ripping it open. He removed the envelope and held it up for Imogene to identify.

She nodded. "That's it. He tried to give that to me, and I wouldn't take it." In the far back part of Imogene's brain, Ange whispered, *You're an eeevil bitch. I love it, Sweetie.*

The Cigar's expression suddenly shifted. He exploded. "Wait. Wait. *She* gave that to *me.* Not the other way around. She's lying."

Eugene looked in the envelope and withdrew ten twenty-dollar bills. He held one up to the light, then a couple of the others. He was professional through and through and immediately knew what Imogene had pulled. He smiled. "Funny money. Good stuff but still forgeries."

"No. Wait. That bitch set me up. Wait. You locals can't arrest for that. I didn't try to pass it. I had it in my pocket. You gotta let me go." He tried to pull away and get loose. The Landry's Laundry man tightened his grip and smiled when The Cigar yelped.

Eugene reached into his dirty pants pocket and pulled out his gold badge. He shoved it in The Cigar's face. "United States Secret Service, you moron. And for the record, mere possession is good enough for an arrest. Take him away."

The Cigar kicked and struggled in earnest. "You bitch, you're done. You hear me? You're dead. I'll get you for this. You wait and see if I don't." His body started to emit a subtle stink, one seated deeply in desperation and fear. Imogene had smelled it on the new fish in CIW.

Suz, who had been standing by watching, turned pale with a hand in a fist held close to her chest. "Oh, my."

Eugene followed the throng toward the front door. He stopped. "Imogene, I'll call you to get a formal statement. And thanks."

"Thanks, Eugene. I owe you. Thanks for coming out."

Imogene would have to change her view of law enforcement. At least a smidgeon. For a brief moment…a fleeting moment she thought of telling Eugene about the dead body buried in her backyard under Mr. Majestic. She had nothing to do with the murder, and maybe Eugene could—

Naw. Not a chance. A cop was a cop. Ange had said *I'd trust my own inflamed hemorrhoid before I'd trust one of those lying, cheatin' peckerwoods.*

That was another one of Ange's bromides that didn't make any sense.

Imogene had pondered for hours what to do about The Cigar and had decided to slip him the fake twenties she accumulated over the last two years working the cash register at Dentco. When you ran a last-resort type operation selling damaged food, you tended to draw in the last-resort kind of folks who prioritized eating over prison and didn't mind the risk-to-results ratio.

She figured The Cigar might not have been smart enough to notice the money as funny, try to pass it somewhere else, and get caught. End of problem. Like Eugene said, they were good twenties. To have Eugene show up after he'd turned her down was nothing more than an odd quirk of fate. They happened but were rare. According to Ange it was the same as *finding a four-carat diamond ring on a finger on a hand shoved so far up your rectum when you coughed the sparkle come out jor mouff.*

Suz stood off to the side one hand braced on a bin, her expression blank, skin pale. "E, what just happened? Those men had guns. Big guns. That homeless man? That ugly fat guy, he grabbed my arm. I thought…I thought he was going to—What just happened?"

"What are you talking about? Nothing happened. Shag your cute little butt to the back, get the mop bucket, and clean up that mess you made. Someone's gonna slip and sue the pants off our illustrious employer."

Suz stared for a moment, her mouth sagging open.

"Suz!"

"What? Oh, right." She took off, hurrying to the back.

Imogene settled on her stool and tried to light a Marlboro. Her hands shook too badly to accomplish the mission. She tossed the cigarette on the counter and threw the lighter across the store. It clattered against the front window and fell in the bin filled with drinks: instant orange juice, lemonade, Sanka, and the like.

Time hit the brakes as the world slowed down, begging her to step off and take a long, permanent pause. She focused on breathing, or the anxiety might pile-drive her right through the floor.

She slid off the stool, walked around the counter to retrieve the lighter, and froze. She returned to her purse, opened it, and took out the now crinkled envelope from Delacorte. After all that had happened in the last couple of days, she needed a shot, an inoculation against the blackness closing in, ready to snuff out life as she knew it. She stared at it, the little bit of hope she held in her hand. The ray of sunlight. Did she want to open it to discover that last little bit of disgrace and shame? Snuff out that ray of hope?

She picked at the edge, got her finger under it, and tore a millimeter at a time, following the seam until the envelope sat opened yet forlorn in her hand. She tried to imagine the words. She wanted the author of the missive to have written something positive rather than what she was so sure to find.

The conflict again hounded her. Did she want to pull the folded note out of the envelope, read it, and, in so doing, toss the last bit of hope onto the trash heap? Live with the debilitating depression that that knowledge would, without a doubt, exacerbate?

Suz came out from the back. "Hey, did you know that the jumbo extra-large can of baked beans is miss—"

Suz froze mid-step, staring at the person who had just come through the front door, making the bell jingle.

From her expression Imogene knew it had to be bad. Really bad. She let the letter drop as her other hand flew to the .38 under the counter. All this happening in a second, one carefully dissected into fractions to make time slow to a tick-tock standstill.

The letter fluttered down.

Suz let out a squeak that rose into a keening wail.

Imogene's hand wrapped around the gun stock, cold and firm.

Suz started to run to the person who had entered.

Imogene's head turned to brace this new threat and couldn't at first rectify the message her eyes sent to her brain.

Regular time slammed back into gear and raced.

Imogene recognized the man who'd entered and stopped raising the gun, waiting for Suz to make it over to him.

Micheal Higginbothom, The Dentco King.

Only this Higginbothom looked like an extra from a disaster movie where the 747 fell out of the sky and landed on him. Someone literally beat him to a pulp. His face, bloated and swollen and lumped in the extreme as if a swarm of hungry bumblebees stung the crap outta him. Had she not known him, she would never have recognized the owner of the Fontana Dentco flagship store. A bandage wrapped at an angle came down across his left eye, giving off a pirate air. His lips looked like flesh tubes about to burst. He carried his arm cast in plaster in a sling. He limped, dragging his foot toward Suz, who rushed to him.

Ange whispered in Imogene's ear. *The dumbass skinflint finally got what was comin' to him. Cheatin' all those hungry people outta food and whatnot. But that right there, that's the work of brass knuckles. Ifn I seen it once I seen it a thousand times. That gangster with the bullshit handle, The Cigar, he did that. Woulda happened to you chickee-baby, you hadn't set up the law to land on him like two tons of wet horseshit. We're gonna talk later about that. I'm ashamed of you for callin' in Johnny Law when you shoulda handled it your own self. I taught you better than that.*

Ange's diatribes grew longer and more frequent each time Imogene moved closer to the edge of that dark abyss.

Suz jumped into Higginbothom's waiting arm. He grunted and groaned;

his bloated lips formed half a smile.

Imogene knew in an instant what had happened. The Cigar found out about a second Dentco and since he put the bite on the first one, why not get the second one ta boot. A twofer, two for the price of one. The Cigar had come from the Bloomington Dentco fresh from strong-arming Higgy-baby when he ran smack dab into Eugene and his two younger thugs from the Secret Service.

She could only imagine the way the confrontation went down at the Bloomington store. Higgy-baby would in no way want to turn over any money for protection. He would try to use his words to talk his way around The Cigar. Higgy-baby got his ass handed to him in a hard-knock lesson in life, one he would not soon forget. He was lucky he was still ambulatory, walking and talking.

Higginbothom eased to a sitting position on the floor, Suz in his one good arm. Both of them crying. All of their hands, three of them, moving over each other as if not believing they still populated planet Earth. It happened that way with perceived near-death experiences.

Ange said, *Oh brother. Whatta couple of cheesy-ass saps. Babe, you gotta get away from them two before some of that syrupy crap rubs off. You gotta stay hard or find yourself back on the top bunk at See-Eye-Double-a.*

Imogene pulled a new lighter off the display and lit up a Marlboro. The nicotine flashed hot in her blood, helping chase away at least a bit of the doldrums.

Ange whispered again. *That dingy broad right there knows your secret. She knows about the Bitch in the Box under Mr. Majestic. What are you gonna do about it?*

"Nothin'. And you can go ahead and butt outta my business. This is my life, not yours."

Imogene realized she said it out loud and clamped her mouth shut around the burning white paper cylinder between her lips. Her aberrant behavior a by-product of severe fatigue.

Too late, they heard her utterance.

The two lovebirds on the floor stopped their lovesick preening and looked up at her.

Imogene shrugged and went back to puffing the Marlboro, thriving on the nicotine infusion that made the daylight brighten and come into sharp focus.

Ange said, *Tell those two idjits ta get a room. That floor right here is nasty-dirty. Not that I haven't done it in nastier places. You know what I mean, Babe? I know you know what I mean.*

This time, Imogene shrugged in response to the in-her-head voice.

Suz struggled to get up. Higgy-baby, now that he finally had Suz—touching her for the first time—wouldn't let her go.

"Come on, Honey." Suz said. "Let's get you back to my house where I can take good care of you."

He suddenly shifted polarity at the new prospect of fulfilling a long-time goal, being with his crush, and letting her help him to his feet. "Imogene," he said. "You're on your own today."

She muttered around her Marlboro that wagged up and down. "Is that anything different from any other day?"

"What did you say?" He, too, had to be on edge over the beating, his lack of courage, and, of course, the pain.

She didn't reply, pasted on a fake smile, and waved.

Suz sensed the confrontation growing in intensity and tugged on him, trying to get him to the glass door and out to her car before the skirmish turned into a pitched battle.

Ange said. *As banged up as that twit is, and wit that broken wing, she's gonna have ta take the top. You know what I mean, babe? Wink. Wink. Ride 'em cowgirl.*

Higginbothom wouldn't let it go. "What did you say? Say it again, Imogene. Go on say it again."

Ange said, *Go on, tell 'em that'll be the only way they'll get 'er done.*

"No, I'm not sayin' anything that even resembles that."

"Say it again, Imogene," Higginbothom said. "I'm tired of you always sniping at me. Criticizing everything I do. Fed up to here." He raised his chin in the air.

Suz had the door open and Higginbothom halfway out. Angrier now,

Imogene shot him a fake smile and waved. "Okay, you want me to say it. I'll say it. Higgy-baby, the condition you're in, she better be the one on top. I'm just sayin.'"

His already large eyes, widening even more the skin struggling to stretch with the purple and red swelling as he grappled to get back into his flagship store. His one good hand clamped on the frame as Suz tugged on that same arm. Suz yelled. "Imogene, shut your mouth. For God's sake's, shut your mouth."

"You're fired. You hear me, Imogene? And I mean it this time. I'm not kiddin' one little bit. You're fired. Get your stuff and get the hell out." His fat lips battered the words into all but indistinguishable blobs punctuated with flying spittle.

Ange whispered. What's the big deal? You were looking for a job when you found this one.

Imogene again raised her hand and waved. "Thanks. I was looking for a job when I found this one."

# Chapter Seventeen

Imogene worked all day, finished her shift, locked up, set the alarm, and drove home more tired than she ever remembered. She turned down Hawthorne, and first thing she spotted was Bernie's car in his driveway. She checked herself and realized she no longer had that urge, that need to be with him. Probably the result of the nightmare of when she relived the evil night that had visited her house twelve years earlier. An evil to beat all evil. The remembrance of just the dream, hours later, still left an acrid metallic taste on her tongue.

On Hawthorne Avenue on the left side, the Widow Weaver stood between her rose garden and her front door with her usual bitter scowl. She hated the world and didn't mind letting everyone know about it. Of course, Suz had a different opinion. She would always say, "Mrs. Weaver's the salt of the earth. You can't find better people."

Wasn't that a fine how do you do? What was Imogene, chopped liver?

Imogene waved at the widow to let her know Imogene was still watching her. Imogene cranked on the steering wheel, turning into her own driveway. She shut down the little red Gremlin and sat for a moment, working up the energy to open the car door, get out, and trundle across the thick grass. Then, the difficult part would be the three concrete steps up to the porch. A regular Pike's Peak in her condition. She wasn't at all sure she could make the short trek that seemed to grow longer by the minute. In the quiet, the car ticked as it cooled.

She lit the thirty-eighth cigarette for the day. Two left. On a normal day, there would be six left to smoke while she sat on the divan and pondered what had happened at Dentco. Pondered her past, something that clung to her like a blood-sucking tick she would never shake loose. Smoke those last six Marlboros, all the while decompressing on the divan, looking out the front window, watching for Bernie. Watching the evil widow through her kitchen window, backlit with a yellow light as she washed her dishes.

In her little car, Imogene took in one long drag on the Marlboro and held it, waiting for the nicotine to do its job. That's when she noticed Higginbothom's antique Studebaker truck parked partway down Suz' drive. Poor ol' Suz had taken the big step and invited him to spend the night. Imogene could only hope that it was based more out of love rather than Suz' most wonderful quality, her overwhelming need to nurture. Higginbothom was a nice enough guy, but there was an important component missing in his character makeup: a total lack of compassion. He also needed a big dollop of morals, which Imogene preferred over his money-driven backbone. Compassion was one of the most important components needed in a healthy relationship.

Imogene let out a long trail of white smoke. The extra boost of nicotine energized her enough to open the car door and spill halfway out, almost going to the ground. She caught the door frame for support. If she hadn't, she would've been on the ground for the rest of the night, too frazzled to stand. She made it to the grass before that little burst died on the vine, and forced her to trudge the rest of the way. She took one step at a time, dragging her other foot up before taking the next. Exhausted.

She opened the door to a house that had been closed up all day. A hot blast hit her face. Stale air. She walked to the refrigerator, took out a Schlitz Malt liquor beer, and sat on the divan. Through the open front door, a breeze made it over and kissed her with a welcome coolness. She put her head back and closed her eyes. She didn't fight sleep; she welcomed the escape.

* * *

That night twelve years ago, Imogene sat upright in her bed, continuing to chain-smoke, going deep into the third pack of the day. This was right after she saw the man with the black leather jacket in the backyard. This was after she dumped the Swiss steak in Tupperware at Bernie's feet, the brown paper grocery sack bleeding red.

She kept the lights off. For some reason, it felt more comfortable that way. The front and back doors were locked, but she kept the window in her room open to the air, or she would surely suffocate. She needed air more than anything else. No, that wasn't true. She needed Wayne to come home from the pool hall. Put his strong arms around her and whisper in her ear that everything would be all right and that he "loved the hell outta her." She loved him more than life itself. She had been a fool for even thinking about stepping out with that dumbass Bernard. She had to tell Wayne, make him understand what he meant to her. The remembrance of that first day he walked into Ozzie's Eats made her smile. She hadn't smiled like that in a good long while. The way he came behind the counter where he wasn't supposed to be. The way he stared at her with those wonderful Gary Cooper eyes.

Nothing in the bright moonlight outside her bedroom window moved; no people, no cars, no dogs and cats. Every now and again, a sleek black-and-white patrol car slid by blacked out, no headlights. On the prowl for the swarthy man in the leather jacket. Looking for the crook who committed a violent crime, the man she saw in the backyard headed toward Mr. Majestic.

The weight from the Iver Johnson .32 pistol that rested in her lap gave at least some solace and peace of mind. The moon rays coming through the window illuminated the shoes she tossed willy-nilly out of the closet and onto the carpet in her mad dive, looking for the gun. Those shoes lay scattered on the floor like ships on a calm sea. Her insides were anything but calm. Wayne would chastise her in his funny way about leaving her shoes out for him to trip over. He had those dern leg braces, after all. He'd been sleeping in his own room for the last seven years after his snoring ruined too many nights' sleep for the both of them. And to be fair their relationship had soured more than a little after he lost the groves and the beautiful house in LaVerne. She would fix that the next time she saw him. Tell him it wasn't his fault and forgive him like she should've a long time ago. If she had to, she would even go to the pool hall, drink beer and shoot pool with him. She wanted him back. She wanted back their old love, wanted it the way it used to be.

Drowsiness took over, and even with the nicotine, her head started to nod. Her chin dipped to her chest twice before she stubbed out the cigarette, more afraid of self-immolation than the swarthy man on the loose in the neighborhood.

Seconds later, she startled awake, still sitting upright on her bed in her bedroom. Maybe it was more than a few seconds. Sleep hung on her like a warm blanket, masking good sense. Where was Wayne? Why wasn't he home yet? She didn't know for sure how long she slept. Maybe a couple of minutes. Maybe a couple of hours.

A whisper of a noise came a second time. The same noise that had awakened her.

The moon had moved around in its nightly orbit, cutting off the direct rays through the window and throwing the room deeper into gray and black gradients where dark shadows lived.

A large object the size of an overturned chair sat in the corner on the other side of the discarded shoes less than ten feet away.

Only she didn't have a chair in her room.

She didn't have anything that matched that size or shape.

Through the open window, a warm summer breeze gently massaged the bedroom and fluttered the curtains. That's when something sinister in nature caught her eye.

Oh, dear Lord, the window screen was slashed open. Her heart jumped into her throat, beating fast enough to snatch her breath away.

"Hey?" A raspy voice said.

She jumped, her bottom coming up off the mattress and back down again. She raised the gun. "Get out of here. Get out right now, or I'll shoot. I'll do it. I'll pull this trigger." Her voice shook so much no one would take her as a threat.

"Help me, I fell. I think I broke me dern leg."

She stuck the gun out further, holding it in both hands that trembled, as if in twenty-below temperatures. "Get out now."

"Don't be silly, come give me a hand."

"You…you get out of my bedroom right this minute." Her finger tightened on the trigger.

The man's face in dark relief, a mask of evil, frightened her to no end. She tried to speak again to demand he leave, that this was his last chance. But the words caught in her throat, writhing in a knot of fear.

His clothes rustled. He was pulling a gun, the one he used to rob and assault a good citizen earlier in the evening, the one the cop had warned her about.

A match flickered close to his face.

The sudden movement startled her. She yanked back on the trigger.

The little gun jumped in her hand.

The gunshot nothing more than a pop.

She tossed the gun to the floor. Her night vision seared from the bright orange flash of the gunshot.

Had the ancient bullet even worked?

The match snuffed out. But not before, in that briefest of a second, she got a good look at him: the swarthy man in the black leather jacket.

Serves him right, coming into an old woman's boudoir, scaring the water out of her.

His shadow eased over and fell to the side. His body purged a horrific grunt.

Alice Putnam rolled out of bed and crawled on hands and knees faster than a greyhound could've done it. Once in the kitchen, she used the counter to rise and stagger to the phone. She couldn't see with the light off and retreated the way she'd come, hand over hand on the counter to the light switch. The bright light blinded her. With her arm up to shield her eyes, she made it back to the phone mounted on the wall and the phone book on the chair below. On the inside flap, she found the number for the police department and dialed.

"Police department, how can I help you?"

"I…I…help me! Please help me!"

"Ma'am, what's the matter? What's your address?"

The stress caught up to her. She slid down the wall in a sitting position and let the phone drop and dangle from the cord. The receiver banged again and again against the wall with a slight knock. The tinny little voice kept talking, demanding information. She spoke through her hands that covered her face and told the man her name was Imogene Taylor and that she just shot an intruder. Shot the man they were looking for earlier. She gave the tinny little man her address.

Hours later, or it might've been two minutes, someone pounded on her door yelling, demanding entry. She couldn't move, frozen in place by fear and dread and most of all a horrible dose of remorse for taking a life. Even if it was one plagued with evil.

A loud noise shook the entire house and made her yelp. They had kicked in her thick front door. Two uniformed men entered the kitchen at the same time from the two different doorways, their guns drawn.

At the sight of the gun she involuntarily let out another frightened yelp and flinched inward, her hands covering her face. She pointed. "Not in here. Not in here. He's in there."

The two officers disappeared, their footsteps telling the tale, thumping the floor across the short span of the living room into the shorter hallway and into her bedroom. She held her breath hoping it had all been a dream. A horrible nightmare.

Of course, *it was* a nightmare. Don't be silly. Sixty-three-year-old women don't shoot intruders in their own bedrooms. Not in this town. Especially not at 744 East Hawthorne. The two officers would find nothing but a jumble of shoes on the floor where she'd perceived an intruder. Dreamt one up. They'd find a silly little bullet hole in the wall, a conversation piece for Wayne to bring up again and again for years to come. They'd laugh about it like they laughed about the above-ground pool used as a lagoon in Gilligan's Island.

Where was Wayne? Suddenly, she needed him more than any other time in her life. Dern his sorry hide. But she would forgive him for being gone at the most inopportune time. Love allowed for errors and encouraged forgiveness. She just wanted him there. She wanted to get lost in one of his hugs. Smell the scent from his gray fedora, the one with the little red feather in the band. Revel in the smoky remains left by his cherry pipe tobacco that permeated his clothes and skin. And even at times, it made his eyes smoky, almost smoldering.

She started to struggle to her feet, using the kitchen counter for support. She pulled the dining room chair over and sat, the stress finally powering down now that the police had arrived. The police. She'd never say a bad word about them ever again. Who in their right mind would rush into a house when they knew there was an armed robber lurking inside waiting for them? Her breathing evened out as the blue uniformed cop reentered the kitchen, holstering his gun.

"Is that the only phone?"

Imogene swallowed hard. "Yes. Is everything okay?" She also wanted to ask if he had actually seen someone in her bedroom. Or was there just a bullet hole in the wall?

The man with the nameplate "J. James" picked up the phone hanging from the cord, depressed the receiver, waited for a tone, and dialed a number by rote. "Yeah, it's Paul Four. We have a one-eighty-seven. We need the coroner and the dicks out here. What? No. And I can't talk right now; the R/P is sitting right here. This is the only phone. Right. I got it."

An acrid, metallic taste from the burnt gunpowder lingered on her tongue. She said, "Officer, would you be so kind as to get me a glass of water, please?"

He complied but didn't smile once, pure professional. When he handed her the glass, she said, "Thank you. Coroner? You said coroner? I thought…I mean I hoped I had only been dreaming and I shot the wall. So…so the man's dead?"

He failed to answer, pulled up a chair and sat across from her at the table. He took out his notebook and wrote notes. Her hand trembled, shaking the water in the glass, the house dead calm. Dead quiet. It creeped her out.

An hour later—she knew it was an hour because she watched the clock on the wall—two men in suits and ties arrived. They stepped into the living room with the officer babysitting her and spoke in low tones.

After that, everyone did their talking, mostly outside on the front porch.

The black arm on the clock continued to make its slow crawl around the face, not holding to normal spans for seconds and minutes. It moved much, much slower now. A long half-hour passed. Out on the porch, one of the detectives interviewed someone. In all the dead quiet, the voices easily made it into the kitchen. The baritone detective kept his voice down to a low mumble that she couldn't make out. But the woman…the woman was none other than the nosy busybody from across the street, the notorious Widow Weaver. She spoke loudly, proud of her words, unaware everyone in the neighborhood thought her rude and socially unacceptable.

"…What did you say?" The widow asked the detective.

He spoke in another jumble too low for Imogene to decipher.

"Yes, the loose woman who lives here has been having an affair with the neighbor, Bernard. Don't just take my word for it. Ask around. They'll tell you the same thing. I saw her at his front door earlier tonight."

"That nasty little witch," Imogene muttered to herself.

The detective interviewing the widow spoke again.

"That's right, Detective." The widow replied, "That's what I said. Her husband came home about an hour before I heard the gunshot. He must've found out about the affair. There's your motive, detective. That's why she plugged him right between the eyes."

Imogene jumped to her feet. "Liar!" She ran toward her bedroom. Her feet pounded the floor. A uniform stationed next to the portrait of Joyce, his thumbs hooked in his gun belt, tried to step in her way to stop her. She bowled him over, continuing on in her mission. Two more long steps, and she was there.

Someone had turned on the bedroom light.

She entered and froze. From out of nowhere came a long, mournful keen. It had to be from her. But her world was too busy swirling down a vortex of emotional pain and agony. "Nooo. Nooo, please God, no."

Wayne lay crumpled against the wall his tanned skin pale and waxy. Eyes open starring off into an invisible oblivion, his soul having fled for nicer climes.

He now sported a third eye in the middle of his forehead that wept a narrow tear of blood. His crippled-up legs in his braces lay akimbo at unnatural angles.

The last thing she remembered was the two cops who crowded the doorway, one on each of her shoulders, dragging her out the same as if she were a harpooned walrus on a beach.

"Wayne! Wayne! That wasn't me. I didn't do that. I didn't, Wayne. I couldn't. Pleeese believe me."

# Chapter Eighteen

Imogene woke with a start, still sitting on the divan, and sensed something amiss. She shook all over, having relived yet again the night Wayne came home without telling her. That night, she waited with a gun in her hand for the swarthy man in the black leather jacket to break into her home.

She had slept upright on the divan all through the night in her own filth, having missed her nightly shower. Her mouth tasted acrid and metallic from the nightmare. She looked out the front window and spotted a baby blue Lincoln Continental parked at the curb.

Sleep clogged her brain the same as sand in a gearbox. She knew the car was significant and… "Oh, dear Lord." She jumped up and hurried to the front door that she left open the night before when she came home and crash-landed on the divan. She needed the air. The cool night air.

The screen door was the only barrier left between an evil man, The Cigar, who had every reason to take Imogene off the board. Exterminate the star witness against him.

She took hold of the thick wooden door, ready to slam it. Just as the screen door opened. In stepped Sam Giancana. The Cigar.

She stumbled back as Ange whispered in her ear. *Don't be a damn panty-waist. You know why he's here. There's nothin' you kin do about it so get in his face. Give 'm that last act of defiance. Flip him the bird and tell him to kiss your white saggy ass.*

The Cigar shoved past her, his shoulder moving her aside. He stepped over and sat in Wayne's chair, his expression smug. He wanted to scare the livin' daylights outta her with his confidence. He accomplished it in spades.

But he'd sat in Wayne's chair, desecrating Wayne's memory. No one did that to her Wayne.

"Get out now before I call the police." Adrenaline pulsated behind her eyes, sharpening every minute detail: his thick gold necklace tangled in a tuft of man hair on his chest, his gray pinstriped three-piece suit, his hair re-coiffed with an entire can of Aqua Net after yesterday's mashing, and most of all, his eyes, gray and foreboding, lacking any sense of humanity. Pure beast.

She tried to walk over to the divan without stumbling; that would let on how fear had gripped her very soul. She fell into the divan, readjusted her bottom, and lit a Marlboro, the first of the day that always brought with it a coughing jag to beat the band. She didn't care, the nicotine her only friend in the room.

From Wayne's easy chair, he stared at her as if she were a Christmas ham and he an unfed lion on a five-day fast.

He pointed a thick finger. His gold wrist chains rattled. "You did me wrong!"

The first inhalations caught in her lungs and made them convulse. She coughed hard enough to pop out her eyes. Hard enough to make her sweat and her face bloat. Her heart pattered and skipped.

The Cigar grinned. "You don't have to worry about those cancer sticks killing you off. Trust me, you won't have to wait long at all. I'm only here so you know what's comin'. I want you to worry, to lose sleep over it. Chew your nails down to the quick. Pull your hair out." He scooted his butt to the edge of the chair to get that much closer to her. Mere inches closer. "In the end, you'll beg me for death's sweet release."

The screen door banged open. In stepped Suz. She didn't enter any further than two feet, afraid of the lion perched, ready to leap. She yelled. "Get out! I called the police. They're on the way. They said you can't be here. They said that you're threatening and dissuading a witness, a felony." When he didn't move, she stomped her foot. "I said get *out* now."

The Cigar slowly stood, straightened his vest inside his suit coat, and then pulled down his cuffs. He checked his manicured nails. "You two bitches don't seem to understand who I am. Or what I'm capable of. I bailed out on your chickenshit little scheme to avoid paying what's owed me. If I get arrested again, I'll just bail out again. You see how this works? You think this hasn't happened before?" He raised his voice, yelling the last part.

He lost his faux congenial air his expression turning to pure hate. "I go to jail, but it never sticks. You know why?"

Ange said, *Don't let the pig run his game on you. Tell 'm he shows his fat snout around here again you'll rip it off and feed it to the crows.*

Imogene took a puff off her Marlboro and, as casually as she could muster said. "You're a pig. You show that snout around here again, I'll chop it off and feed it to the crows."

Suz and The Cigar both looked at her, stunned. Harsh and violent words incongruent coming from a seventy-five-year-old woman who drove a little red AMC Gremlin, who smoked two packs of Marlboros a day, and who clerked at Dentco. An old woman who under the circumstances should've been scared right out of her big panties.

Out front through the picture window a fast moving black-and-white patrol car slid to the curb, brakes screeching. The uniformed driver jumped out and ran to the porch. He flung open the screen door and entered.

The pig stood and once again pasted on a fool's grin. He turned and put his hands behind his back. "Remember what I said, ladies. I'll be back and the next time I damn well guarantee you won't see me comin'. You can count on it."

The cop, D. Harold, handcuffed him and escorted him out to his patrol car just as another cop car slid up to the curb. The two cops talked.

Imogene couldn't sit any longer; anxiety forced her to stand. She paced in front of the picture window, watching The Cigar sitting in the backseat, comfortable as you please. The sad part about it was she knew that feeling, the one about being cuffed and trapped in the back of a cop car. It was anything but comfortable.

Suz came up behind her and put a hand on her shoulder. "It's going to be all right, E. The police will protect us."

Imogene smiled. A little chuckle slipped past her lips. "You are wonderfully and beautifully naïve, my pretty friend."

Out front a third car slid up to the curb, a plain Dodge government car. Out stepped Eugene who hurried over to the two cops and joined the animated conversation.

Imogene puffed and puffed, pacing in front of the window. She said, "The worst part of it. You want to know the worst part of it?"

"Tell me, E."

"The worst part of it is that nosy wretch the Widow Weaver is getting a ringside seat to all this drama. She'll put the kibosh on me again if she gets half a chance. Rat me out. Send me back to See-Eye-Double-a."

Suz's expression sagged.

"What?" Imogene asked.

Suz shook her head, not wanting to give it up.

"What, tell me."

"E, Mrs. Weaver passed on five years ago while you were ah…gone on that extended vacation."

The words filtered through Imogene's brain and shook her to her core. More so than the frightening contact with the pig.  The implications staggered her. She made her way to the divan on wobbly legs and plopped down. What the hell was happening to her?

Suz hurried over, knelt, and took Imogene's hand. "E, are you okay?"

No, she wasn't okay. For the last two years, since she'd been out dragging around her unwanted tail, she'd seen the Widow Weaver in her front yard as she stood there and glared at her. Saw her in her apron and gloves tending her rose garden, saw her at night through her kitchen window washing her dishes. And now Suz said her the widow had been dead and gone five years? Six feet under with the worms doing the rest of the job, wiping her off the face of the earth.

Imogene grabbed and clutched Suz's hand as her other hand serviced the Marlboro. She spoke as she exhaled a lungful of smoke. "Suz, tell me true. In your garage…I mean, last night, did we really…with the…box. Did that all—"

Suz gripped her hand and nodded. "Yes, that all happened, and I'm trying hard to forget it. I think it's best you do as well."

Ange chimed in. *Now's a good time. Take this bitch out. Remember what I said about the only way to keep a secret? Do it right now, Imogene, and then drag her sorry ass into your bedroom. Hide her body under your bed until later. It's a perfect alibi. No one will believe you did it, not with the cops right out front.*

"Sweet baby Jesus, would you shut up."

Suz pulled back as if slapped.

Imogene patted her hand. "Sorry honey, not you."

Suz's expression looked like she had just eaten something sour. Imogene patted her hand again. "It's okay, dear. I just need some sleep, that's all. I promise you I'm okay."

"I hope so E, you and I are tethered at the hip now over what we did last night."

The cute little neighbor was also worried about the secret, only vice versa.

Imogene said, "You know Imogene is spelled with an I and not an E?"

Suz's huge smile warmed Imogene's heart.

"Of course I do. For my best friends, I do this silly little thing. I assign random names. I guess you could call them pet names. I hope that's all right?"

"I'm your best friend?" This revelation shook Imogene more than the threats from the pig but in a different way. Imogene glowed with new hope and happiness that gave the threats from minutes earlier more bite. She had something to live for and Imogene didn't want anything to happen to her new best friend.

"Don't be silly; of course, you are." Still on her knees, she moved in and hugged Imogene. She stayed in the hug. Suz's body warmth and heartbeat brought tears to Imogene's eyes. Imogene could've stayed that way forever. She choked out a whisper. "Kid, you can call me whatever you want."

The front screen door opened. In stepped Eugene and the police officer D. Harold.

And with them, the real world returned with all its stark reality.

Imogene pulled out of the clinch. She turned her head away and swiped at her tears.

D. Harold took the information he needed for the police report and left.

Eugene sat in Wayne's easy chair, the same place The Cigar had sat. The irony of it wasn't lost on Imogene: how good and evil moved on the same ethereal plane, bumping and colliding, the same yet absolutely different.

Eugene rocked in the easy chair, staring at Imogene, gathering his thoughts. Suz sat in the chair just below Joyce's portrait.

Eugene finally spoke. "Imogene, I've known you going on three years. I know you well enough to realize you are not going to take my strong advice to go into witness protection. Don't you see, without you the US attorney doesn't have a case against Giancana. That means Giancana only has one option to stay out of prison."

Ange wanted to chime in. Imogene suppressed her comments, tried to anyway. *Don't you dare crawl into bed with this mangy dog, you'll get fleas. And think about it E, you do this you can never come back to C block. You'll forever be segregated. Marked as a pariah. You'll be a K-nine. A keep-away. You want that kinda stigma? I don't think so.*

Ange had heard the "best friend" comment, the thing about the pet name and now called Imogene E for the first time. That same warm glow returned and swept through Imogene's body. She had two best friends. What more did a girl need in life?

Imogene said. "What about Suz, here? She going to be offered witness protection?"

Eugene's expression fell. "No, she wasn't the one Giancana tried to coerce into passing the funny money. That was only you."

"Then I say ta hell with all ya all. Suz doesn't go, I don't go."

"Imogene, you're not being reasonable. Think about this for a minute. We can't protect you if you don't let us."

Imogene snuffed out her Marlboro, bumped out another, and lit it. "I'm not budging on this, Eugene. You might as well mount up and ride off into the sunset." She tried for light and breezy and fell short.

Suz got up, came over. She sat next to her and put her hand on Imogene's. "E, now logically you know this is the right thing to do."

"Don't even think about turning those big brown eyes on me. I'm not

Higgy-baby. My mind's made up. I won't let the likes of Sam Giancana send me running for the hills. I'm sittin' my big butt right here. Let 'im come and do his worst. I'll deal with it. You wait and see if I don't." She wanted to add that she and Ange would deal with it but she'd already spooked Suz enough with the Widow Weaver thing. Hell, it spooked the hell outta Imogene. She had to put a lot more thought into it after everyone left her alone.

"Now," she said, "if you two don't mind, I have to take a shower and get to work." She stood and walked around the coffee table. From the new angle in the center of the living room, she could see more of the front yard. D. Harold still sat in his cop car out at the curb, writing his report with Giancana in the backseat, his bloated face thrust forward bumpin' his gums not letting up with the constant barrage of berating language.

Off to the right on the other side of the little red Gremlin stood Higginbothom, his face still damaged, purple and red, his arm in a sling. He stared at the animal in the back of the patrol car and trembled, scared out of his wits. Higginbothom would never forget the beating he took from that man. The pain and fear Giancana instilled in him would be there forever.

Imogene ground her teeth. The very idea that a pig like that could ruin her friend. No way was she going to run and hide.

Let the bastard come. She'd be ready for him.

# Chapter Nineteen

Imogene unlocked the front glass door to Dentco, turned off the alarm, and immediately took her seat on the stool behind the counter beside the cash register. She lit up a Marlboro and tried to swallow down the knot in her throat. One put there by the fear and horror she relived from the day before when she slipped the Cigar into the envelope with the funny money. Then, the confrontation that ensued. The obstreperous language. The way he chomped at the bit to get away from the men who held him, trying to get at her to do her dirty. She had never seen such wanton love of violence. For him, it came as a need, a bloodlust unfulfilled.

She puffed and puffed, finishing the cigarette in record time. She bumped out another and lit it. Out in front, Amy Chin from the Lotus Tea House and Massage Parlor hurried over and entered Dentco. She stood on the other side of the counter, her eyes brimming with tears.

Her eye where The Cigar had beat her was much better, the black and blue turning to yellow. She held out a plain envelope and bowed. "We are in your debt, mama san. We owe you for your great service. For what you did for us."

Amy didn't realize that the day before, Imogene had, in a similar fashion, held out the same kind of envelope, offering it to The Cigar. Imogene shivered at the similarity.

Ange said, *Sweet baby bald-headed Jesus palomino can this shit get any schmaltzier? Have the bitch bow again and give her a swift kick in the ass. Tell her we're real women over here and not curbside floozies who'll just roll over and offer themselves up at the first sign of trouble.*

Imogene let the envelope thick with cash in Amy Chin's hand hang between them. "I don't want your money. What I did was for me as much as for you. We all have to work together to stay safe." She didn't know where those words came from. Stay safe? What a shit sandwich. Nobody was safe anywhere. Your number comes up, that's it, you're D. U. N. as Ange would have spelled it out.

A tear rolled down Amy's cheek. The poor naive girl thought it was all over because The Cigar had gone to jail. When in reality the real trouble had just begun.

Out front and across the way Ibrahim from Cherry Liquor came out the back door to his store lugging three cases of Schlitz Malt Liquor headed for Dentco. Off to the right, Hank from Hole in One Donuts came out of his shop carrying three pink boxes that contained a dozen donuts in each. Three dozen. As if she could eat all those before they turned stale. It was the thought that counted.

*"Well, for the love of mike. I'm gettin' all choked up here. Not. What's with all these schmoes and their gratitude? I'm gonna hurl, E. I swear I'm gonna toss me cookies all over your good shoes."*

At the same time, Suz pulled up in her Volkswagen painted red with black spots like a ladybug. For Imogene, it was a step too far on the cutesy-o-meter. But not for Suz, it fit her like a glove. She got out and came in the store. "Hi Amy, how goes it?"

"Hi Suz. I'm trying to show our gratitude for what Imogene did for all of us yesterday and she won't take it."

Suz put her hand on the outstretched envelope still extended in Amy's hand and lowered it. "I know Imogene. You'll stand there all day. She'll never take that money. It's just not in her."

The bell over the door rang again. In walked Hank and Ibrahim with their gifts.

*Hey, look, if we were standing in some raggedy-assed manger, these three buffoons could pass as three wise men.* Ange guffawed loud enough for all to hear. Or at least Imogene thought she did.

Everyone laughed and talked, happy the stress The Cigar caused had dissipated. Everyone but Hank had an apple fritter. He said he'd never eat another donut the rest of his life. Just the thought of it made his stomach churn. The life of a fry-cook.

Imogene began to relax and enjoy the good company. She had not realized until that moment these nice folks were all her friends. She didn't have the stomach to tell them it wasn't over yet. Not by a long shot.

All three, one by one, said their goodbyes and left.

When the doorbell jangled after the last one, Suz lost her smile and turned to Imogene. "E, Mike is serious about firing you this time. He sent me over to run this store. And to run you out if you're here."

"Yeah, yeah. If I had a penny. You can go ahead and go over to the Bloomington store. I got this."

Suz came around the counter. "Maybe you should go home for a couple of days and let him cool off. Hey, what's this?" She bent over and picked up a crumpled envelope on the floor.

Imogene had already gone back to staring out the front window like she always did when no customers shopped in the store. She turned too late. Suz had already opened the envelope and pulled out the letter. "Hey, gimme that. That's mine. You have no right—"

Suz backed up her eyes large as a baby doe's. "Oh my God, E."

Imogene's stomach dropped clear to the floor. Suz had desecrated her envelope, her touchstone that contained the last vestige of *hope*. Hope she so dearly needed the last couple of days. Imogene would never again find so perfect an example of hope sealed in an envelope.

She leapt off the stool and snatched the letter and envelope from her. At the same time, Imogene held up her hand. "Wait. Wait. Don't say a word. I haven't looked inside it yet, and I don't wanna know what it says. You understand. I just don't. So, don't you say a word about what you read." The request came out more of a demand.

But Imogene did know what was written in the letter. Life had never gone her way, not with her dad, not with being thrown in with all the others of the great unwashed masses to work at Ozzie's Eats, not with the loss of their groves and the wonderful house in LaVerne and most of all, not with the loss of Wayne, the love of her life. There wasn't any way the letter could be anything else but a rejection. That's just the way life worked.

She folded and smoothed out the rumpled letter face side down and returned it to the envelope.

"E, I didn't know that you—"

Imogene held up her hand. "Da, da, da. Don't say it. Don't say another word. Please Suz, keep out of this."

Imogene reached under the counter, took out the stapler, and stapled the envelope shut.

But it was too late. She had witnessed Suz' expression, her reaction when she looked at the letter. Though the question begged was she just excited that Imogene had simply written a book? Though there was nothing simple about it. And that it didn't matter it was a rejection? Or did the letter say something else. Now the touchstone, instead of hope, had turned into something more in the realm of a horrible little itch she could never reach.

"Ah, dern you, Suz." She tore open the envelope, cutting her finger on a staple, and unfolded the letter, marring the paper with blood droplets. For the third time in two days, she was staggered. Her knees wobbled. She backed up and sat on the stool, one hand going to the counter to stabilize her swoon or she would've continued on down to the dirty Dentco floor.

Her breath came hard. Words by the ton spilled out of Suz' mouth at a hundred miles per hour, none of which made any sense in Imogene's heated and addled mind. Imogene controlled her breathing and looked at the letter a second time to make sure she wasn't seeing things.

Delacorte Publishing
   John Catskill, Senior Editor
   1750 Broadway, 19th Floor
   New York, NY 10019
   212-555-2613

Mrs. Bea Taylor
   1926 Cherry Avenue

Fontana Ca. 92316

Dear Mrs. Taylor:

Normally, Delacorte doesn't accept unagented manuscripts. But in this case, I am so pleased you sent us Peekaboo POTUS. What a gem of a novel. I have never read anything like it. The unique voice, the story—over the top yet plausible as presented—a seventy-five-year-old woman who creates a plan to assassinate a sitting President; quirky and yet full of verve and creativity. Such detail. Such controversy. The main character's love for Wayne comes through as genuine, making this action-packed thriller a romance as well. A novel that will cross multiple genres and pull in a wide audience. As you can see, we are very excited about this project.

Your query letter, though, did not give us enough information about you. Who is Mrs. Bea Taylor that she can have so much information and background to write such a tone-perfect novel? Amazing. Truly amazing.

Please tell me you're working on a sequel; this could be a wonderful series.

Do you have an agent? We are prepared to make an offer on this soon-to-be best-selling novel.

Please call me at your earliest convenience.

John Catskill
  Senior Editor
  Delacorte Publishing

The air turned thick around Imogene and warbled like a songbird underwater. How could this be? Her little bit of hope just paid off big time. Hit triple sevens on the slot machine of life. That wasn't supposed to happen. All those days in C block how she wished so hard it hurt, wished that the warden would call her in and say the whole thing was one big mistake and she was free to go. That particular hope, the most important one of her life, had never materialized. Why now? What had changed?

She turned to Suz.

Suz took her in a hug. "Ah, E, you're crying. You poor ol' dear. You're so happy you're crying."

Imogene pried Suz away from her and shook the letter in front of her face. "You don't understand. You know what this means?

"It means yippee my best friend is a famous author."

"No, you don't get it. But I do. It means the arrest gods giveth and the arrest gods taketh away. This right here means someone's going to discover that body in my backyard buried under Mr. Majestic, and I'll go back to C block for the rest of my life."

"Oh, pshaw. Don't be a Gloomy Gus. No one's going to find that box. Why would they? Only you and I know about it, right? And I promise you I'm not telling *a soul*. Wait. Did you say you haven't even opened this letter yet? I mean, before I found it on the floor? E, you have to call this Catskill guy and talk to him like right now. Right his minute. We gotta hear what he has to say. Let him make you a lavish offer. Have you started on the sequel? Can I read the book? Please let me read your book. I *am* your best friend, right, E? Oh, my God, am I in the book?"

Imogene held up her hand and closed her eyes. "Please, you're giving me a headache with all the jibber jabber."

Imogene needed to find a quiet place and stare at a wall for ten or twenty-four hours. She'd taken in too much stimuli in the past two days. She was full to the brim about to overflow. A state that might dump her in the babbling idiot category, talking to herself and answering.

Suz put her fingers up to her mouth and twisted, mimicking locking her lips and throwing away the key. She pulled the desk phone on the counter over and handed Imogene the receiver. She took the letter from Imogene's hands that quivered and dialed the number to John Catskill, Senior Editor of Delacorte Publishing.

No. No. No. Don't do this. I can't do this. Please no.

This was stress Imogene didn't need. Not piled on top of everything else.

And yet she let it happen and took the receiver by rote as her eyes watched her best friend dial the New York number.

New York. Imogene was about to talk to someone in *New York City*.

Her mouth turned dry with anticipation and anxiety. She had her back to Dentco's glass door and front window.

The phone rang on the other end. New York. Little Alice Putnam was going to be talking with someone important. A publisher interested in *her* work.

The phone on the other end rang.

From behind her came: "Imogene Taylor, I'm arresting you on a parole violation for consorting with known felons."

Someone on the other end of the phone answered. She slammed it down and pivoted on the stool to find the fat Nancy Do-right standing there with her hands on her hips.

The other shoe had dropped just like Imogene thought it would. You couldn't mess with the arrests gods and not get burned.

# Chapter Twenty

Three hours later, Imogene still sat on the concrete bench in the local county jail, waiting to catch the chain to CIW. The night Wayne died, she thought she'd hit rock bottom. At the time, she hadn't known what was in store. The horrible time-crushing wait sitting in that CIW prison cell. Watching time flutter by without so much as a wave or a smug smile. Sitting in that small, smelly prison cell, twiddling her thumbs day after day. Now that she'd lived through those ten years and with the prospect of another fifteen, this new twist in life about ripped her guts out. She had never been so low and depressed. A ton of pressure sat atop her, making it difficult, if not impossible, to breathe. The parole violation she dodged for the last two years had come to fruition and meant she'd spend the rest of her life in prison. And for what? According to the parole agent, Imogene had consorted with a member of organized crime by handing him an envelope that contained forged money. Even though the report read that *The Cigar had handed it to her*. Didn't matter according to California law.

In the world that Nancy Do-right inhabited, the fact that Imogene had not reported the first contact with The Cigar fit the criteria perfectly. She'd "consorted with ex-convicts." It wasn't fair. The Cigar had come to her and not vice versa. But Nancy was technically correct: Imogene had not reported the contact. The only thing that kept Imogene from curling up in a fetal position on the highly polished and waxed floor was what had happened when Nancy put the cuffs on her. What was said in that moment. How it shifted Imogene's world right under her feet. She still thought about it. How it couldn't possibly be true. Her mind rejected the possibility.

Imogene resigned herself to her fate standing in Dentco amongst her friends while the cold steel bracelets encircled her wrists. The girls from the Lotus Tea House and Massage somehow sensed the problem next door and came over to see. This compounded Imogene's humiliation. The seven girls stood in a throng watching and haranguing Nancy Do-right.

In the back of Imogene's mind, she kinda knew this rolling disaster was on its way down the hill with Imogene standing in its path, unable to jump clear.

The click of those cuffs was the same as the cold steel door in CIW slamming shut for the last time with fifteen more years in the offing.

Ange whispered in her ear. *Ain't this just the most wonderful thing? The dynamic duo rides again. This is gonna be great, E. You wait and see if it ain't gonna be the best of times and not the worst of times. Time will pass by just like that.* Ange snapped her fingers. Her smile dissipated. *I miss the shit outta ya, babe.*

Nancy had grabbed hold of Imogene's arm to escort her out to the G-ride, the baby blue Dodge parked out front. A car she would've seen if Suz hadn't distracted her with that dumbass letter…and the phone call that never went through. The arrest and parole violation didn't have to happen if Imogene could've seen the witch pull up. Imogene coulda taken it on the lam. Slipped out the back door and over to Madam Wu's Pleasure Palace, hid under one of the broken-down beds that smelled of baby oil and sweat and sex. Ugh. But Fate, that evil bitch, wouldn't let her catch a break like having her book published.

Imogene said in a hoarse whisper, "You think I can get my old cell back with Ange?"

Nancy stopped moving her toward the door to look at her as if she had three heads. "With who?"

"Angela Ledger. You know, my cellie. You read my file. I double-bunked with her for close to nine years."

Nancy looked around, then back at Imogene. "What the hell are you talking about, girl? You never celled with no Angela Ledger. I never heard of that convict. You were the powerhouse in C Block. They put every new fish that rolled into CIW with you. So you could get their minds right before they mixed them in with Gen Pop. You were the grand dame of CIW." She lowered her tone so none of the others could hear. "And the warden of CIW called me personal like and asked that I give your case a little extra attention. He really wants you back." She winked.

This new revelation gut-punched her. How could that be? It couldn't. Nancy was messing with her head, had to be. Without Ange, Imogene would've never made it through the ten-year bit. They would've found her at morning roll call hanging from the neck by the bunk blanket.

Yeah, this was just Nancy playing her gotdamn mind games.

Imogene sat on that concrete bench in county playing the arrest over and over in her head, trying hard to compare it with the memories of all ten years in a ten-by-eight-foot cell. Trying to remember all the times she and Ange played checkers, smoked Bugle Boy, laughed and cried.

And cuddled and spooned.

Another hot thought rose up in her befuddled brain, one ironic in nature. Imogene had deserved every bit of this parole violation. There was a dead woman buried in her backyard under Mr. Majestic that no one knew about. She started to chuckle. The other sad sacks waiting to catch the same chain from county over to state stared at her as if she'd lost her feeble mind. This goaded her to laugh even harder. She laughed until hot tears ran down her cheeks.

"Imogene Taylor?" The jailer called her name.

What did she care about getting fingerprinted and photographed? Her life was over. She had nothing else to live for. What was the rush? Now, she had nothing but time. She stopped laughing and sat back down. What if Nancy had not been blowing smoke up Imogene's dress. What if Ange really had been a figment of Imogene's imagination? A safety valve to let off emotional pressure. Fifteen years without Ange...well, that just wouldn't do.

Wait. Even after she got out on parole, in the last two years, Imogene had heard Ange's voice clear as day. She even visualized Ange each and every time she spoke. Saw her expressions, her mannerisms. How could she do that if she never met her? She couldn't, not if Ange was nothing more than a ghost.

No. Nancy was just running a game on her, had to be.

"Imogene Taylor." The jailer said more intently this time. He came to the bars and looked in the cell. "Taylor, get your ass up here before I come in after you. And you won't like it if I do."

Imogene stood and trundled over. "Yeah, that's me."

The jailer, a fat slob who'd dined too many years on the jail's all-starch diet, took a Forge key from his belt and opened the cell. "You're sprung."

"What?"

A few other women, all cons, wandered over. "How can she be?" one said. "She's here on a violation. Those are stainless steel, unbendable commitments. What's up with that?"

The slob jailer shrugged, "Ask your cellie here. The feds are letting her out. Got a writ of habeas."

All the women now stood. "Snitch. Rat. You cheesed-eatin' rat."

Imogene hurried to the opening and shot through. She muttered to the jailer on the way past, "Thanks for nothin' asshole." She was trying to rehabilitate her con image, didn't like harsh vulgar language, but she was back behind concrete walls and bars...and when in Rome.

Eugene waited for her outside the West End Sheriff's station in the parking lot. He drove her home. Neither spoke during the entire trip. She had only sat on the concrete bench in a holding tank but still sensed the filth all over her body in a sickening film. Decent folks were never meant to have that experience. She wanted to cry even then over still having a tail and that her rescue from the jaws of despair was only temporary. As soon as she stepped out the barred gate, the clock started ticking, counting down the time when she'd again be pulled back in on a violation. Prison for the rest of her natural life. Nancy had told her as much.

They rode from the jail to Imogene's house on Hawthorne.

Eugene pulled up and stopped out in front. "Stay safe, Imogene."

She said, "Thanks. Sorry to put you through all this."

"Wasn't your fault."

They sat quiet in the car letting the silence communicate for them.

Finally, she said. "You never did tell me what the 'L' in your middle name stands for."

He smiled, "That's a government top secret."

"Come on, it's me. Come down off that high horse and spill it."

"Lemuel."

"Oh, sweet Jesus."

"Yeah, that's why it's a secret."

More silence, this time due to the fat elephant sitting between them.

"Is he back out?"

Eugene looked away from her and stared out the windshield. "Yeah. Bailed out even though I tried getting a no-bail hold for threatening a witness. His high-powered mouthpiece brought up that…well, let's just say he convinced the judge."

"Cause I'm a con, right? You can say it. We're second-class citizens. No victims involved, right."

He reached under the front seat, pulled out something in a rumpled paper bag, and slid it across the bench seat without saying a word. He was taking a huge risk doing this for her.

"I already owe you too much, Eugene."

"When the system's not working for you, you have to work the system."

She pointed to the bag. "I take that and use it. It'll be the same as pulling the trigger on myself. I'll go in for the rest of my natural life."

He shifted his gaze from looking out the windshield to looking at her eyes. "At least you'll still be walking and talking."

"You've never been in. You don't know what it's like."

He looked back out the windshield. "You're right, and I can't even imagine. You do what you think is best and I'll back you the best I can. Please take it. I'll sleep better."

"I take what's in the bag, I'm linked to you. I'll pull you down right alongside me, and you'll get a taste of the inside for yourself. Thanks for everything, Eugene." She leaned over and kissed him on the cheek. The kiss out of character for her. She left the bag on the seat, got out, and closed the door. Before she turned to cross the street to her house, she looked down the driveway toward the Widow Weaver's house. A diminutive Hispanic woman stood in the kitchen window at the sink washing dishes. Imogene's mind definitely needed a tune-up. She didn't have time to worry about the small things, especially with The Cigar and his cronies after her. She walked across the street to her yard, her driveway conspicuous without the little red Gremlin.

"Dern it to hell."

They had inadvertently left it parked at Dentco, and Eugene had already driven away. She needed to get back to work or risk having her mind spin at such high RPMs she'd explode. Only she had no way of getting there, barring calling a taxi. Out of instinct, she looked up and down the street. Four houses down, a baby-crap mustard-colored sedan sat at the curb. The car didn't belong in the neighborhood. She walked back down her drive and into the street, not taking her eyes off the single occupant behind the wheel, a woman with a blond bob haircut and button nose.

The OC, organized crime, had yet to allow women among their ranks especially their torpedoes. Imogene came around to the open driver's window. "Hey, would you mind giving me a ride over to Cherry Avenue in Fontana to the Dentco?"

"Excuse me?"

Imogene didn't wait to converse further. She walked around, opened the front passenger door, and got in.

"What are you doing? Get out of my car. Who do you think you are?"

"Really, you wanna play this stupid game? Come on, let's just cut to the chase. Start this baby up, and let's get rollin'"

"Ah, hell." The woman started the car and made a U-turn.

She could've been the same age as Joyce, Imogene's daughter. No, probably Imogene's granddaughter. Definitely too young to be futzin' around in this kinda violence. You try and pet the hyena you're gonna get mauled. And The Cigar and his buddies were a barrel full of hyenas.

They rode in silence until the woman said, "My name's Ruth, and I'd appreciate it if you didn't tell Eugene you made my surveillance."

"What is Eugene to you?" She had deep blue eyes and perfect alabaster skin. She'd be eaten alive in CIW.

"He asked for a favor. I work for the US Marshal's service. I took time off to cover you until the trial. Eugene's trying like hell to get it sanctioned so I don't have to use my vacation time, and then this'll all be on the Government's dime."

"Let me guess, the Feds look at this as a twofer, two for the price of one. I'm an ex-con who did time for murder. I'm a non-human in their eyes, and if Giancana takes me out you can take him down for something more than a cheesy forgery beef. And I get taken off the board in the bargain. Am I close?"

Ruth looked from the road to Imogene and back. "Eugene said you were one smart cookie."

Ange spoke for the first time in an hour. Imogene was beginning to believe she really made it all up in her half-crazed mind, and, knowing the truth, ran off Ange.

*I'm ashamed of you E, takin' up with the enemy like it was nothin' atall. You're not a cheese-eatin' rat. For God sake's, ya shoulda caught the chain and come back here with me. I woulda protected ya. You know that?*

But Imogene didn't know that. In fact, she wasn't sure about anything anymore. The Widow Weaver dead and gone, the bitch in the box buried in the backyard under Mr. Majestic, and now the cops are acting like they have always had a backbone and a heart and soul. Up was down, and down was up.

*If you're gonna play your cards this way then go on, do it, ask her the big question. Bet ya you won't like the answer.*

"Hey…ah, you're not just using me as bait, are you? You will stop him or his cronies when you see 'em and not wait for something to happen first, right?"

Ruth looked from the road once again, her eyes expressing incredulity. "Imogene, I can't believe you'd even ask that question. You have entirely the wrong idea about law enforcement."

*Yeah, right, that's why they threw your skinny ass in prison for ten years. For an accident. Right? Go on, tell 'em about that accident. Tell her how Johnny Law stole a whole decade from ya. And that was no accident. Mama, please.*

Imogene turned in her seat and watched the passing landscape as she thought about all that had happened.

Fifteen minutes later, Ruth pulled up in front of Dentco and let Imogene out. From inside Dentco came Suz' muffled scream. "Imogene! They let you out." She ran from inside the store to the front door.

Before Imogene closed the car door, she stuck her head back in the car. "Thanks for the ride. And thanks for doing this. Over there at Hole in One, they got some killer apple fritters and dark sludge Hank calls coffee." She shut the door, turned just as Suz made it over, and took her in a hug that forced the air from her lungs.

The Dentco now seemed comfortable like a long, lost home. After the discovery of her true friends, she was the happiest she had been in twelve long years. How could that be? Not with the executioner's blade hanging over her head in the form of a buried box, and with a whack-a-do parole agent after her butt, chasing Imogene with a vengeance. And, of course, the worst part, organized crime vowing to take her out. She hugged Suz for a long moment, reveling in the warmth of friendship. They walked arm in arm into Dentco. Imogene broke away from Suz, went over behind the counter, and reached for the Colt .38. She put it in her dress pocket, then took her place on the stool as if nothing had happened and waited for them to come to her. What else could she do? While she had waited for Wayne to come home from the bar or the pool hall, she had become enamored with reruns of Bonanza, a western with the Cartwright family defending their ranch. With the Colt in her dress pocket and the bad guys, the men wearing black hats coming to get her, she couldn't help wishing she had friends like Adam, Little Joe, and Hoss Cartwright backing her play.

*"What's the matter with you, girl? You don't need those white trash make-believe characters, not when you got me. I got your back, girl. You know that from when we ran C-block. Now quit your belly-achin' and man-up. Put on your big girl panties and at least pretend you can't wait for 'em ta come get ya."*

Suz came over and stood next to her, beaming as if she had yellow canary feathers sticking out her mouth. She reached over, picked up the phone, and handed her the receiver. Suz read from the letter, her lips silently moving as she dialed.

"No," Imogene said. "I'm not ready. I can't do this right now." The words came out of her mouth, but she still held the receiver, clutching it until her knuckles blanched white.

The phone rang.

Suz whispered. "Go get 'em, E."

On the second ring, a woman on the other end picked up. "Delacorte Publishing, how may I help you?"

Imogene uttered a word but only a croak came out. She tried to put the phone down. Suz stood too close and held it up to Imogene's ear.

The nice woman in New York said, "Hello?"

"Ahem, yes, this is Imogene Taylor. May I speak with Mr. Catskill?"

"What's this regarding?"

Suz had her ear right next to Imogene's, listening. She whispered, "Mrs. Bea. Tell her, Mrs. Bea Taylor."

"Oh, right. I mean, this is Mrs. Bea Taylor."

"Oooh, hold on, please." The phone clicked and immediately picked up.

"This is John Catskill. Is this really Mrs. Bea Taylor?"

Imogene wanted to faint dead away. Suz put a hand on Imogene's back, supporting her.

"Yes, it's me. I...I got your letter."

"Oh, my goodness. I mailed that weeks ago. I thought you'd never call. I am so glad you called. You haven't shopped Peekaboo POTUS to anyone else yet, have you?"

"No."

Suz prodded her back. "The offer. Ask about the offer."

"Wonderful. That's absolutely wonderful."

"I was kinda surprised you liked it so much."

"Liked it! We love it here at Delacorte. Do you have an agent? Let's get this show on the road. Let me give your agent a call."

"No, I'm sorry, I don't have an agent."

"No problem, any of them will jump at the chance to represent you. Can you come over to my office today, and we can discuss the book? We'd love to meet you."

"Ah, no. I'm a…in California."

"Oh. Hmm, that is an issue, but not a large one. We can send you a ticket. Before we go any further, let me get your address and phone number."

Shame flooded in. Imogene was an ex-con who worked at Dentco in Fontana. Who was she to think this man would continue to like her book, or her for that matter once he found out that horrid little truth?

Suz prodded her again.

Imogene shoved the phone receiver away, disgusted with herself, ashamed that she would even hope to be someone she wasn't. This had all been a big mistake.

Suz took the phone. "Hello, this is Suzanne Davis. I'm Mrs. Bea's literary agent." Suz looked at Imogene and shrugged. Imogene nodded and whispered "Hell, if I can be an author, why can't you be an agent? Go for it."

Suz smiled hugely and then wiped her expression clean, shifted to serious. "I'd like to discuss the offer you mentioned. What number are you thinking about?"

Imogene couldn't hear the response. Suz wilted, screwing her eyes shut; her hand slapped the counter and stayed there for support. She put the phone to her chest, opened her eyes, and whispered, "Seventy-five thousand."

It was Imogene's turn to swoon with lightheadedness. She swayed on the stool, glad she was sitting down.

"Well?" Suz said to Imogene with urgency.

Imogene tried to push the words out and couldn't. Suz's expression shifted back to blank as she again spoke into the phone. "I'm sorry, we aren't in the same ballpark."

Imogene grabbed her arm. "Are you kidding me? Take it. Take it."

Suz shrugged her off, listened, and then mouthed, "One hundred."

Imogene thought she might pee herself. "A hundred? Are you kiddin'?"

*"Wake up, E, this is all a dream. It's not for real. Remember you're on your way back to See-Eye-Double-ya. Tell these two buffoons ta quit yankin' on your*

*dick. Let's get back ta real life and start plannin'. We gotta be ready for when that asshole comes for us. You know I'm the only one here talkin' true. We gotta lay a trap for this asswipe before he sneaks up and back-shoots ya."*

Ange took the bite off all the excitement, but Imogene wouldn't have any of what Ange was sellin'.

This time, Suz didn't ask Imogene what she wanted to do. Suz shook her head to no one but herself. "I'm sorry, but we're thinking in the high two-hundred range."

Suz listened and then wilted yet again and lay across the counter. "Yes, let me speak to my client and I'll get right back to you. Yes. Yes, today. I'll call you right back." Suz hung up and let out a squeal that hurt Imogene's ears. Suz jumped up and down, clapping her hands like a kid in kindergarten. "Three hundred. He said that was his final offer and that it has to be for a three-book deal."

Imogene muttered. "Sweet baby Jesus. Wait. More books. I couldn't possibly write another book. That last one sucked away part of my soul."

# Chapter Twenty-One

The mustard-colored car with Ruth the US Marshal followed Imogene home in her little red Gremlin. Ruth kept her distance and if Imogene had not been looking for her she would not have even noticed. Was it a good thing to have a cop so close for hours at a time with Suz' mom buried in the backyard?

Three hundred thousand dollars rattled around in her head, making her a little crazy. How could it not? More money than she had ever seen. More money than in any of her dreams of Utopian wealth. But just as quickly, the idea of writing two more books elbowed its way in, covering the elation, smothering it in a black cloak.

Before she made it to that part of the equation—the obligation to write another book—she would first have to dodge The Cigar and at the same time juggle the threat of going back to C Block behind Nancy Do-right's campaign to do Imogene wrong. After all that, if she survived, writing another book would be child's play.

Too many problems swirled around and around, giving her a category-five headache. The smart play would be to put that whole book mess out of my mind and concentrate on one critical problem at a time. Deal with one, then move on to the next. Tick them off with a little check mark, no different than going to the Alpha Beta Grocery store.

Imogene showered and put on a comfortable ratty house dress that belonged in the ragbag. She pulled an ice-cold Schlitz Malt Liquor out of the refrigerator, sat on her divan, and smoked the last six cigarettes in the second pack of the day. Allowing her mind to relax and take in all that had happened. The most important thing being what Nancy Do-right had said about Ange not being real. If Ange wasn't real and the sightings of the Widow Weaver weren't real, then—

*That's right, it means you've gone around the bend. You've gone a little soft in the head. No big deal: it happens to the best of 'em. Now come on, quit your messin' around and get yo ass back here ta me at See-Eye-Double-ya. I miss the hell outta ya, girl. We kin spoon ta our heart's content up on the top bunk just like we used to.*

For two year,s Nancy had harassed Imogene and made her life miserable with idle threats. Why *wouldn't* Nancy make something up like the thing about Ange? Do it just to harass and jibe a parolee? Sure, that was it. What she said about Ange had to be a fairytale to get under Imogene's skin. That had to be it. And she did it only because Imogene let her. She again pushed out the thoughts of all that book money and wondered why Suz hadn't come over to do another one of her little jigs like she did in Dentco after she called back and confirmed the deal.

Maybe Imogene should've been more worried about losing her grip on reality, but first things first. More important, above all else, was not going back to the joint. Anything after that took a backseat. She set the .38 Colt on the divan next to her and covered it with a throw pillow.

She salted the rim of the beer can, sipped and smoked, and watched out the window. Suz wouldn't be able to hold out. Before too long, she would be over pounding on Imogene's front screen door. Even though Imogene had told her, she wanted time to absorb it all. If she came over, Imogene would just turn her around and send her home. Tell her again tomorrow morning was soon enough.

But gawd-dern it, it was fun to think about all that money. "Wayne, you see me now? Wish you were here."

She looked the other way down the street. Maybe she'd make some coffee later and take it out to Ruth sitting in her car, just past Bernie's house. Out there protecting and serving. But then what would Ruth do if she had to pee from all the coffee? Ruth would have to come in and use the john. Would that violate surveillance protocol? Of course, it would.

The alcohol in the beer took the edge off and she finally started to relax. Out in the front yard and street nothing moved, no cars, no people, no stray pets. Quiet town USA.

Maybe it had all been a dream. If she wrote all that happened in the last few days, put it in a book, no one would believe her.

All of a sudden, off to the right came Suz in a rush. Another woman trailed along behind in denim pants, the kind cut low, showing far too much waistline for prudence's sake. Navel and half her hips showing. Her peasant blouse was white with ruffles and elastic that accentuated her breasts. Three bead strands hung down from around her neck, rattled and swung across healthy cleavage, tanned and freckled but not nearly corralled well enough. The woman's hair, dyed platinum blond, rose in a 60s up-do beehive. The whole getup froze her in a past era, one that said this woman was unable to change with the times. With all the sun-winkles, the wild hair, it was difficult to decipher an age. With the garb and the make-up the woman was trying to pull off mid-forties but had to be in her mid-fifties. Maybe even older.

*E, take a look at that fool. Tell her dis is 1973, girl. Tell her ta pull her head outta her ass and get wit the program. Join us here in the real world.*

Suz didn't wait to be asked; she pulled the screen door open and walked right in with her friend on her heels. Suz looked pale, her expression neutral and, at the same time, close to going into shock. She moved over to Wayne's easy chair and plopped down. Her pretty brown eyes seeing Imogene but not necessarily registering anything other than what swirled around in that cute little brain.

Suz's friend came in with a swish of beads and smiled to beat all, a smile that made her eyes mere slits. "Hi, I'm Thelma."

Suz choked out some words. "Thelma, sit."

"Oh, my land. You don't have to say it like that. I'm not your pet." She sat in the chair underneath Joyce's portrait.

The only light in the house came from the hall in front of the one bathroom. Imogene preferred the shadowy dark that emulated her life. The dim yellow shone on one side of Thelma's face. She looked vaguely familiar; at least her features did. She could've easily fit up on the stage in the 60s TV show Rowan and Martin's Laugh-in. Maybe that was where Imogene recognized her from, a throw-back twinge of recognition. The '60s. Back when Imogene sat in C-block's group hall watching television with the other cons. That entire decade gone, wasted. Corralled no better than a beast in a throng of other beasts. Smelling their B.O. and starchy food farts.

"Suz, you going to tell me who this is?"

Suz stared at Imogene and, without looking away, said, "Thelma, tell my best friend Imogene what you told me a few minutes ago over at my house."

The "best friend" tag always gave her a little twinge, a warm feeling. She never had a best friend before.

"Of course." Thelma looked at Imogene.

"It all started when—Well, my mother was dying, you see, and I took a trip to go see her one last time, clear across the continent of these great United States. In New England. Boston. I'd never been on a plane. This was, oh, twenty-odd years ago. Jets were still brand new. 1953. Yes, it was in '53."

Imogene looked from Thelma to Suz. Suz put her index finger to her lips to shush Imogene's questions, then pointed to her ear, wanting Imogene to just listen. Suz now looked angry. Maybe even beyond angry. Incensed.

What the hell was going on?

Thelma continued on unfazed. She picked up her beads and twirled them as she spoke. "I got on the plane nervous as a cat." Rattle. Rattle. "At the time, I had never so much as taken a train or a bus, and I now found myself on this…in this big long aluminum tube with wings. A beast too large to fly. At least not so high in the air like that. To fly at all, really. It was like something out of a cheap sci-fi magazine. How could something that had to weigh forty tons get up in the air and carry all those people hundreds of miles? It just wasn't right. It went against nature. The plane didn't have any feathers. Truth be told, I was scared outta my wits. I only tell you this part, to be fair, to show you I wasn't myself. I shook like a leaf in a high wind, and I sweated right through my blouse."

Imogene took a long slug of Schlitz Malt Liquor and wished she had some pruno, a prison alcohol concoction Ange used to make in a plastic bag hidden in the cell toilet, strong with a lotta wang to it.

*You think I'm a few tools short of a toolbox? This woman here is a total whack-job, Imogene. Tell her to get the hell outta your house 'fore some of it rubs off on ya.*

Truly, Imogene had enough problems without Suz draggin' in some fruit loop off the street. She trusted Suz and decided to let the crazy street person carry on. Maybe just a little more. There had to be a reason why she brought her into the house.

"I climbed all those stairs up into the belly of this huge silver beast and then just walked right in, dumb as you please. In a kinda daze, I found my seat. Then they wanted me to strap in just like they do to the loonies in the looney bin. You know, just before they shoot you all up with Haldol, that makes you babble and drool." Thelma waved her one hand, with the other she swung her beads. "Sure, I knew all about flying, that it was supposed to be safe and all, but this was just how I felt. I had a hard time wrapping my mind around it."

*Exactly what mind is she talking about? This gal is cuckoo for cocoa puffs.*

The irony of hearing Ange tag the woman as crazy made a lump rise in Imogene's throat and again question what Nancy had said about Ange. That she had never really been there in C-block. Which meant she was never there at all. Past or present.

"All this new stuff, the plane, the seat belts—the other passengers who got on and acted like this wasn't a big deal—made me want to yell, 'You dumbshits, how is this going to work? You think we're all just going to rise up into the air and fly like birds? Are you kidding me? Are you all outta your ever lovin' minds?'"

Thelma had risen up in her seat and now calmed, easing on back. "Anyway, all this mess made me have ta pee. I had to pee bad but was too afraid to unbuckle and get up. I stayed sitting strapped in like they insisted. Just like Dr. Frankenstein insisted when he strapped down the monster before he reanimated him with electricity. Right? Are you with me on this? Am I right? That's another thing. Why would Dr. Frankenstein strap down the monster? He didn't know he was going to be a monster once he put the juice to him. Right? So why strap him in? So, that just begged the other question: why were they strapping *us* into our seats? Right?"

"Thelma?"

"What? Oh, yeah. Sorry. I sometimes get off track. Anyway. I strapped in like everyone else. That day I was a lemming ready to go off the cliff with everyone else because in the end when it was all said and done, I really did need to see Mom. At this point I'm a real nervous Nellie. And I may or may not have smoked a doobie in the airport bathroom before I boarded. You know just to settle the nerves. I wanna put that out there, so you'd know where I was coming from. Anyway, this huge, ungodly beast rolls down the runway, and at first, it struggles into the air like it can't make it. Like it's not going to make it. I hold my breath the entire time and claw the armrests. Everyone around me just sits there calm as you please, reading books or magazines, or eating Planters peanuts with those packages that had the peanut in a top hat and cane dancing without a care in the world.

"Now, here's where the story starts to get a little weird."

*Just now it's getting a little weird. You look "weird" up in the dictionary, and you'll find a picture of this looney bird, the one sittin' right here.*

"This man, a guy sitting across the aisle, stared at me like I had a big zit on my nose or something. I mean, every time I looked, I caught him staring and then looking down at his watch as if he had a very important meeting coming up. A meeting up in the air at the top of the world? Yeah, right.

"I was sitting mid-plane in a window seat trapped against the wall. After about an hour, or it might've been a couple hours…I don't wear a watch. I don't want time as a friend or worse an enemy. You ignore her, and she leaves you alone. You know what I mean?" She held up her arms as an example. "Look, I'm only fifty-five, and I sure don't look a day over twenty-five."

*Huh, thought she was sixty-eight or better. Whatta you think, E?*

"Anyway, I couldn't take it anymore. I just had to pee or burst my bladder. I walked down the aisle, my legs making me out like some kinda drunken sailor. I make it to the bathroom door and look back. That same man followed me, walking right at me real fast with something big in his hands, the size of a suitcase. But it was this cardboard box. His eyes were trying to tell me something. To watch out that some unknown danger was creeping up on me from behind." She shivered, shaking off the fear-filled memory.

"I didn't know what to do. I jumped into the bathroom and closed the door. Tried to close the door.

"The man stuck his arm in and blocked it. I fought with him to get it closed. He said in this frighteningly harsh voice, 'I'm trying to help you. Stop it. Listen to me, we don't have much time. Get down on your knees before it's too late.'

"'Let me alone, or I'll scream. I swear I'll scream.' Then he did something really strange. He shoved into that small bathroom that big box. All the cardboard pushed me away from the door. His arm snaked in, grabbed onto a red handle sticking out, and jerked it. The box exploded into nothing but yellow, lots and lots of yellow that smelled of rubber, and squeezed me hard against the wall. It filled every open space. I couldn't breathe. Couldn't get my lungs to work."

Thelma stopped and looked at Imogene for a reaction. Imogene sipped her beer, no longer interested. She just wanted the stupid story to end, get the two visitors the hell outta the house. She needed peace and quiet to think.

Suz said. "That's not the whole story; go on, tell her the rest. What was the yellow thing, and where was the man from?"

Thelma nodded. "The yellow thing was a life raft. He'd shoved it in with me and inflated it as sorta giant cushion. I couldn't move a muscle. He'd slammed the door before it inflated. I was stuck. No one could get in or out of that bathroom." She paused again and swallowed hard as if the retelling caused her great angst.

"Thelma?" Suz said.

"Okay. Okay." The words gushed out of her. "The man was from the future. He was sent back there to keep me alive. The plane crashed. I was the only one that survived. I found out later that I was a princess from a forgotten planet banished here forever. My people are, to this very day, still out there looking for me. There, are ya happy now? I said it. You're sure not laughing this time, are you, honey?"

Imogene didn't think it was funny either. Not in the least. "Suz, thank you for this brief interlude from the real world, but I'm tired. Could you please just—"

Suz held up her hand. "Wait, that was just the basis for what I really wanted you to hear. Thelma, tell her the other part."

"What other part? Oh, you mean that I'm your mother."

The beer slipped from Imogene's hand and fell to the floor. Foam roiled out the two holes, an imitation of how her brain felt squishing out her ears.

# Chapter Twenty-Two

Imogene swallowed hard. "You're Suz's mother?"

Suz shrugged and sat back in Wayne's easy chair. Smug, now that Imogene had her brain stretched the same as Suz had.

Thelma said, "Yes, I don't understand what the big deal is. I'm not some kinda ghost risen from a grave."

Imogene looked at Suz and pointed to the wall in the direction of the backyard. "What we…I mean…the person back there isn't who we thought. She's someone else entirely?"

Thelma looked at the wall where Imogene pointed. "Who? What are you talking about now?"

Suz ignored the questions and said, "It's true, this is my mother. I've been questioning her for over an hour. She has all the right answers about me and my father, the house, and its eccentricities. She's convinced me beyond any doubt. She saw Dad's obituary in the papers and came back here to pay her respects. And *apparently,* she's been in contact with Dad over the last couple of years." Her voice caught, "And Dad never said a word about it."

*Does she mean good 'ol Mom came back from her long, lost planet where she reigned over the Lilliputians? Left them just to come to the funeral of a mere peon? And E, you think you're crazy?*

Imogene ignored Ange. "Are you okay? I mean, I'm so sorry your dad was talking to your mother and not telling you."

"He told me she was dead! So, no, I'm not okay." She took a couple of deep cleansing breaths.

Thelma opened her hands flat and stuck them out. "I'm sitting right here."

Suz stood, ignored her mom. "I'm tired. I know you are, too. Let's deal with all this mess in the morning."

"Hey, wait a minute. You can't drop a big smelly stink bomb in my lap, run off to bed, and expect me to sleep tonight."

"Thelma, would you please wait for me next door? I have a couple of things I need to discuss with Imogene."

"Not until you quit calling me Thelma and call me Mom."

Suz's lips turned to a straight line. "*Mom*, please?"

Thelma stood, her beads rattling. "Fine, I'll make us some herb tea and double chocolate brownies. You used to love double chocolate brownies." She went out the screen door. They watched her traverse Imogene's property headed for Suz's house.

Imogene spoke first. "I guess we're now sure that's not your mom out there in the box?"

"I guess so. I don't know what to do about it. My brain hurts just thinking about what all this means."

"I don't see how this changes anything."

"What are you talking about? There's an unidentified dead woman who has family looking for her. I can double-dog guarantee you that right this minute, they're wondering what happened to her. These are people who need closure in order to get on with their lives. I know I would."

"That woman has been in that box since Heck was a pup. No one's looking for her now."

"Doesn't matter, E. Her people will still carry her around in their pockets the same as loose change, always ready to rattle around." Suz shivered. "I can't image the constant pain and anguish."

*Tell her ta try shootin' a spouse, huh, E? Tell her to go ahead and try that, see what kinda bite anguish kin take outta her ass. She's got nothin' ta bellyache over. Go on, tell her, E.*

Ange interrupted more and more. Probably caused from all the fatigue and stress.

"What are you proposing? That we dig her up, clean off the crate, put her back in your garage, and call the police?"

Suz eased back down into the chair. "When you put it that way, it does sound a little cuckoo."

"Speaking of cuckoo, you sure that wingnut's your mother? No offense."

"None taken. I can see for myself she's not all there. Probably why she ran off." She paused and turned contemplative. "E, I can't live with myself knowing what we did. I just can't. That poor woman out there in the box deserves so much more. Her soul is going to wander forever if we don't do something. At least find out who she is."

*Aha. The apple* doesn't *fall too far from the tree, slash, crazy person, does it, E?*

"I think I prefer that you call me Imogene."

"Really?"

"No, not you. I'm sorry, it's late. I was just talking to myself. Why don't we do this? Why don't we sleep on it like you said? Then tomorrow, you and I will try and identify who's actually out in the box."

*What did I say about a secret? This whole thing is unraveling and smells like three-day-old fish. You shoulda taken care of her when you had the chance. When you had the cops as an alibi, like I told ya. You'll learn to listen to me. You used to listen to me, E. I dictated that entire book to you.*

Imogene stood and ushered Suz to the door. That's when Imogene noticed for the first time in a long while the part of the door jamb the police splintered twelve years ago when they kicked it in. Bernie, the neighbor and reluctant boyfriend, fixed it while Imogene was in jail fighting her case. He did a great job splicing the wood to blend it in but had not repainted it. The frame was painted white and the splice was still natural wood color.

Suz stopped. "How are we going to find out who she is, E? We're not policemen."

"Trust me, I know all about this kinda stuff. I did tons of research to write the book."

Suz's concerned expression shifted suddenly to a smile. "Can I read it, E? You said I could read it. I won't be able to sleep tonight anyway, please?"

The smart play was to keep Suz's hands and mind busy so she didn't get a pang of conscience and phone the police about the unknown woman in the box.

"All right, dern it."

Nobody Imogene knew had read the book. No one except John Catskill from Delacorte. The book become a part of her, a shy friend she didn't want to expose to undo criticism for fear of deep emotional trauma from the chiding, the ridicule, and, worst of all, the derision. Sending it to Delacorte had been the single most difficult thing she had ever done.

And as luck would have it, Catskill ended up loving her shy friend composed of fifty-two chapters and four hundred and twenty-one pages.

Imogene hustled into the bedroom and came back with the only carbon copy. A thick sheaf of papers bound together with a fat rubber band. She planned to type a second copy, a clean copy, but life just barged in and knocked her on her ass. Typical.

Suz glommed onto to it. "Oh, thank you. Thank you, E." She clutched it to her chest. Her blouse would be marred with blue from the carbon.

Suz' child-like innocence made it easy to distract her with the manuscript. An errant mother giving a child a piece of candy to keep her quiet.

Imogene had the screen door in hand, trying to push her obstinate friend out. "And don't show it to anyone. And I mean no one. Not even your mom, you understand?"

Suz's expression shifted once again back to consternation. "You really think we can figure out who's in the box? E, we don't even—"

Tired of the game, she wanted to put a hand on Suz's face and shove her out. Instead, she took another verbal piece of candy from her make-believe candy bowl. "Why don't you go home and think about what you'll buy with your portion of all that money?"

Suz froze. She tried to push back in. Imogene held her foot against the bottom edge.

"What money, E?"

"Your fifteen percent of the three hundred thousand for being my agent. That's forty-five thousand to you."

Her mouth sagged open. "Oh, no, Imogene. I couldn't take money from you. We're best friends. That would be wrong on so many levels."

"You're taking it if I have to cram it down your throat." She wanted to pull back the harsh words as soon as they flew past her lips. She wasn't angry at all about the money. Suz earned it and then some. She just wanted to be left alone to think and Suz wasn't cooperating.

But Suz only laughed. "Oh, quit playing the hardcore ex-con. I love you, E. See you in the morning." She stepped back out of the way. Imogene closed the door. Suz walked across the grass and headed to her house, holding the manuscript as if a delicate newborn child.

All of a sudden Imogene realized another huge problem. Once published, everything in the book would be made public. During the writing, she never thought about that component. The idea of publication just wasn't part of the equation. Why deal with problems that weren't there and never would be? Right? Now, everyone who bought a book would…Oh, dear lord.

The book contained just about everything Eugene said in regard to the presidential protection team. He swore her to secrecy, never to tell a soul. He never thought a seventy-three-year-old woman (her age when she was finally released from CIW) would ever have cause to tell anyone. Imogene was a safe place to vent long-kept state secrets. Or at least he thought she was. After all, she made the Secret Service's "Take a wingnut to lunch" list.

Perfect. Just perfect. Something else to worry about, to add to the long list. When life tackled you, everyone else piled on and chanted nah, nah, na, na, nah.

She didn't like Eugene at all at first, but he was the kinda guy who grew on you like licorice jelly beans. Now she liked him a lot. Respected him for his strong moral fiber and ethics. He was risking his career to keep her safe and even called in markers from friends to help out. How could she stab him in the back?

She would talk to Catskill about Eugene's information used in the story, delete it somehow. Maybe go back into the book and modify that part. Every written word now bubbled up from memory. The manuscript, a tight weave that if messed with, the entire sweater would unravel and fall apart.

What a gawd awful mess. Even the good things now started to unravel.

Imogene got three more beers from the fridge and regained the regular spot on the divan, smoked and drank, forcing mind and body to take on one problem at a time. The first most important one being Suz's conscience. She wouldn't go too much longer before ethics and morals forced a call to the cops. Tell them what Ange so eloquently referred to as *the bitch in the box buried under Mr. Majestic.*

When she finished the three beers, she found a ball of twine in the kitchen junk drawer and threaded the beer cans together. She tied one end to the screen door handle on the inside and pushed the cans behind the chair. She sat back on the divan, picked up the Colt .38, and clutched it at her side, hidden in the folds of her dress. She left the solid wood door open because it opened inward. The screen door opened out and would give a second or two more notice with the cans banging. She was nothing more than a big lump of cheese sitting on the divan baiting a rat trap.

She put her head back and let sleep take her. She wished like hell to return to simpler times. Back when she rode in the truck sitting next to Wayne as they flew down the highway leaving Arkansas far behind. With the bag of money in a flour sack under the seat, the entire wonderous world lay open and waiting. The warm wind blowing in her hair. She smiled and tried to transport back to that place.

* * *

Morning. Beer can clatter startled her awake. Someone pulled open the screen door. In an instant, her heart jumped up into her throat. She raised the Colt, aimed it at the empty doorway before anyone came through. In that instant, an image flashed in an overheated and tired brain: Wayne on the floor of the bedroom. She shot him as she came out of a deep slumber. No one should ever shoot first and ask questions later.

In stepped Suz, first looking down and to the left at the beer cans tied to the door. Imogene jerked the gun out of view, putting it back under the throw pillow. Her heart thumped hard at the prospect of almost having shot her best friend in the world, a young, naïve waif half Imogene's age.

Suz smiled, "That's a great idea, E. No kidding. But what if I was someone evil? Sure, you'd be awake, but what then, huh? He'd have you. The police wouldn't get here in time. They wouldn't even know you were in trouble."

Imogene nodded. "Why don't you make some coffee? I'm gonna take a shower." Difficult issues processed better in the shower.

While writing *Peekaboo POTUS*, anytime that deadly affliction called writer's block took up residency, the hot shower spray did the trick. Somehow, the divided attention reopened the creative portal on the right side of the brain.

Hours earlier, she fell asleep before answering Suz's question about how to identify the poor murdered woman in the box. A shower would be just the ticket to float those answers to the surface.

"Wait. Wait. First, I wanna talk about your book. I read the whole thing. I only got to bed a couple of hours ago. It's absolutely wonderful."

"Oh, dear lord. It's too early for this kinda crapola." She rose and stood atop knees that cracked and wobbled. Old age was hell. She didn't want to hear anything about the book. Hated that someone else got a peek into that part of her soul. The barfed-out words on over four hundred-and-twenty-one pages were enough to sour anyone's stomach. Words that had no right to be called art or even story, for that matter. The book was really nothing more than a character study. Who wanted to read about an old woman who works at a Dentco with delusions of knocking off the President? Ridiculous.

Imogene walked past Suz who followed her into the bedroom talking a mile a minute, saying how much she absolutely loved the book. How it was a parable of the problems in today's society. Went on and on about how it had so much depth of character and story.

Imogene rummaged around in the bureau drawers, looking for a decent pair of underwear just in case Suz followed along into the bathroom, continuing to yammer on.

No way would Imogene let that happen.

She found the best pair and swore to get the Woolworths to buy new ones. Out of the closet, she pulled down a dress mid-range on the acceptable scale and headed for the bathroom.

And still, Suz talked on: "You know what I thought was so fantastic about this story? It's how you painted a glorious picture with such a subtle hand, the idea that our town paralleled almost exactly the one in the Andy Griffith TV show…well, that was just masterful. You know, Mayberry, you did that on purpose, right? Truly brilliant how you showed the contrast from the small town living to what actually goes on in Washington D.C., the corruption, the degradation. Worst of all, the constant deception. And, oh my goodness, the satire of that failed attempt to assassinate a sitting President was sensational. So authentic and real, as if it would be possible to really do it just that way.

"Overall, the end result was such a great metaphor for how humans are killing off the world a little at a time, and the folks in Mayberry just keep on doing what they have always done. Unaware, not paying any attention to their own demise, rising up to slap them in their faces. I'm telling you, Imogene, that this book is nothing short of stunning. I'm not kidding. I can't believe I know someone with such depth of creativity. And originality like…like *The Tropic of Cancer* by Henry Miller. Yeah, just like that book."

Imogene entered the bathroom and turned around. Suz bumped into her. "Oh, sorry."

What she said in that last part blew Imogene's mind. Stunned her. She didn't try to put any of that kinda crapola into the book, the metaphor, the parable, the satire. None of it. She only told a story to relieve her angst caused by the government locking her up like an animal in a zoo. And it had worked; she never would've gotten through her stint in the joint without that little project. It wasn't until they gave her a tail and released her that she finished it. That tail being the sole motivator. The government's way of never letting go.

But now that Suz brought it up, pointed those things out like large written words on a chalkboard, it was too dern obvious.

Imogene's mind wasn't focused as she stood in the bathroom holding the door, trying to close it on Suz. Instead, she quickly traveled a hundred miles per hour going over each chapter, seeing the story she wrote from an entirely new perspective, the one Suz presented.

Sweet baby Jesus. She might be right.

Imogene said, "You do realize you and I are kinda in the exact same spot as those folks in the book? We live in the town of Mayberry, and we have the bitch in the box under Mr. Majestic and The Cigar coming after us to end our days in the most violent way possible."

Suz's mouth sagged open, her turn to be stunned. "You're absolutely right. We somehow brought Washington, DC, problems to our little Mayberry."

Imogene reached out, put her hand on Suz's chest, and gently pushed her outside the bathroom door to close it.

"Wait, E." She grabbed her arm. "The way you depicted Wayne…Well, I've never read anything more tender and touching. So loving. Something so honest and real. I can only wish that someday I'll find that kind of love."

Tears filled Imogene's eyes as her throat closed off with emotions. She made one final effort to move Suz back. She complied. Imogene shut the door. She stood forehead against it wishing with all her heart Wayne was still alive. That very minute still in his bedroom smoking his pipe and calling out like he always used to, "Imogene?"

"Yeah, Wayne?"

"Love you, Imogene."

* * *

Thirty minutes later Imogene came out, skin more pruned than before, the water heater having run cold.

Suz sat at the opposite end of the divan from where Imogene usually sat. The Colt in her hand rested in her lap. From her expression, Suz wasn't happy about finding the gun.

"E, I think this whole mess is out of control and we should turn it all over to the police while we still can. Before somebody gets hurt. You have a gun right here on the couch. What if your parole agent suddenly popped in on one of those spot checks and finds it? Off you go back to prison. This time for keeps. They won't let an armed and dangerous parolee loose, not again. Even though I know you're not dangerous. But they don't know that. I don't want you to go to prison, E. And I also don't want anyone to hurt you."

Imogene came around the coffee table and sat in her usual spot. Suz had left a large mug of now tepid coffee on the table. Imogene picked it up, sipped it, and stared at her friend. "Let's talk this whole business through, okay?"

# Chapter Twenty-Three

Imogene sat on the divan, sipping cold coffee, talking with Suz, her only friend in the world. Imogene held out her hand. "Give me the gun."

Suz stared at her, waiting for Imogene to relent. When she didn't, Suz handed her the gun, now slick with sweat. Suz didn't like guns, and it showed. Imogene shoved it down between the cushions out of view, but it was still easily accessible.

The first day when Wayne picked her up out in front of Ozzie's Eats and whisked her off to parts unknown on that wonderful adventure, Imogene had wanted to toss the gun from the flour sack out the window. After what happened to her father, guns left a bad image seared into her brain. But at the time, Wayne told her, "This is a hard lesson learned: you never need a handgun until you *really* need a handgun." She acquiesced, believing him more than adequately sophisticated with life experiences she had yet to encounter. What did she know back then, right? She should've gone with her first instinct.

That same gun would be the end of her ideal man, Wayne.

The end of her life as she knew it.

The thought of him gone yet again made a lump rise in her throat. She didn't ever want to get over him. Keep him safe in her heart for eternity.

Here she sat with another gun close at hand, a harbinger of violence and grief. And yet, it truly was the only way out of the predicament. If The Cigar came for her, what else could she do? And he would come for her, of that there was no doubt.

*Violence begets violence. Been that way E since the dawn of time. Get over it.*

She picked up a new pack of Marlboros to cover her not so latent emotions and banged it against her palm to seat the tobacco in the slender paper cylinders inside. She meticulously tore off the cellophane, opened the pack, and bumped one out. The first of the day. All the while, Suz watched like a curious third grader. Imogene held the Zippo lighter, ready to flick and light the cigarette pinched between her lips. "It's going to get real ugly for a minute or two."

"What're you talking about?"

"You'll see." She flicked the Zippo, lit the cigarette and inhaled a huge breath just to get it over with fast. The coughing jag took hold. Hard. More so that morning. This time, a lung might even cough up. Bloated, red-faced, watery eyes like every morning with that first puff. "I'll quit these evil bastards tomorrow. I swear I will." She finally caught a breath and stared at Suz. "There, now let's talk."

"That's so attractive, E."

Imogene stared.

"Okay, you said you studied all this crapola and know where to start because I have to tell ya, I'm out in the weeds on this one."

Imogene sat back and puffed, enjoying the hot infusion of nicotine that straightened everything out and put an edge on the world. "For those lost ten years in the can I had all that extra time on my hands. I read manuals on how to investigate homicides, on forensics, and interrogation techniques. I read books about the law, courtroom procedure, and, most important, the rules of evidence. The first thing you do at a murder is secure the crime scene."

"We did that already. We moved it and buried it all under two feet of dirt."

Imogene ignored the snarky comment. "Next, you identify the victim."

"There's our first big problem, one as wide as the Grand Canyon. We thought it was Mom, which made Dad the prime suspect. But all that water got tossed out the window with the baby last night. When right out of the blue, Mom showed up."

Imogene chuckled. "You mean from the planet Krypton."

Suz didn't respond. Maybe a line had been crossed. In every circle or clique at CIM, disparaging comments regarding mothers brought on the red-eyed beast of revenge. Moms were forever and always taboo.

Suz finally let a smile creep out. "Yeah, and you think I'm happy about it? But really, if you take away all that Fruit Loops stuff, she's not a bad person. She's kind and generous."

"Never said she wasn't."

"Then how do we identify the woman in the box?"

"There are homicides that have been investigated without knowing the victim's identity. It can be done as long as we have a starting point."

"As in?"

Imogene took the cigarette from her lips and blew out a long stream of smoke. "We found her in your garage, and like you said, that still makes your dad the prime suspect. We backtrack in time and try to discover a woman in your dad's life after your mom left. Then see if she abruptly disappears."

Suz looked out the front picture window mentally traveling back in time to suss out the brain food Imogene tossed her way. After a moment, she rose without a word, walked to the screen door, opened it, rattling the beer cans, and left.

She walked to her house, a woman on a mission.

Imogene smoked the Marlboro and drank cold coffee, the taste dampened by the cigarette smoke. Another reason to quit. The clock on the wall ticked past fourteen minutes. They would both have to leave for work soon.

Suz reappeared in the front yard and headed to the porch, carrying a dusty old box with a black felt tip marker written on the side in her youthful script, "Dad stuff." She opened the screen door that rattled the empty beer cans and entered.

The box strained her arms and bulged at the bottom, threatening to burst the contents all over the ratty gold high-low carpet. She sat down on the couch close to Imogene and set the box on the carpet at her feet. She stared at Imogene. "I still find it hard to believe Dad could kill a woman. Then put her...entomb her in a box in our garage. Not my dad. He wasn't like that. I'm tellin' ya he didn't do it."

Imogene smoked and stared, not having a problem with it. Not after living ten interminable years with violent women who, on the outside of their skin, acted like anyone else.

Until they didn't.

Until something or someone pushed the wrong button that made hot blood rise into their eyes and pulsate until sated with someone else's life.

Truth be told, Imogene was one of those women. Twelve years ago, she pulled the trigger. A simple and easy two-pound pressure with the index finger. In that fraction of a moment her entire life shifted. She got tossed into another world she still fought to exit. To find a way back. But once awarded a tail the journey became nothing more than an impossible dream.

Suz waved her hand to clear the smoke in front of her face that hung in a fog bank around the couch. The years of nicotine tainted everything in the room. Greased the walls with a thin film, permeated everything cloth. Turned the entire living room into a giant cigarette filter. Imogene wanted to quit and couldn't. The craven desire had her by the throat and wouldn't let go. Just like her tail.

Suz opened the flaps on the box and took out one of fifteen big business ledgers, the kind with green cloth covers and red leather bindings. Old. Dusty. On the cover and binding of each, Suz's father Mel had written beginning and ending dates. "These are diaries Dad kept. He was a lonely man. I didn't know how lonely until I found those letters from Mom and now these. He loved Thelma dearly. It took a chunk out of him when she left. I found the part where she went to see her dying mother and never came back. When she left he gave up on every social aspect of life. He sorta turned into a robot just going through the motions, eating, sleeping, working, paying the bills, and making entries in these darn books. Looking back on it now, I realize I didn't have a normal relationship with him. I guess I thought all the kids I hung out with had fathers who acted like mine."

*There it is right there. He did it; he killed whoever was in the box, no doubt about it. Those books, call 'em "The Anatomy of a Hometown Killer," are the evidence you need. Classic John Wayne Gacy, Jeffrey Dahmer, Ted Bundy. Give the girl a cigar to figure it out. If there's smoke, there's fire. Dig deeper, E, you'll find more.*

"These weren't in the garage, they were in his bedroom closet all the way in the back. I didn't want to read 'em. Thought I never would but kept 'em anyway. Now I guess there's no choice."

"Do you really think he would log how…I mean, would he write about a dead woman stored in the garage?"

"Based on what I've read so far, the raw, unflinching emotion where he doesn't hold anything back? I'm guessing there will be some sort of explanation. There just has to be. How could something that large be in his garage without his knowledge?"

"I suggest we adjourn. Head over to our respective jobs and read some of these while sitting at our Dentco counters checking out the customers."

"E, Micheal said that you're fired."

"Pish-tosh. I need this job or get thrown back in the can on a violation. Come on, let's get going."

Suz followed the red Gremlin in her VW bug, the baby-crap mustard-color government car, with Deputy Marshal Ruth following behind her. A short conga line of women fighting the evil that men bring into the world.

Suz didn't take the turn-off to the Bloomington store; she followed along to the Fontana Dentco.

In seven more miles, Imogene slowed. North on Cherry Avenue, almost to the store, a small brigade of cop cars intermixed with yellow police line tape blockaded the street and surrounded Cherry Liquor. Imogene's stomach knotted, and bile rose in her throat. She punched the steering wheel and gritted her teeth. She didn't have to be clubbed over the head to know exactly what happened.

She continued on and parked in front of Dentco, something Higgy-baby said never to do. "The close parking spots are for customers only. All employees are getting paid, so they can park and do the walking."

"Yes," Imogene told him, "but we're not employees until we clock in."

"Imogene, sometimes you give me the galloping trots."

She got out of the Gremlin, stood, and stared back at Cherry Liquor. Suz stepped from her ladybug and came over. "Whatta think's going on over there?"

Imogene turned, glared at her, and said nothing. God bless the blissfully ignorant.

Suz's hand flew to her mouth. "Oh, my God, not Ibrahim?" She bolted before Imogene could grab her shoulder. Suz ran across the parking lot. A tan and green deputy sheriff stopped her at the perimeter, too far away to hear the verbal exchange.

A fat tear for Ibrahim rolled down Imogene's cheek as she bumped out a cigarette and lit it. She turned, unlocked Dentco, and switched off the alarm.

She sat on her tall stool behind the counter and let life come for her. She no longer possessed confidence in her ability to take on all comers. Grief did that to a person, fizzled every bit of confidence and ambition, took them both out behind the barn, and shot 'em in the back of the head.

Now, *she* was even thinking like Ange.

Three of the Davis ledgers sat on the counter. She took the one with the oldest date, opened it, and started reading. Twenty minutes passed. The mundane—the inanity of the words, the same as a heavy sedative. She shook off the need to curl up on the floor and catnap. She lit another Marlboro, heading too quickly toward the self-imposed two-pack-a-day limit. How could a person ever quit smoking if life kept kicking a girl while she was down?

Out the front window, across the expansive parking lot, over by the side of Cherry Liquor, Hank and Amy Woo stood next to Suz, talking to a plainclothes detective in a suit, giving him their statements. The fool, you never take interviews together; you always separate them. In a court case, that lame-headed move would be grounds to impeach those witnesses and, in most cases, a huge win for the defendant. For ten years in the joint, she read law books in the law library, gaining enough education to be equal to an effective criminal defense attorney. But also learned the old adage: a woman who is her own lawyer has a fool for a client.

Imogene took the Colt from her dress pocket and hid it in a half-empty box of Lucky Charms cereal. She kept the box close at hand by the leg of the stool. If evil did descend, deciding to take a chance and enter Dentco, she would, cool as you please, pick up the cereal box and pretend to be snacking. Her hand reaching in as if searching for the hidden prize.

She forced herself for the umpteenth time to focus on the mundane words in the ledger that described the unceremonious everyday activities of an emotionally and socially crushed neighbor, Mel Davis.

But the event, still in progress across the parking lot, kept pushing to the forefront, blotting out all else. Burning anger rose out of grief fueled by the death of a good friend, Ibrahim. A useless, senseless death. The Cigar had killed him for no other reason than to cause hate and discontent. To send the message that he was coming for her.

With Ruth parked out in front of the Hawthorne house, The Cigar couldn't get at Imogene. He did the next best thing to cause pain and mental suffering. It worked.

Ruth, the US marshal, appeared in the window, walked to the door, and came in. She pointed over to Cherry Liquor. "You know what's going on over there?"

Imogene seethed. Of course, she knew. She said nothing.

"It's no longer safe for you out in the open. Sitting there on that tall stool, big as you please, in front of God, everyone makes you a stationary duck in a carnival shooting gallery. To keep you safe, we need to get you under wraps. Secreted away in a motel far off the beaten path. Come on, let's go."

Imogene reached, took a stale Big Hunk candy bar out of the box on the counter. Unwrapped it and took a bite. Chewed. The normally soft nougat, now hard, gave her dentures an unneeded challenge. She spoke around the candy. "Nothing's changed. In fact, I don't need you around anymore. My friend got hurt because of you. Giancana couldn't get at me, so he did the next best thing. As long as you're on me, more of my friends are gonna die. So don't take this the wrong way, but Honey, hitch up your big-girl panties and take a hike. You don't. I'll call the papers and tell 'em how the government's wasting money protecting an ex-con, a murderess who works at a Dentco in Fontana of all places."

Ruth stood in front of the counter, grinding her jaw muscle. Imogene took another Big Hunk from the box. "Take one. On the house. Then please, get the hell away from me."

Instead, Ruth reached for the phone on the counter. Imogene slapped a hand down on top of hers. "Sorry, phone's for employees only."

They glared at each other for a long moment.

Imogene broke the stand-off. "If the justice department still wants their bait for Giancana, tell 'em I'm all in. Tell 'em to throw a wide net around me and then just wait for him to come take me."

*Thatta girl E. You tell 'em how the cow eats the cabbage. Tell 'em to take a long walk off a short pier. Screw these G-men. Well, G-woman.*

Ruth let out a tight little grin. Not a smile. She nodded, turned, and fled at a gait this side of a jog.

Imogene resumed reading the ledger but again couldn't stop her mind from running out of control. She had not seen her friend Ibrahim over there, dead on the duckboards behind his counter. The blood, thick and coagulated in between the slats. But in the place of that image, her over-active imagination supplemented him with other dead bodies seen in manuals and photos of forensic crime scenes. But the worst one of all, the most frequent image that popped up was that of Wayne dead on the bedroom floor with a third eye in his forehead. One she put there with the little .32 Iver Johnson pistol.

She slid off the stool, grabbed the wastepaper basket and threw-up her coffee and the little bit of Big Hunk she had choked down. She tore off a handful of paper towels kept close at hand for emergencies and wiped her tears and mouth.

Across the way, Hank hurried toward his donut shop. He closed, locked the door to Hole in One, and put up a Closed sign. Seconds later, the interior lights went off. An ostrich with his head in the sand while the wolf sat alongside free to take a bite outta his ass at any time.

Amy Woo came next, fleeing the unseen horror show at Cherry Liquor. She disappeared out of view. When the door to the Lotus Tea House and Massage parlor slammed closed, it shook the wall and shimmied Dentco's front window. Svelte and delicate little pigs hiding in their glass house.

Over next to the police line, Suz slowly ventured back. She came in and wandered behind the counter, holding a stack of ledgers in her arms. She sat on the only other tall stool and stared off into space, her words robotic. "You saw what was going on at Ibrahim's. Why didn't you come over? You know what happened to him, don't you? He was our friend. Why didn't you come?"

Imogene stared, afraid if she said a word, sobbing tears would choke and burn her eyes, reveal feelings she trained to keep under control. Showing weakness at CIW left your throat open to be clawed out. And she learned a long time ago weeping was a waste of time. She liked far better to harbor a violent rage for Giancana rather than give over to grief like he wanted her to. She fought the urge to yank the Colt out of the Lucky Charms, walk to the back room and let the TV have it. Shoot the hell outta of it.

Suz opened a ledger on her lap and pretended to read. "With all your experience you must've guessed what happened, right? But I'm here to tell ya, you don't know what I saw over there. You really don't."

A rude and unfriendly comment. Imogene said nothing. Couldn't if she wanted to.

Tears ran down Suz's face and dripped on the open page, smearing the perfect blue cursive ink. "E, bloody footprints came from out of the liquor store. That's what was tapped off, those shoe prints. The murderer went from the store out to the street where that *a-hole* got into a car and fled. Bloody damn shoe prints. Can you imagine what must've happened to poor old Ibrahim to have caused those shoe prints?"

Imogene reached over and put a hand on her back to console her. Suz leaned into it. They sat there for several minutes.

Suz said, "We told the cop about Giancana. He said they already knew about him and checked his alibi. Apparently, he was at an all-night poker game in his suite over at the Holiday Inn on G Street with plenty of witnesses. But we all know what happened. Don't we, E?"

Imogene swallowed hard several times. The first words to her friend came out in a croak. "There's nothing we can do for Ibrahim. It's too late for him. But if you want to do something to keep your mind busy, give me a hand here and read. We can only deal with one problem at a time, and this is one we can at least have some control over. One we can do something about."

Suz's head whipped around. "Seriously, just like that, you're throwing Ibrahim over?"

"I'm not throwing him over. You should know me better than that. The law will never get who's responsible for what happened over there. And it doesn't do any good to fret about it. We're talking about the law of the jungle here, and you're not at all familiar with how that works."

"What are you talking about?"

"The Cigar will get his. The men like him always do. His own kind will eventually take him down. One class A predator thinning the herd on the way to the top of the heap."

"You call that justice?"

"I call it the real world in our little Mayberry."

"Wait. You're saying you believe there are two worlds living side by side, coexisting in the same universe, and we've somehow crossed over."

Imogene shrugged. "Call it what you may. It is what it is. Nothing we can do about it but try and protect our own backsides. What I do know is that we buried a dead woman in my backyard. We need to deal with it."

Suz stared. She finally gave up, nodded and started reading. She now accepted the true way of the world, the one in which she now existed. The same world where Imogene resided for the better part of the last decade and a half. The one she knew best.

Imogene went back to reading her ledger but felt Suz's eyes linger on her for several long seconds before again looking down and turning the page.

Two hours later, they had made a dent in the stack of ledgers. The mundane life of Mel Davis was easy to scan, to speed read through. His days were all the same: Up in the morning, shower, breakfast, drive to work, lunch, drive home, dinner, a little TV, and bed. He watched the same TV programs every night. All the different extraneous words used to tell the same story made Imogene want to scream. The only halfway decent stuff was what he wrote about Suz growing up. His observations depicted a deep and admiring love. Imogene grew to understand Suz better, as if she was her own child.

Imogene's eyes ached from strain. "Hey, what happened to your mama last night? Is she still at your house? We can ask her if—"

Suz's head jerked up to look at Imogene. "Ask her what? If she knows of a woman daddy may have killed, stuffed in a box, and buried at the bottom of a crapola pyramid piled in the garage?

"Don't be silly. We could ask her if…yeah, you're right. It sounded better in my head."

"Mom disappeared. She wasn't there when I got home from your house last night. I don't know where she got off to. She doesn't have a car or any money. She has to be on foot."

"Terrific."

"What?"

"Nothing."

In that moment, if they had dropped what they were doing and gone looking for Thelma, things might have turned out differently.

# Chapter Twenty-Four

Imogene sat on the divan drinking the Schlitz Malt Liquor and smoking the last Marlboros of the day, watching old man time slither by outside the house pretending no one noticed him. But Imogene did. She recognized him for what he was: a petty sneak thief.

Ruth, in her baby-crap colored government car, was conspicuous in her absence. Eugene and the assistant US attorney must've taken her good advice and widened the net to allow what was going to happen, happen. The thick green front door stood open; the screen closed with the beer cans tied and ready to sound the alarm. At first rattle, Imogene had to be ready to draw down on the intruder and shoot first or be shot. A dire situation unfair in its creation, yet every bit as real as the nose on her face. How had things spiraled out of control so quickly?

Earlier in the day customers flocked to Dentco, making it difficult to read the ledgers. Most of them bloodthirsty lookie-loos tired of standing across the parking lot at the police line hungry for information not forthcoming. They came into Dentco looking to munch on gossip and instead found the well dry.

Odette showed up and said not a word about the ugliness surrounding Cherry Liquor. She stocked the bins out front the same as if murder and mayhem visited their neighborhood every day. George arrived and opened the double doors at the back of Dentco. He drove in the forklift with three pallets of dented and damaged food he brought over from the warehouse.

Life continued on as if nothing had happened to poor Ibrahim.

Across the way, Hank never reopened.

Lonely, perverted men came in their cars, parked in front of the Lotus Tea House and Massage Parlor. They got out, shook the locked door, got back in their cars, and left, their deviate itch left unsated.

The ledgers revealed nothing out of the ordinary. Nothing at all was mentioned about any crapola in the garage, including the large box.

Back at the Hawthorne address, eight o'clock came and went. Night outside grew darker.

Nine o'clock rolled in without fanfare. At nine-fifteen, Higginbothom's truck pulled up out front and parked. His shadow sat in the dark, staring straight ahead. Why didn't he get out and walk over to Suz's house, his girlfriend? Commiserate. Let her lick his wounds. His face still banged up to beat the band, courtesy of The Cigar and his brass knuckles.

All day at Dentco no one even brought up Higginbothom's name or thought to call him, tell him what went on across the parking lot at Cherry Liquor.

The phone on the kitchen wall rang. Rang and rang.

And was unanswered.

Eugene. Had to be. No words to anyone needed to be said. Let 'er ring.

Higginbothom finally got out and walked across the thick grass, his shoulders slumped more than normal. He didn't veer over to Suz's house. He came straight on and mounted the three concrete steps to the concrete porch. He stuck his face into the screen, trying to see inside to the left, over to the divan. His expression more like a bank robber with a woman's nylon over his head. "You there, Imogene? Can I come in?" He didn't wait for approval, opened the door. The beer cans rattled. He looked down at his feet, consternation over the cans plain in his eyes.

He took a seat in Wayne's easy chair. He looked as if he'd lost his last friend. The swelling and bruising on his face had faded some. No longer purple and blue, more yellow and brown.

"Can I help you with something?"

He stared at her and said nothing.

After a time, he finally said, "Did you work your regular shift at Fontana?"

"I've never missed a day of work. You know that."

He nodded and again turned silent.

"What's going on? Why are you sitting in a chair in my house? Shouldn't you be next door wooing the beautiful young and vivacious Suzie Q?"

His eyes stared right through her.

Ah, crap. Something happened.

"What's going on, Mike, what happened?"

He started to talk and stopped. His face bloated red with anger.

"Aw, for crying out loud, spit it out."

"Someone stole a big truck."

"And?"

"A monster truck. They drove it through the window of the Bloomington store. Totaled it. Smeared Spam and sardines in tomato sauce all over the floor. Looks like a slaughterhouse. Imogene, I'm ruined."

"Pish-tosh. Your insurance will cover it. No big deal. It's a minor setback and nothing more. You still have your flagship store. And more important you still have me to run it."

*E, in the Big House, this twinkle toes would get his ass handed to him. Why you wastin' your time on him. Tell him ta hop on his horse and ride.*

Higgy-baby shook his head.

"Oh, sweet baby Jesus. You don't have insurance, do you?"

He shook his head again.

The tight, penny-pinching fool. He accounted for everything that could happen except for a demented killer named Cigar, tearing away at Imogene's friends. The Cigar now rose to the top of the list of problems that needed addressing. Even before the woman in the box.

"Why'd you come here, Mike?"

"I went by the Fontana store and couldn't find my Colt I kept under the counter. I need my gun, Imogene."

*Hah, this cheesehead will just shoot off his own big toe. Go on and give it to him, E. This will be worth the price of admission. I can see the title of the movie now. The nine-toed cock-eyed cowboy of Calico County rides again. Go on, give him the gun, E. The Cigar rubs his ass out, they'll have The Cigar for murder. Problem solved.*

"Shut up. He's my friend."

# CHAPTER TWENTY-FOUR

"What'd you say?"

"I said I didn't move that gun. If it's not there, I don't know where it got off to."

Over by the front door, the beer cans rattled. Imogene's hand automatically moved between the cushions, fingers wrapping around the grip.

In walked Suz, clad in Levi cut-offs not suitable for public consumption and a yellow tank top. Did she change into those kinds of clothes when she saw Higgy-baby pull up in his truck?

Higgy-baby tried to control his anger over the destruction of his Bloomington store and couldn't. Suz read his emotions wrong and went to him. Or maybe she *didn't* read them wrong. She moved into his arms, sat on his lap, and buried her face in his neck. She put her lips up to his ear and whispered. His chest rose and fell more slowly as his anger quelled. They kissed, one that didn't have an ending.

Imogene stood on creaking knees, stalled a moment to stabilize a wobbly balance, and walked to the door. She had enough of that syrupy crapola to last a lifetime.

Out on the porch, she sat on the cool concrete steps, smoked Marlboros, and enjoyed the night. Darkness, a friend who never judged. If a car came down the street the short distance to the divan left plenty of time to retrieve the Colt between the cushions.

Off to the right, over by Bernie's, came a rustling in the shrubs that bordered the houses in the front yards. Huh, a few days ago, the mere thought of Bernie coming over would've lit a spark in her chest, warmed her face. Now nothing. Nada. Zip. She was officially over him. Thank you, Cupid, for removing that dern arrow from her haunch.

From out of the night, Thelma appeared like an apparition from an alien world. She wore that same goofy smile, her eyelids slits. She walked past, headed for Suz's house. She raised a hand, "Hi-ya."

"Wait just a minute, girlie. Come back here."

Thelma returned and took a seat a little too close for comfort, forcing Imogene to slide over a few inches.

"Beautiful night, isn't it?"

"Don't gimme that crapola. Where've you been?"

"Out for a stroll. We don't get many nights like these in Alaska. And please, I really don't appreciate your tone."

"A stroll through the neighbor's shrubs? You been gone twenty-four hours. That's a helluva stroll."

She shrugged. "It's dark. I lost my way for a minute. I think." She winked as if a long- dusty secret lay between them. "Then I found you sitting here. I thought I'd gone the wrong way. Earlier tonight…I think it was tonight…I got lost and walked a couple of miles." Thelma's stomach growled the same as if a bobcat sat two feet away.

"Why didn't you walk on the sidewalk instead of across the front yards?" The memory returned. The story she told the night before. The one with the yellow life raft in the plane's bathroom. The one with her as a lone survivor. The part about being from another planet. The way she told it with the confidence of a politician. As if no one in their right mind would dispute the facts as given.

Another shrug. "Does it really matter? I'm hungry." She stood, her long two strings of beads rattling. Wait. Two strands? Weren't there three? She'd somehow lost one. How does a person lose a strand of beads? Hey, those were the same clothes she wore the night before.

"Can you please sit for just a minute, I wanna talk."

Another growl from her stomach sounded off. That same angry animal. "Do you have something to eat?"

"This'll only take a minute."

The two in the house, Suz and Higgy-Baby wouldn't appreciate someone rummaging around in the kitchen for a late-night snack, not while they snacked on each other. She just hoped the snacking didn't devolve into hot monkey sex right there in Wayne's easy chair. One could only hope Suz at least still had on her shorts. What they were doing to Wayne's easy chair was sacrilegious.

"Suz told me that in the last couple of years, you've been in contact by phone with your ex-husband."

"What's with the big interest in Mel? I don't get it. You and Suzanne think he was some kinda big mystery. He wasn't. I'm here to tell ya he wasn't. Sure, he was kind and nice and…and… He was…he was just Mel. I loved him dearly. He's dead. I'm sorry and sad but, oh my gosh be-gosh, let the poor man rest in peace."

*E, tell this crackpot to call up to the mother ship and beam her sorry ass outta here. This here's too much crazy for a Friday night.*

Imogene reached out, took her by the hand, and pulled her back till she again sat on the step. "I lived next to Mel for a lot of years, and I'm sad that I never got to know him better."

"Okay, and?"

"One time, this was quite a few years back, I met this woman who had just come out of his house. I would really like to reconnect with her, but I can't remember her name."

"Whatta ya think I am, some kinda gypsy who can see in ta the past? How the heck would I know? I'm hungry and have ta get going."

"I'll make you a hotdog sandwich with mayo on wheat and a vanilla malt if you sit here a little longer and talk about the women in Mel's life."

Thelma's eyes glazed over at the thought of food.

"I'd like ta help ya, really I would, but I don't know of anyone. And to tell ya the truth, I think I mighta broke him. I don't think there was any woman after me." She said it without guile or hubris.

"What did ya talk about when you called him?"

Another shrug. "We mostly talked about Suz. What else did we have in common?" Her voice caught. "I was a fool for runnin' off like that. I missed her growing up. I missed her whole life. Now, she's a young woman who looks at me like I'm trash. Maybe I am. Maybe I do deserve that kinda treatment. But I'm here now, ready to make amends."

"What else did you talk about when you called him?"

"You're a cold and callous shrew, aren't ya? I just laid my heart at your feet, and you ignore it. I didn't call him. He called me. He wanted me back."

"So he was lonely?"

"What do you think?"

"Just calm down a little. We're only a couple of friends sitting here chatting and enjoying the evening."

The beer cans rattled as the screen door opened outward. Suz exited with Higgy-baby's arms all over her. "E, would you mind putting Mom up for the night?"

Ah, man.

*If you say yes, you're gonna hear this cuckoo clock sounding off all night long. She might even get ascaired and crawl into bed with you. Wink. Wink.*

"I don't mind stayin' over here while you and your young beau do a little scoodlypoopin'. Imogene here has already offered to make me a hotdog sandwich and a malt."

"Sure, why not." Then Imogene whispered to Suz, "I can sleep on the divan."

"Thanks, E. I owe ya."

"You just remember that."

They both moved aside so Higgy-baby and Suz could use the steps. The two walked across the yard slowly, not in a big hurry at all. Higgy-baby's hand eased on down and cupped Suz' right butt cheek. Gave it a squeeze. Trashy. Lurid and salacious and yet at the same time erotic. A pronouncement of what was yet to come.

They continued crossing the thick grass.

If the use of a room and a hot meal stood in the offing, it made no sense not to get paid for it. Information being the currency of the day. "Thelma, what do you know about all that junk and crapola in the garage? Suz and I have been working like dogs getting rid of it."

Had the question flown Imogene too close to the sun? In this case, the sun being a secreted woman's dead body buried under Mr. Majestic. Would Thelma ask questions about the question?

"Mel was a hoarder, pure and simple. No big secret there. We gonna get after that sandwich? My stomach thinks my throat's been cut. I could eat half a caribou haunch my ownself." The Queen of Krypton climbed the three steps up to the porch and looked down upon Imogene.

Imogene took the steps up, her knees screaming, demanding respite.

Thelma asked. "What's so important about all that stuff in that darn garage?"

"Why? Did Suz say something about it?" Imogene opened the screen door about to step in.

"No, but your neighbor Bernard asked about a big box. Asked if it was still there. Asked me right in the middle of his down stroke. If you know what I mean. That man's a regular Tom Jones. I'll tell you what."

Imogene let the door bang shut. She bellowed. "Suz! Get your ass over here, now!"

# Chapter Twenty-Five

Suz walked outta the dark, holding Higgy-baby's hand. "What is it, E? We're kinda tired and need some rest."

*Yeah, right. And if you believe that, I gotta dead woman in a box I'll sell ya. Right, E. Go on, say it just like that. Go on tell her "rest," our achin' ass. We can smell the pheromones from here.*

"It's something about our box."

"Our what? Oh. Oh, my." She suddenly looked all around to see if anyone else stood close enough to hear, someone who could suss out the root of their secret. "What about it?"

"I now know the 'who,' and the 'why.'"

Suz's hand flew to her mouth. "Oh, dear Lord." She turned to Higgy-baby. "Honey, I'm really sorry, but I'm gonna need a rain check."

"What? Why?" He glared up at Imogene, who stood on the concrete porch with Thelma looking down on them. He was angry over the night's missed opportunity to jump Suz' bones. "If it's that important, maybe I should stay."

Suz tugged on his arm. "Please, babe. This is women's stuff."

He looked from Suz's eyes to up at the porch. "Imogene, you give me the galloping trots, you know that?"

"Yeah, I guess I am like a plate of rancid oysters. Thanks for that."

He stomped across the yard over to his truck, got in, and screeched the tires, leaving. In the sudden quiet, Thelma's stomach growled again. "I'm hungry."

Suz mounted the steps. She reached into her shorts pocket and came out with a wadded-up twenty. "Here, go home and order a pizza."

Thelma snatched it away. "Thanks for nothing. I was promised a homemade hotdog sandwich and a vanilla malt. Tomorrow, I'm going back to Alaska. People are a lot nicer there." She stomped off, disappearing into the darkness to the east.

"Wait," Imogene said.

Thelma reappeared as if she bobbed to the surface in an inky black pool of crude oil. "Yeah?"

"When you were over at Bernie's, did you happen to see his wife?"

Thelma waved her hand, "Ah, ta hell with you. I thought you changed your mind about the sandwich." She turned to leave again.

"Mom, please?"

Thelma turned around. "Nah, his poor, infirm wife died nine or ten years ago. I think that's what he said."

Imogene whispered, "Sweet baby bald-headed Jesus."

Thanks, Mom. I'll be over later, and we can talk. Please don't leave again until we talk, okay?"

They both waited for the door to slam at Suz's house.

Suz turned. "Tell me."

Imogene opened the screen door and went inside.

For the first time since the thing with The Cigar started she was afraid. Not of The Cigar but of her neighbor, Bernard. What he was capable of. A kind of evil that lay dormant waiting to reappear. The kind of embedded evil residing in the house right next to hers that she had missed for too many years.

Inside Imogene took up her regular seat on the divan and lit a fresh Marlboro from the one that hung from her lips, chain smoking. Her hand automatically moved between the cushions feeling for the Colt.

Gone.

Her hand moved all up and down the cushion crack. "Ah, crapola on a cracker."

*I got it, E. I got it right here. I got yo back, you don't have to worry.*

"Shut up, you got nothing."

"What?"

"Please just sit."

Suz took her regular seat in Wayne's easy chair and knew enough to wait a few moments for Imogene to gather her thoughts.

Higgy-baby had taken the gun. Maybe that was a good thing. If The Cigar did something to him and she had kept the gun, especially after he asked for it, that level of guilt would be the last straw. It would kick her over the edge into that yawning abyss. A perpetual fall into an endless darkness. Hell wasn't brimstone and fire; it was darkness with a total lack of anything at all.

Imogene sorted out the words in her head. Words that didn't make sense, and at the same time, they did. "Out there on the porch, not two minutes ago, your mom told me where she's been for the last twenty-four hours."

"Where?"

"She was next door makin' the beast with two backs with Bernie. *With Bernie of all people!*" Imogene shouldn't have been jealous, not over someone who stores dead bodies in the neighbor's garage. But she was just the same. Thelma rolled into town and wasn't there but a day or two, and she…well, for some weird reason, it didn't seem right.

"She was doing *what*? A beast with two backs?"

In Imogene's overheated mind, Ange, with a cockeyed grin, made a circle with her index finger and thumb while moving her other index finger in and out in a lurid fashion. *Right, E. Am I right? Ol' Bern was over there attacking her mom's pink fortress.*

Imogene said, "Well, there's no nice way to put this. I once overheard my daddy talking to a friend, and he called it…ah, batter-dipping the corndog."

"What? With my mother?"

As if that was a big surprise. Heck, Suz had intended to do the same thing with Mike that very night had Imogene not intervened.

"I…I figured she had talked to Bernie when you asked Mom about his wife, Dot. But…are you sure about the other?"

Imogene took in a deep breath and told Suz everything right from the start about her and Bernard Lowery. Told her about Bernie's wife Dorothy and how Bernie kept his squeeze Delores stashed over on Campus Avenue. Told her about Bernie's bi-weekly sojourns and even told her about the worst part. How Imogene had also coveted thy neighbor. But in her own defense, she had yet to taste that poison fruit. She left out the part about the day she had made the decision to step across his threshold, to "batter-dip his corndog," even though he had Delores over on Campus. Would've but was interrupted by the cop telling them of the swarthy man in the black leather jacket on the loose in the neighborhood. Armed and dangerous. That last part, the nudge that sent Imogene home to get her gun and sit up, waiting for Wayne to come home.

Suz sat back in the chair. With each lurid revelation, she sat a little closer to the edge. When Imogene finished, Suz jumped up. "So, you're saying my mom...*My* mom was over there with that...that pig...and he told her about a box stored in our garage?"

Imogene still couldn't quite wrap her mind around it either. She had for too long dreamt about Bernie. Not only the sex, but also living a wonderful life together. One that, at the time, precluded *him* from spending all *his* extra hours over at the pool hall on Fourth Street. What a horrible little fool she'd been.

She swallowed down deep emotions that threatened to strangle her, "Suz, I know who's in our box."

Suz backed up until her legs touched the chair. She fell into it. "It's his wife, Dot, isn't it?"

"Who else could it be?"

Suz shook her head. She stood again and paced back and forth. "This kinda thing never happens. This isn't supposed to be happening at all. None of it. Especially to us. Not at my house. Not at the house next door to you, E, not in this kinda quiet neighborhood." In a flash, her stunned expression suddenly shifted to anger. "And my mom went over there and had sex with him? You know this for sure, E?"

"No. Now, just wait a minute. I don't know for sure. Of course, I don't. How could I?"

But she knew. Suz needed to be talked down or risk a much larger problem with her friend storming over there and punching Bernie in the nose. Not a wise thing to do to a stone-cold killer. "Sit. Please just sit down, and let's think this through."

"I'm not gonna sit down. Tell me what Mom said. Every last word. Don't leave anything out. I'm not kidding, E. Don't you leave out one dern word, or I'm going next door and yank a few kinks into her until she tells me the truth."

"We don't even know if—" Imogene got up, moved around the coffee table, and passed the easy chair where Suz sat. Imogene blocked the exit by closing the big green front door. "—if it even is his wife Dot, who's out there in the box."

But it was. Nothing else made any sense.

Suz bolted out of the chair. She came over and stood in front of Imogene. "Don't change the subject, E. Tell me right now what she said, or I'm going over to ask her myself."

"Okay, look. You and I both know your mom's…a little off. You admitted as much. She's not hurt in any way from her encounter with him. She's a big girl making her own choices. No one can fault either of them."

"Last chance, E, tell me true."

Imogene put her hand on Suz's chest. Pushed her back a little away from the exit. "Based on what your mom said, yes, she had carnal relations with Bernard Lowery."

Suz's jaw locked, the muscles worked grinding her teeth.

"Wait. Now, wait just a minute before you go off half-cocked. We're in this thing up to our eyeballs. We take a wrong step we'll both end up in C-block for the rest of our lives. Trust me on this, Suz, I know what I'm talking about."

Suz pushed against Imogene's hand. "Get out of the way, E. I'm going over there to rip out his throat."

The viciousness of the threat, incongruent with the quiet, demure Suz, took Imogene's breath away. Imogene shoved hard. Suz took two steps back to keep from falling.

"Going over there is childish and immature. You're neither of those things. It's also exactly what a man would do. A bullheaded, foolish move that will accomplish nothing and will, without a doubt, exacerbate a problem already out of control. Is that what you really want?"

That got to her. Some of the anger bled from her expression.

"Think, kid, do you want immediate satisfaction like a man? Or do you want to take a step back, think about it, and then act like a couple of white witches and really stick it up ol' Bernie's patooty."

She took a moment. Her eyes hardened. She finally nodded. "Let's break out the flying monkeys. What'll we do first? Put all that glorious jailhouse education to work, and let's figure out a plan."

Imogene said, "First, I'm going over there, knock on his door and get invited in."

"Wait, that's not a good idea. No. That's not happening. It's too dangerous."

"We gotta find out for sure if Dorothy's still alive. I was in prison for ten years and haven't seen her after I got out. When I have talked to him, he talks like she's still alive and in the house. And he still makes his clandestine rendezvous over on Campus with Delores, but that might just be to keep up pretenses. Keep Delores on the hook so he doesn't have to commit. Why would he change that part of his life that's been working so well for him? When's the last time *you've* seen her?"

Suz' scrunched up her face. "E, I've *never* seen her. I only know about her from talk around the neighborhood. Gossip that's she's totally disabled from a massive stroke and has been forever."

"Talk around the neighborhood or just from your dad?"

Suz eased round Imogene, backed up, and sat back down in the easy chair that rocked. Imogene retook her seat on the divan.

"Yeah, you're right, E. We really do need to watch our step with this whole business."

Imogene let out a long breath in a sigh of relief. Suz finally understood the complexity of the situation.

"You know, E, I didn't think anything about it at the time, but in one of Dad's ledgers, he wrote that he "owed the neighbor a big favor." She made air quotes.

Imogene snapped her fingers. "Then our theory checks out. That's what's called circumstantial evidence. Now we just need to find out for sure if poor ol' Dot is next door and still kicking. Or out back in a box under Mr. Majestic." A sad cliché. Dot, if still alive, couldn't move a finger, let alone kick.

"It has to be her. Who else could it be?"

The last time Imogene had seen Dot, that was…was gawd dern it, going on twelve years ago. About as long as the body had been in the box. Bernie had only talked about her when they spoke in the front yard the few times after Imogene got out of C-block wearing her tail. Dot, being nothing more at the time than a shameful roadblock that kept Imogene from making a total fool of herself and advancing a dream of a relationship. Now, she was glad the tail had kept her safe. Suz was right; who else could it be?

Suz said, "No, I thought about it. No way are you going over there. It's time we called the police."

She just slipped back to the bad option. Imogene was beating her head against an invisible wall over her best friend's inability to see the fallout from that nuclear option. They needed to take care of the problem themselves.

"Okay, then. You tell me. What are we gonna tell the police?"

"We can call anonymously, tell them the man at that address killed his wife. That's all it'll take. Let them figure the rest of it out."

"Two things. What if, for some reason, his wife died from natural causes?"

"Wait, that's right. Yeah, she's been sick a long time. It could've happened just like that. Because of what happened to Ibrahim, that taste of violence, we automatically thought the worst of Bernie.

"But how does that explain why he chose to bury her in our dad's garage? You seem to have all the answers. Why do you think he would do something like that?"

"For the money. Murder is always about money, sex, or power. Dot had to be on state disability. She dies, the checks dry up. That goes the same for a natural death."

"Of course. That has to be it. Doesn't mean he killed her, though, right? The cops can still tell if she died of natural causes or was murdered, right? What was the second thing?"

"If either one of us goes over there to see if Dot's still alive, it'll tip our hand for sure. No matter how delicate we play it, if we go next door, he'll know we're onto him. He'll come for us. He has to know we found the box in the garage. He had to have seen us all those nights working out there with the lights on. The big circus out front with that cloud of locusts hauling away all the junk. In fact, he has to be wondering about why we haven't already blown the whistle on the dead body. Right this very minute he has to be waiting to see what *we'll* do next. It's odd he hasn't already been over here asking, poking around. If I miss my guess any minute now, he'll be knocking at my door."

"E, you really have a devious mind the way you pieced together this whole mess. Now I see how you came up with all that great stuff in *Peekaboo POTUS*. But you're absolutely right. You can't go over there and ask to see Dot. Not if he already knows we found the box. If he is a killer, it'd be like a matador waving a red flag in front of a man-killing bull. In this case, a woman killing bull. But at the same time, you've just walked us back into the same corner we were in when we started. What are we going to do?"

"Go get that big flashlight in your garage and the two shovels."

"Ah, come on, you gotta be kidding me?"

"Nope. We don't have a choice. We gotta see if Dot's really in the box."

# Chapter Twenty-Six

Two hours later, after the last house light in the neighborhood winked out, Imogene and Suz exited the backdoor, dropped down the ten concrete steps to the backyard, and made their way once again to Mr. Majestic.

The full moon stood high overhead illuminating the entire block with a muted white glow, creating eerie shadows where they normally wouldn't be. Imogene quietly talked to Suz, trying to calm her down to keep her mind off the dastardly deed at hand. Grave digging. Imogene shivered on the inside. It wasn't that cold. "Keep the flashlight off until we get under the tree. Then, while one digs, the other can hold their hand over the beam."

Suz, one step ahead, waved her hand behind her. "I know. I'm not a fool. Don't treat me like some middle-grade snot nose."

Suz jumped and let out a little eek. Eight steps later she did it again. Edgy as a cat on hot bricks.

*This gal's het up so bad she's gonna have ta change her jonnies or change her name to Skidmark Sue.*

Behind the garage, they found Mr. Majestic just the way they had left him when they buried the box, the coffin that contained their poor neighbor, Dot.

The Hass avocado tree rose up into the night, 35-40 feet, a towering monolith. A dark beast ready to devour anyone that approached. A fairytale way of thinking. Two hours before midnight, that's the way Imogene looked at her old friend, as a beast. The branches had not been pruned for twelve years and instead of a well-manicured fruit tree, Mr. Majestic stood at the ready—wild and willing to take on all comers. More useless imagination running amok.

The long branches, thick with healthy dark green leaves, draped down to the ground, creating a massive dark tepee. Imogene reached in and gently moved some aside and waited for Suz to duck and enter into the inky blackness.

In a harsh whisper, she said, "Are you kidding me? No way am I going first. I know I'm being silly…but that's just the way it's gotta be. No ma'am, no thank you, and kiss my country buttock."

Imogene didn't want to be first, either. Stupid as it sounded, even after surviving being locked up like an animal with other animals in the zoo, fear over this silly misadventure still gripped her heart with an ice-cold hand. Not a fear of the boogieman but of the very real possibility The Cigar could be in there waiting, hatchet in hand. Mr. Majestic was the perfect place to hide while surveilling the house at 744 Hawthorne. Imogene wanted a piece of the man, do him dirty like he deserved, but the inky blackness somehow elevated his evil and wickedness. No wonder horror stories used the dark as a vehicle to pound fear deep into the farthest reaches of the subconscious. The absolute quiet didn't help matters. It worked in the same manner, gawd awful in its foreboding. Sweat rolled down into her eyes and stung.

*That girl right there needs to be in her flannel bunny jammies with a cup of hot cocoa and graham crackers, the useless wrench. Here, tell her get outta the way, I'll go in first.*

"No, you won't. I'll go in before you do."

"Okay, then go. You don't have to be sarcastic about it. We're friends, E, don't let this come between us."

"Harrumph." Imogene ducked her head and entered, forcing down her fear and allowing her anger toward The Cigar to fester and rise up. She held up the shovel, entering like a knight jousting an unseen foe. Her feet shuffled, rattling through the heavy carpet of dead leaves. Inside, the new form of darkness had an unsavory feel, almost thick like unsolidified chocolate pudding. Again, with the overactive imagination. The humid, fecund odor of rotting leaves smelled like musty death.

"Get in here and turn on that dern light." Imogene held her breath, waiting for an attack from any direction. The Cigar wouldn't use a gun. No, that wasn't personal enough. He'd use a garrote, flip it over her head and across her neck. Or a long-bladed hunting knife thrust up under her rib cage and into her heart, causing a piercing pain so great her eyes would pull in all the light from distant stars as her soul left her body.

Suz came in. The branches closed up, further enhancing the eerie darkness.

The large camping flashlight came on. Imogene held up her arm to its blinding effect as shame for having been a scaredy-cat sauntered in and took up residency.

No emissary of death stood by waiting for them. What a fool she'd been.

"Right here," Suz said, scraping the dead leaves away from the grave. "Should be much easier to dig this time; the dirt's loose."

"You go ahead. In this case, youth before age. Every bone in my body is already sore as heck." Imogene, against her better judgment, pulled the Marlboro pack from the pocket in her dress and lit one. Her hands shook from the adrenaline that had just started to bleed off. The nicotine instantly righted her boat, tightened every nerve. She reached up and held on to a thick overhead branch, fatigue starting to take its toll. She shook each orthopedic shoe, in turn to get out the mulched leaves.

Suz didn't complain about the work arrangements and shoveled. "The last time we were here, we just plopped that ol' box down in the hole. This time, we gotta drag it out, and I don't know how you and I are going to accomplish that. We might need some ropes and pulleys."

"We just need to get the dirt off the top and open it. I wanna another gander at who's inside."

Suz stopped digging. The light wasn't bright enough to illuminate the shadows covering her eyes. "We might as well take her out from under here. We're going to turn her over to the cops, right?"

Imogene was tired of the game defending the position to leave the cops out of it. "Look—" She closed her eyes and counted to ten, allowing the sudden rise of anger to subside. "Do you know the term aiding and abetting after the fact? Or the penalty for destroying evidence in a homicide investigation? Or half a dozen other laws we violated in your garage the moment we opened the box and didn't immediately call the police? When we buried her here, we precluded any solution other than keeping her a secret for all eternity. Unless, of course, you want to go to prison? Am I getting through to you this time?"

"Yes, you are. You don't have to be a butthole about it." She threw the shovel down. "Your turn to dig."

"I'm sorry. Suz, I'm sorry. It's just late. I'm tired, and with all that's going on…well, I shouldn't have snapped at you."

Suz picked up her shovel and started digging again. After a time, she finally spoke again. "You know, the only way I could do this at all is to pretend you and I are in a movie." She looked up and smiled. "And you know, right there when you snapped at me…well, it reminded me a little of *The Treasure of Sierra Madre*. When the men started fighting amongst themselves over all things, greed. Do you know what scene I'm talking about?"

*Hot spit and Monkey vomit, can you believe this girl. She ain't right. She's gone and fallen down. Maybe hit her head on a rock.*

This time, Ange had it right. *Thunder and Tom Walker*, what's that girl talkin' about? She's thinking about a movie while digging up a desiccated body in a box under a tree.

Suz's thought was an emotional defense mechanism. Imogene had read about it in *The Psychology of a Killer*. The book said in similar situations, killers tended to foster those types of emotions to keep the victim calm.

"Yes…ah, that was a hellava movie. I loved it."

Suz's smile tarnished some. If Imogene could see her eyes, she knew she'd see pain and disgust over being patronized. Imogene's words, a hammer when she should've used kid gloves.

Imogene tried to make up for the unmistakable tone she'd used. "Here, let me help."

"No, I got this. You just go on and keep supervising. Apparently, I'm not worth spit."

"Please don't be that way."

From out of the darkness someone else said, "I can help. I don't mind helping."

The voice outside the drooping branches caused them both to jump out of their skin. Imogene's heart took off at a gallop. "Sweet baby Jesus."

Suz moved over to where they had entered with the shovel raised at the ready. "Who's there?"

The branches parted. "It's me, silly." Thelma stuck her head inside the tree. "What in the name of God's little green acre are you two idjits doing out here in the middle of the night, diggin' under this tree? Have you lost your minds?"

*Hah, this from the lifeboat lady in the plane's bathroom.*

Suz looked back at Imogene, not knowing what to do. What to say. What kind of explanation could possibly work. Not one came to mind. They'd been caught.

*Look, gals, she's a wingnut. Jus' tell her the truth. If she does spout off, no one's gonna believe her. Right?*

Ange told it straight. The truth was the only option.

*That or club her over the head like a beached catfish and stick her in the box. Put Bernard's new girlfriend in there right alongside the dead wife. It has a sort of symmetry to it, doesn't it, E? But to be an honest Abe, we're gonna need a bigger box.*

Ange didn't know words like symmetry.

Imogene said, "It's a long story. Do you think you could go up to the house and wait for us? We'll be in directly and tell you the whole sordid story."

"Dear lord and murderation." She took the shovel from her daughter Suz and started digging. Her two strands of beads wiggled and rattled. Her platinum beehive hairdo pulled in the ambient light and glowed as if she were some sort of alien. "There's only two things you two idjits could be doing out here in the middle of the night. One is looking for a coffee can filled with cash that you somehow forgot where you buried. I've done that myself. No shame in it. And the other is a body. I'm guessing a body. Come on now, lend a hand, or we'll be at this all night."

In Imogene's head. Ange laughed and laughed.

Suz picked up the other shovel and helped. In no time at all, they struck the top of the box, the makeshift coffin. In another few minutes, they got all the dirt off the top and from around the rim. Thelma stood back, leaning on the shovel, breathing hard, obviously waiting to see what happened next. "Well, is someone gonna open it?"

Imogene came over, took the shovel from Thelma, and stuck the rounded point under the edge of the lid, the box two feet below the dirt level. She pried. The wood and screws creaked and screeched. The lid popped up with a puff of rancid air.

Thelma waved her hand in front of her face. "Whewee, that smells like a beach full of dead fish."

Imogene popped the lid off the rest of the way; her eyes automatically averted, her mind not wanting to see Dot in that condition. Almost as if the grave diggers had become voyeurs desecrating a place where the victim had an absolute right to privacy.

*We're all gonna be barkin' in hell for pokin' Mr. Grim Reaper in the eye and thumbing our noses at him. I'm here ta tell ya, he can't take a joke.*

Imogene picked up the big camp flashlight and directed it into the gaping maw.

The woman lay with her head resting on her knees almost as if taking a nap. All her skin was nothing more than wrinkled crepe paper, beige and splotchy brown. The muscle underneath had melted away, revealing strong bony outlines obscuring any and all physical identification.

An abrupt groan slipped from Imogene's mouth. She took a step back. And another.

"E, what's the matter?"

"Suzanne," Thelma said, "the woman's never seen a dead body before. How did you two yay-hoos know to dig in this spot? Who is she?"

"E? Are you all right?"

Thelma sidled over to Suz. "I don't think this gal is a good influence on you, Honey. Maybe you should find some different friends."

"Mom, can it? E, talk to me?"

Imogene's arm rose without a command to do so. She pointed. "That's not Dot."

"What are you talking about? Of course, it is."

"Dot always wore her hair in a bob it was easier to care for…when you're…when you can't move a muscle. Look at the length of this woman's hair. If she were standing, it would be all the way down to her—"

Thelma said, "It's common knowledge that when you die, your fingernails and hair continue to grow."

*Oh, dear Lord, E. Did you hear this twit? The cheese has done slid off her cracker. Hair doesn't grow after you're dead. Especially not a foot and a half—ta two feet. Sweet baby Jesus.E, you think this woman's mother had any children that lived?*

"What?" Suz asked. "I can see you thought of something. Talk to me, E."

"It's Poppy. I'm a doddering old fool for not seeing it the first time we opened the box."

"You two idjits opened this box before, and now you're back out here doing it again? And people say I'm crazy as an outhouse fly."

"Shut up, Mom. Poppy, who? What are you talking about?"

"Poppy Liu. She was the in-home nurse for Dot. It has to be. Poppy's the only woman I know who had long black hair that…glistened like a raven's wing." Imogene flashed back to the day Poppy came out of Bernie's house wearing her white nursing garb replete with the white nurse's cap set atop of all that beautiful black hair. She walked out to the curb to wait for her ride to pick her up. That was the last time Imogene ever saw her.

"Gosh darn it," Suz said. "We're for sure back to murder again. I don't care what you say, we can't let this pig get away with it. He has to pay. Someone has to speak for Poppy Liu. Stand up for her." A fat tear rolled down Suz's cheek. Her nervous system couldn't take this kind of pounding. Suz, with her kind, gentle soul, cried over the violent death of a woman she didn't even know and had never met. Suz was a genuine human, too good to be friends with the likes of Imogene.

Imogene closed the lid. Depression and despair filtered down from above, darkening the night even more. "I need some sleep. Can we please—I'm begging you here, Suz—can we please wait till morning before we make any kind of decision on what to do?"

Thelma took a step forward. "I don't know what's going on, but I think I figured it out."

*Yeah, sure, she's right. And a dog's nuts glisten in the moonlight?*

"Mom, please, not now."

"Don't shush me. I know what I'm all about. I've been around the block a few times. And if that man next door did the dirty to this ol' gal then someone needs to give him the big adios. If you know what I'm sayin'."

"Mom!" Suz turned to Imogene. "Yes, we will revisit this tomorrow and decide. We are all too tired to make an informed decision tonight. Let's all go sleep on it."

Imogene nodded with her chin toward Thelma. "She's a wild card; you'll have to keep her on a short leash."

"I know. You don't have to worry."

Thelma, indignant, said, "I'm standing right here. Trust me, I want no part of this little bughouse chess match you two got goin' here. I just can't believe I traded fluids with that man next door."

"Oh, dear Lord. Come on, Mom. Let's get some sleep, it's late."

Imogene eased the lid down on the box, tamped down the nails, and whispered. "So sorry, Poppy Liu."

# Chapter Twenty-Seven

Imogene took two beers out of the fridge. She wanted the entire sixpack but needed to have her wits about her in the morning. In the morning, huh. It was three-thirty. No options at all presented themselves. None. The complex dilemma encompassed her parole, the box under Mr. Majestic that contained a dead nurse, all of it mashed in with two people she had no chance to control—Suz and her whack-a-do mom—left no options whatsoever.

In the books Imogene read in CIW, the interviews with homicide suspects, most all of them said that once cornered after the first killing they more often than not chose to kill again to extricate themselves from a problem that continued to expand exponentially. Kill witnesses or those who would try to restrict their freedom. That was the only option left. To kill more people to keep the secret. To keep from going back to prison. The threat of prison loomed more heavily than any other time in the last two years. But she wouldn't do it. She couldn't. She'd let the game play out, let the cards fall as they may. Move over and let that evil bitch fate take the wheel and drive them both highspeed right into a wall.

She sat on the divan, stared out the big picture window, smoked one last Marlboro and chugged the first Schlitz Malt Liquor. The alcohol and nicotine fix relaxed her frayed nerves. Joyce in the portrait on the wall stared down, judging, casting an aura of shame.

"I didn't do anything wrong. What are you so het up about?"

Talkin' to a picture, what next? She leaned back and closed her eyes, trying to conjure the only thing that gave any solace at all: Wayne's smile, his gentle words. His touch. She choked on the emotion that rose up in her throat. Tears forced their way out of closed eyelids and ran down her cheeks.

*Knock it off, ya sad sack. Quit your bellyachin'. At least you're not in C-block, stuffed into a huge concrete box and steel bars with hundreds of smelly-assed women who do nothing but complain. Consider yourself lucky. Buck up or I'm gonna find someone else ta talk to. Girl, you've turned into a real downer.*

Imogene pushed Ange's voice out of her brain and concentrated on that first day Wayne came into Ozzie's Eats. Came behind the counter and stood not inches away. Did it for her. He loved her the moment he laid eyes on her. He told her so a million and one times over the years. It always hurt her that she couldn't reciprocate. She didn't love him at first sight but did come to love him dearly over the first days and weeks they were together. How could she not, him with those Gary Cooper eyes, that warm smile, the way he touched her as if fragile as porcelain?

That was better. Her breathing evened out as sleep sauntered in. She really needed to get up and take a shower. She smelled of Mr. Majestic and death.

* * *

Beer can rattle startled her awake. Daylight filled the living room through the big picture window, bright, almost blinding. In that diced-up second, she flinched from the light. Her hand, all on its own, stuck down between the cushions, looking for the gun that wasn't there. Her mind telling her this was it, that it had to be The Cigar. The ever-elusive Lady Luck had flopped her way for too long.

That frozen second moved on. The person who failed to knock or ring the doorbell stepped into the house. A man.

At first, she didn't recognize him. Her mind had already accepted her fate and pasted on this visitor's face a past memory of what The Cigar looked like.

She shook as a shiver coursed through her body. This was…this was her neighbor Bernard Lowery. What was *he* doing in her house? He had never come over before. At least not while Imogene was home. She chuckled at the irony. How, in past daydreams, she had wished for such a stupid thing. Now that it happened, she could only cringe.

Bernie wore brown tweed pants that matched his ecru sweater vest. His long-sleeved shirt was baby blue. On his feet were penny loafers sans socks. He had a gold colored chain bracelet on his wrist. Tasteful and understated. He smiled with those killer dimples. But his eyes…oh how his eyes looked evil. And most of all determined.

"Hello, Mrs. Taylor. I haven't seen you in a while and I thought I might pop in to see how life has been treating you. I hope you don't mind the intrusion."

The conversation from the previous evening echoed loudly in her brain. *He knows that they know about the box.*

And how come he hasn't come over to find out why they had not called the police? He waited as long as he could, the pressure building up to a breaking point. He couldn't wait anymore.

Then, all on its own, the information from the book about interviewed killers popped up. What they had said about being cornered, about if confronted with no way out, they'd kill again and again to keep from being discovered. Leaving behind a daisy chain of carnage and mayhem.

Imogene was about to become a part of that daisy chain.

*Get up right now. Go into the kitchen, grab a butcher knife with a fat blade, and gut this pig before he has a chance to make his move. E, do you see that lump under his sweater at his waistband. He's got himself a gat. He's gonna do you in. Shoot your ass. Don't sit there like a lamb with her neck exposed. Get your ass up and act. Don't you dare go down without a fight. You hear me. I'll never forgive you, E. Move. Now!*

Bernie moved slow as molasses on a cold morning over to Wayne's easy chair and eased down. Ange was right about the lump; he had a sweater bulge that could be a weapon.

Sweat broke out on her forehead and ran down into her eyes, stinging. Let it sting.

This was Bernie the neighbor. He wouldn't try anything. Not in broad daylight. Not with neighbors close enough to hear a scream.

But she wouldn't scream. She wouldn't give him the satisfaction. Her anger rose, tamping down fear the way it was supposed to work. She moved her bottom to the edge of the divan, preparing to leap. Her old body, muscle and bone, telling her it was not a good idea. But leap at what? That she didn't know. Maybe just at him if he did pull a gun.

"I've seen you and Suzanne Davis working late at night in her garage. I was sorry to hear about her father; we were quite good friends, you know."

"Hmm, is that right?"

"That's right. Based on what I saw, he left quite a mess behind."

She forced a smile. "I guess that would depend on your definition of quite a mess.

His smile broadened covering his teeth, making it more a grin. "How is your job working out? It's at Dentco, right?"

She nodded, firing back her own faux smile. She searched her memory. Had she told him she worked at Dentco? Or had he followed her? How could he shoot her and expect to get away with it?

*Don't you dare play dumb. You're an ex-con, a murderess, a no one. Nobody's gonna care if this turd wipes you off the board game of this screwed-up life.*

"Heard about that awful business with that liquor store. Did you know that poor soul who was killed?"

"Yes, we were *quite* close."

Her mocking him tarnished his smile a bit.

*That's it, E. Your only chance at this is to get him angry enough to make a mistake. Don't watch his hands; watch his eyes. They'll tell you when to move. Keep it up, girl. Get him mad as a hatter, then run for that butcher knife.*

Ange was wrong and knew better. You never take a knife to a gunfight.

Movement caught her eye. Out the front picture window, a car pulled to the curb, a blue Chevy Vega.

In this situation, safety came in numbers. A man in an immaculate blue pinstriped suit and tie got out and looked around as if confused.

Come on, whoever you are. Come up to the porch. He looked like one of those religious zealots who peddled the Word door to door. That was all right. Anyone would do.

He had some kind of papers in his hand. No, it was a manila envelope.

"What are you looking at?"

"No one. Somebody's out front but it isn't anyone I'm familiar with." There, let him know there will be other witnesses to kill if that truly was his end game.

The man in the pinstriped suit looked up and down the street one more time, then his eyes happened on something in the area of the porch. The address number, maybe. He stepped across the sidewalk and into the thick grass. He walked almost to the middle—

"Did you and Suzanne find anything of interest in the garage? Mel kept everything, you know. He was a real pack rat."

She turned her attention back to the killer sitting in Wayne's chair. "Yes, don't I know it. The man never threw anything away. The garage was filled to the brim with nothing but junk. And yes, you're right, there were some interesting items. Some real archaeological finds." She winked at him. Let him interpret it any way he wanted. She remembered what Suz had said the night before about poor Poppy and that someone had to speak for her. That emboldened Imogene to say what she did and to wink.

Blue pinstripe stepped up on the porch.

"You didn't happen to have anything over there in the garage, did you?"

The fool visibly squirmed. "Why, no. Why would I store something over there when I have my own perfectly good garage?"

"Hello?" Blue pinstripe stuck his face close to the screen door.

"Hello, come on in." Didn't matter at all who he was as long as he came in and stood by.

Beer cans rattled. Blue pinstripe stepped in, looking down at an oddity he evidently had never seen before, a redneck burglar alarm.

"Just one moment." She held up a finger and quickly disappeared into the kitchen. In two seconds, she reappeared with a thick-bladed butcher knife, held down by her leg covered in the folds of her dress. She sat back down on the divan. Now, bring it on, Bernie. Go ahead and try something.

Blue pinstripe stood by the chair under Joyce's portrait and looked around the house, taking it all in. He turned his attention to Imogene.

She asked, "Can I help you with something? You want to sit down and take a load off?" She said it while staring into Bernie's eyes that said he understood the game, the intent.

Blue pinstripe said, "Yes, thank you. I flew into LA, and there was quite a bit of traffic driving here. Are you Imogene Taylor?"

"Yes, that's right. Airport? You drove in from the airport to come and see me?" Now, she looked at him more closely. The man had a narrow face with a nose too large in comparison to his other features. His skin carried that pasty hue found in office folks who rarely ventured out into the sun. His blue eyes, though, lit up the room with an excited air as if he'd stumbled upon a buried treasure.

"My name is John Catskill, and I have here the contract that—"

"John Catskill from Delacorte?"

*Hah, Imogene, don't that just beat all? Who woulda thought this turd woulda floated to the surface on a day like today. Ain't it just your luck? Huh? Ain't it, E.*

Catskill must've read her expression. "I'm sorry to intrude like this. Is this a bad time? I wanted to get ink on this contract for *Peekaboo POTUS*. I'm sorry for not calling first."

Bernie must've realized his window of opportunity had slammed shut. He struggled to his feet. "I guess I'll be going now so you two can conduct your business." He kept his one hand on the bulge under his sweater vest, holding it in place.

From the kitchen, a harsh baritone voice said, "Sit back down, asswipe. No one's going anywhere. Everyone shut up and sit down." In stepped The Cigar with one of his thug-uglies who sported a long-ago-broken nose. A real mouth-breather. Both carried guns in extended hands. Black dangerous-looking guns that could only represent one thing.

Death.

# Chapter Twenty-Eight

Fat Cigar wore his usual crushed velour warm-up suit, this one light gray. His thug buddy stood over by the TV and looked on with emotionless eyes as if he didn't care what day it was, let alone what it would feel like to take a life. Imogene had run into his type in C-block. Stone killers all. The gun in his hand played a game, moving from person to person waiting for the command to engage. Bark out fire and death.

The Cigar shoved Bernie in the chest. "I said sit down." Bernie fell back in Wayne's chair. Instead of fear, a normal reaction under the circumstances, he showed anger. Vehemence.

Poor John Catskill slunk back in the chair, trying to get small, holding the manila envelope with the contract against his chest. "What's going on? Why do you have guns? Mrs. Taylor, why do these men have guns?"

"Just take it easy," she said. "They're not after you. They've come for me."

"Seriously," he said. "Is this the Jake Bannon in your book that you buy the plastic explosives from?"

The Cigar looked at his employee. "I told these people to shut up. I guess they need a lesson."

The thug took a giant step forward.

Imogene screeched, "No, don't."

The thug pistol-whipped John Catskill from Delacorte across the forehead. Knocked the bejesus outta him. The thunk, the same sound as knuckles thumping a watermelon. He turned limp in the chair, his head off to one side, his eyes slit with just the whites showing. Blood from the gash ran down his cheek to his chin and dripped onto the blue pinstriped suit.

*So much for being an author, huh, E. Too bad. But it was fun while it lasted. Right? Wasn't it fun while it lasted?*

"Why don't you do something instead of just talkin' your crap all the time."

*Just say the word, and these asswipes are toast. I'm not kiddin'. I'll wipe the floor with 'em.*

The Cigar smiled. "Who you talkin' to? You gone off your nut or somethin'? Me being here like this scare the water outta ya? That it? Well, good. You haven't seen nothin' yet, girly. It's about to get dark and ugly."

Beer cans rattled. In stepped Suz.

"Nooo. Run, Suz. Get the hell outta here."

Too late. The thug grabbed her by the arm and jerked her up short. She clawed his face and slapped him in quick succession, then pulled away. She backed up slowly, careful not to trip.

The Cigar laughed. "Heh, heh, heh. No problem, just more for the party. I'll take care of all your friends here first. Make you watch. Whatta ya think about that, huh, grandma?"

"I'm sorry, E. I didn't know what to do. I saw that blue Vega out front and thought it might be trouble, so I just came over. I'm too shook up to think clearly. Let me get by you, I need to sit down."

"Don't sit over there," Cigar said. "Get your ass back over here. Do it right now. You don't want to make me mad. It'll just make what's going to happen a lot worse." He took several steps forward.

Suz didn't listen, determined to sit on the divan next to Imogene. She passed in front with her bottom not inches away from Imogene's face. Suz's hand on the bottom hem of her top pulled upward.

There in the waistband of her shorts was the Colt .38.

In one motion, Imogene grabbed the handle of the Colt, yanked it out, shoved Suz down, and screeched like a barn owl. "All right, all you sons of bitches, let's dance."

Staccato gunfire filled the small living room. Blue/gray smoke billowed in the air.

Imogene gritted her teeth, aimed at The Cigar, and yanked back on the trigger. The gun jumped in her hand. The bullet hit Cigar in his tub of a stomach with a thump. He grunted as his body accepted the lead gift. She raised the barrel and fired again. And again.

Staccato gunfire filled the small living room. More blue/gray smoke billowed in the air.

The Cigar's gun went off, blowing out the window behind the divan.

Bernie had stood and tried to get the gun in his waistband clear, but it hung up on his sweater vest. The thug had aimed at Imogene to defend his boss but now saw his imminent demise if he didn't handle the closest threat. He swung his gun in an arc and fired again and again. Six feet away, Bernie's body jerked and twitched. Blood misted around him in a halo.

Imogene lined up on the thug about the same distance as the phone book on the chair in the back of Dentco, where she'd practiced with the Colt. She fired three more times. The thug back-stepped with each shot and fell against the TV—over the top of it. His head struck Joyce's portrait, and it fell down on top of him.

The raucous noise ended abruptly with three dead men on the floor, the billows of gun smoke evening out into a smooth fog bank.

All of it had occurred in two violence-filled seconds.

Imogene stood, the gun extended, her mind having given up on her. The only thought, no matter how hard she tried to move away from it, was how the now vacant spot on the wall where the portrait used to be was so clean. And how that meant her living room was in dire need of a paint job.

Suz stood up with tears streaming down her face. "Imogene, are you okay? Did you get shot?"

Imogene slowly turned to look, not seeing her friend. Suz took the gun from her hand and eased her friend down onto the divan. Imogene brought two fingers up to her lips.

"What, you want a cigarette?"

Imogene kept her fingers at her lips.

Suz sat down and lit two Marlboros, put one in Imogene's mouth, the other in hers. She'd never smoked before but knew she needed something or go absolutely batshit crazy.

The nicotine infusion brought Imogene up from a dark place and sat her back on the divan with her best friend. Why were there three dead men in her living room? "Oh, sweet baby Jesus, that wall needs paint."

Suz coughed and choked on the cigarette smoke and laughed. "E, that's all you're worried about?" She slapped her leg and laughed some more.

"Suz, honey. You're going into shock. None of this is funny. Not in the least. People died…I…I killed people here. I'm going back to prison."

Suz held up the gun. "No, you're not. There aren't any witnesses. I did all the shooting. That's what we'll tell them. This was self-defense." She used her shirt to wipe away any fingerprints and then put her arm around Imogene. Imogene leaned into it. Couldn't get enough of her best friend, who had just saved all of their lives.

Suz buried her face in Imogene's shoulder and spoke, her words muffled. "E, I have never been more scared in my entire life. I had the gun but knew I couldn't pull the trigger. You saved us all." She started laughing even more.

She had lost her head.

Suz said. "Did you yell that on purpose?"

"Yell what? I didn't yell anything."

Suz pulled away to look into Imogene's eyes, craving the truth. "You yelled, 'All right, you sons of bitches, let's dance.' That's what your main character Maybelline said in your book before she shot it out with the Secret Service."

"I did?"

"Yes, you did."

John Catskill came around, his eyes rolling in his head, iris, whites, iris, whites. He stood on unstable legs, his hands going to his face and almost making it when he spotted the carnage and mayhem that lay at his feet. He fainted dead away.

Police cars with their sirens blaring skidded to the curb out front, parking behind the blue Vega.

The blue uniforms with guns drawn ran across the thick grass.

Suz yelled. "All right, all you sons of bitches, let's dance." She threw her head back and laughed a crazed woman's laugh. Imogene joined her.

# Author's Note

During my two tours on the SWAT team I was given training in executive protection put on by the Secret Service. The instructor told us many marvelous secrets from his past while assigned to the presidential detail, one of which concerned the crazies who sent the President threatening letters. The crazies were investigated and assessed a threat level. Then, when a president visited a city, those crazies who rated couldn't be rounded up and detained because it violated their civil rights. Instead, agents from the Secret Service were assigned a crazy whom they picked up and took to lunch on the government's dime. This factoid was, in part, how this story was spawned.

The genesis of this story is based on something my grandmother once told me. I lived with her for two years. At seventeen, I punched out my overly abusive stepfather (later, I found out I could've shot him and still been justified). I moved in with my gracious grandmother, Alice Putnam, who lived alone after her husband (my grandfather) Wayne passed away. He smoked a pipe and took pictures of the Thanksgiving Day parade with his new camera and tried to pass it off as being real to us and his friends. He had two citrus groves in LaVerne and lost them both to blight and weather. They did visit Universal Studios and talked about the Gilligan's Island set ad nauseam.

All alone, my grandmother sat on her divan (not a couch, never a couch), day after day, and smoked one Marlboro after another in a two-pack-a-day habit. The neighbor next door on the west side did have a wife who had suffered a major stroke. She never spoke or moved, for that matter, ever again. The devoted husband took care of her. Being the Nosy Nellie, my grandmother spotted the neighbor sneaking out late at night on a regular basis. She never confirmed that he had a woman stashed over on Campus, but that was the rumor. A rumor she may have started. The house on Hawthorne was just the way I described it. There was a portrait of her daughter (my Aunt Joyce) hanging on the wall above the TV. But Aunt Joyce didn't die in a motorcycle accident; she passed years later of breast cancer. She was, however, the one who told me about a motorcycle accident involving her best friend, who succumbed in a most brutal and violent manner in the accident described herein.

Grandmother drove a little red AMC Gremlin, and there *was* a huge ancient avocado tree in the backyard behind the detached garage that she had me water once a week.

In Yucca Valley, where I worked as a detective in narcotics, there was a house fire. When the fire department extinguished the blaze, they found a dead woman in a box in the garage. It was the owner's long-missing wife. He had even moved from the house where he originally reported her missing, brought her along, and stored her in the garage. Had there not been a fire, he would've died a natural death before anyone discovered his heinous deed. He ended up committing suicide—if memory serves. I'm sure the incident is easily located on Google.

Cherry Liquor is a real place. As was Dentco, owned by my best friend's parents. I used to visit frequently and knew how the operation worked. There *was* a massage parlor right next door and, when as a cop (please don't read anything else into this), I had reason to talk with the nice women. They *had been* victims of a robbery and didn't report it to the police for various reasons. They did cook their meals on a Hibachi in the alley around back.

My father adopted my brother Van. He's more my brother than my other brothers (sorry about that, li'l bros). His mother's name was Thelma and she was a little eccentric, but not to the extent I painted her in the story. Her physical description and clothes came right from memory. She was one of the most kind, caring and loving people I ever knew. And that's saying something.

After I moved out of my grandmother's house, I moved in with my dad, whom I had been estranged from as a boy. I lived with him from age nineteen, while working as a cadet at Ontario Police Dept., until I attended the Sheriff's academy. I woke one morning to music being played on one of those keyboard machines that had recorded harmonies and odd noises. Thelma was playing and singing (she couldn't carry a tune in a bucket, but God bless her for trying). This wasn't the odd thing about this event. The odd thing was that she had used spray paint cans and painted everything in the living room gold. And I mean everything, furniture, lamps, everything. It was like waking up and stepping into a scene from Charlie and the Chocolate Factory.

So, when asked how I think up some of these wild tales…well, there you go.

# Acknowledgements

I would like to thank the wonderful folks at Level Best Books for their great work and attention to detail.

# About the Author

During his career in law enforcement, bestselling author David Putnam has worked in narcotics, violent crimes, criminal intelligence, hostage rescue, SWAT, and internal affairs, to name just a few. He is the recipient of many awards and commendations for heroism. *The Blind Devotion of Imogene* is the first novel in a trilogy. The next novel in the series, *Imogene's Grand Fiasco*, is due out next year. Putnam is the author of the acclaimed and bestselling Bruno Johnson Crime Series. Putnam lives in the Los Angeles area with his wife, Mary.

SOCIAL MEDIA HANDLES:
  Facebook.com davidputnambooks
  Instagram.com davidputnambooks
  Twitter.com dave Putnam

AUTHOR WEBSITE:
  www.davidputnambooks.com

# Also by David Putnam

Dave Beckett Series:
*A Fearsome Moonlight Black*
*A Lonesome Blood-Red Sun*

The Bruno Johnson Series:
*The Disposables*
*The Replacements*
*The Squandered*
*The Vanquished*
*The Innocents*
*The Reckless*
*The Heartless*
*The Ruthless*
*The Sinister*
*The Scorned*
*The Diabolical*

www.ingramcontent.com/pod-product-compliance
Lightning Source LLC
Chambersburg PA
CBHW020622110726
47899CB00002B/610